A Sherlock Holmes Alphabet of Cases

Volume 2
(F to J)

From The Notes of
John H. Watson M.D.

Edited by
Roger Riccard

First published in 2018 by
The Irregular Special Press
for Baker Street Studios Ltd
Endeavour House
170 Woodland Road, Sawston
Cambridge, CB22 3DX, UK

ISBN: 1 901091 70 8 (10 digit)
ISBN: 978 1 901091 70 0 (13 digit)

Cover Illustration: **Sidney Paget** illustration of Holmes from
The Hound of the Baskervilles (1901).

Typeset in 8/11/20pt Palatino

About the Author

Roger Riccard's family history has Scottish roots, which trace his lineage back to the Roses of Kilravock Castle near the village of Croy in Highland, Scotland. This British ancestry encouraged his interest in the writings of Sir Arthur Conan Doyle at an early age. After successfully authoring the novels, *Sherlock Holmes & The Case of the Poisoned Lilly*, and *Sherlock Holmes & The Case of the Twain Papers,* he then went on to create a dozen short stories of the famous sleuth and his faithful companion, Dr. Watson in a two-volume set: *Sherlock Holmes: Adventures for the Twelve Days of Christmas* and *Sherlock Holmes: Further Adventures for the Twelve Days of Christmas.*

He has also had his work featured at the Museum of London's *Sherlock Holmes Exhibit* and been included among the best Sherlock Holmes authors worldwide, contributing to several Sherlock Holmes anthologies.

Having earned a Bachelor of Arts Degrees in both Journalism and History from the California State University, Northridge, his career has progressed from teaching into business, where he has used his writing skills in various aspects of employee communications. He has also contributed to newspapers and magazines and has earned some awards for his efforts.

He currently lives in a suburb of Los Angeles, California with his wife, Rosilyn, and their 'kids'; Chocolate Labrador Retriever Tootsie Roll, and cats, Bela and Amanda.

Other Books by Roger Riccard

Sherlock Holmes & The Case of the Poisoned Lilly

Sherlock Holmes & The Case of the Twain Papers

Sherlock Holmes: Adventures for the Twelve Days of Christmas

Sherlock Holmes: Further Adventures for the Twelve Days of Christmas

A Sherlock Holmes Alphabet of Cases Volume One: A-E
(A 5 Star Review Recipient from Reader's Favorite)

To my Rosilyn,
My Greatest Adventure

Note to the Reader

As with all the stories I put forth about the world's first consulting detective, Mr. Sherlock Holmes, I must give thanks and credit to his original chronicler, Dr. John H. Watson. While not all his notes are complete, or in some cases, orderly, those which were left to Mrs. Hudson's care and subsequently entrusted to her niece, my 'Grandma Ruby' of New York, in the early days of World War II, have provided the essential facts of the tales herein. I have attempted to flesh out historical and geographical details via internet research and networking with other Sherlockians and British associates. I beg the reader's indulgence for any errors and trust that the stories herein shall be entertaining in and of themselves.

Roger Riccard
Los Angeles, CA USA

Contents

Foreword

David Marcum

I initially became aware of Roger Riccard in 2012, when his first book, *Sherlock Holmes and the Case of the Poisoned Lily*, was published. I was quite happy, as the story sounded very much like something produced by Watson, and left for later generations in his tin dispatch box.

I've been collecting Sherlock Holmes stories since I was a ten-year-old boy in 1975, and over the last forty-three-plus years, I've accumulated, read, and chronologicised several thousand of them. I only care about the ones about the *true* Sherlock Holmes – no modern day settings or parodies, no stories where Holmes is more Van Helsing than consulting detective, and nothing where he's broken and damaged instead of being heroic.

In spite of my insistence on adventures about the legitimate Holmes, I've been willing to overlook aspects of some stories that aren't quite right in order to satisfy my ongoing starving hunger for more narratives. Happily, however, every once in a while, someone comes along who absolutely understands Holmes and Watson, and I know that I can settle back and enjoy those tales without having to worry about any sudden and incorrect intrusions. One of these authors that I absolutely trust is Roger Riccard.

When I read his first book, I didn't know if there would be more. Many authors – especially Holmes authors – have just one story in them, and then they're done. I was pleased when, the next year, another of Roger's stories appeared on the website of the famed and beloved Sherlockians Carolyn and Joel Senter. This story, *The Case of the Twelfth Drumming*, showed that Roger did, in fact, have access to more of these adventures, and that he hadn't been lured into the weeds of presenting Holmes in some shocking way to satisfy modern insensibilities. This was a solid story. I became increasingly interested in seeing what else he would produce.

I wasn't disappointed. 2014 brought *Sherlock Holmes and the Case of the Twain Papers*. And then he became more ambitious, with the first of his themed short story collections. In late 2015, he published *Sherlock Holmes: Adventures for the Twelve Days of Christmas*, containing six stories. A year later came the sequel, and the remaining six stories, in *Sherlock Holmes: Further Adventures for the Twelve Days of Christmas*. This remarkable collection has Holmes investigating a myriad of different situations. Each story is unique, rather than being twelve clichéd variations of the twelve Christmas gifts, as might be offered by a lesser author. They cleverly work in the various aspects of the *Twelve Days of Christmas* without being too cute, or too painfully on-the-nose. (And it was wonderful to see the publication of *The Twelfth Drumming* as part of this collection – showing that Roger clearly had a plan from way back.)

In early 2015, I had the idea of assembling a new Holmes anthology, featuring authors that I knew or admired. The royalties from this project go to the Stepping Stones School for special needs students at Undershaw, one of the former homes of Sir Arthur Conan Doyle. The initial idea for a small book of a couple-of-dozen Holmes stories, at most, initially grew to a three-volume hardcover set of sixty-three stories, the largest collection of its kind ever assembled. And after that, the planned one-time event became an ongoing series, currently at ten massive volumes, with two more in preparation. We've raised over £20,000 for the school so far.

Early on, I was able to track down Roger and invite him to the party. Sadly, he couldn't participate in the first books, as he was deep in a project – which I was to learn was the first of the Christmas volumes. However, he and I stayed in touch, and by later that year, he was on board to contribute to one of the anthologies. Since then, he's been a great supporter of that project, as well as additional collections, and I can't thank him enough.

And now Roger has found an ambitious new project, *A Sherlock Holmes Alphabet of Cases*. Volume I, containing stories related to A through E, came out last year, and now we have Volume II, with F through J. This should keep him busy for the next few years, and I realised that, when all of these stories are written and counted up, he'll have over forty of them, which is well on the way to equaling and surpassing the pitifully few sixty original Canon adventures brought to us by Dr. Watson's original literary agent, Sir Arthur Conan Doyle. I personally can't wait to read and re-read every one of them, and to discover what future surprises are in story for us from Roger's pen.

This book is a really strong collection, ranging from the early days of Holmes and Watson's partnership (*The Italian Gourmet*) to a time when Holmes had retired (*The Judgement of Dr. Watson*). *The Fool and His Money* is wonderful as well, and I especially like *The Gunsmith of Sherwood*, as my father, John Marcum (a former sheriff for a time), once traced our ancestry back to Nottingham, where there was a very distant ancestor, Sir John Markham, also a sheriff ... of Nottingham.

My personal favourite of this set, however, is *The Mysterious Horseman*, with an amazing surprise ending that I wish I could have shared with my dad – he would have really appreciated it too!

But enough of that. You have five new adventures waiting for you. I've just read them, and I know how good they are. Soon you will too. Enjoy!

The game is afoot!

David Marcum
May 2018

11

The Adventure of the
Fool and His Money

Chapter One

At the end of my first year of association with the consulting detective, Mr. Sherlock Holmes, I found myself tracked down by an old comrade of mine from the Fifth Northumberland Fusiliers, a fellow officer named Alexander Sinclair.

Alex and I had grown close after spending several weeks together while I was treating him for a severely broken leg, sustained in a fall from his horse during a minor skirmish against a gang of bandits in India. I was fortunate to be able to save him from amputation and he had felt beholden to me ever since.

His letter reached me at 221B Baker Street on Boxing Day 1881. I had gone out that morning to replenish my supply of tobacco. Upon my return, I was informed by Holmes of its arrival.

"There's a letter on the desk for you, Watson," he announced from his position in front of the fireplace where he was reading the morning paper as he lounged in his familiar mouse-coloured dressing gown.

I put away my Ship's tobacco tin and retrieved the letter. I was pleasantly surprised at the return address. Sitting down across from Holmes, I reached for my penknife to open the envelope when a thought occurred to me.

"Over the past year you have demonstrated some astounding powers, Holmes," I declared. "I confess that I am at a loss as to your thought processes which lead you to arrive at such accurate conclusions on apparently trivial observations. Please tell me what you can about this letter, for I am still very curious as to how you perform this trick."

I held the letter out to him. Reluctantly he looked around the edge of his paper at me in an attitude of impatience, with narrowed grey eyes and furrowed brow. After a few seconds he sighed, folded up *The Times*, set it on the table and picked the letter from my hand as if he were snatching a ball away from a dog.

"How many times have you heard me tell a client that I am not a magician doing mere *tricks*? Pure observation and deduction, Watson, *that* is the basis of my craft. It is the result of a disciplined mind and an accumulation of knowledge as to cause and effect."

He perused the envelope carefully, examining it from every angle, feeling the texture with his thumb and middle finger, holding it up to the light of the nearby lamp, even sniffing it.

"Wait," I pleaded. "Slow down and let me make notes as you explain this process." I retrieved a pad and a pencil from the desk and returned to my armchair, entreating him to talk me through each step he was taking.

He sighed heavily again and started over. "Are you quite ready now, Doctor?" he asked, like a schoolmaster with an inept pupil.

I nodded my assent and he continued once again. "A visual examination of the envelope shows it to be among the better quality stationery available on the market. Not top of the line, but hardly hotel standard. This tells me the sender is fairly well off, or at least has access to someone who is. The texture and weight of the paper confirms the quality and also allows me to determine if there are any enclosures other than the letter itself, such as a ring or a locket. This allows me to surmise that there is but a single sheet inside."

"I see," I commented between my scribbling. "But why did you use your middle finger instead of your index finger to feel the paper?"

"Ah, you made an observation instead of just watching me work. That's progress at least," he answered, somewhat sarcastically, I thought. He continued, "A man's index finger has a tendency to have tougher skin because it is used more than the other fingers. Thus the middle finger has more sensitivity to feel finer variations of texture."

"Interesting," I noted on my pad. 'Please, go on."

Raising it up in the air again, he said, "Holding it to the light also adds to the judgement of the quality. It is finely woven which makes it strong, yet allows the paper to be thin. Not so thin that I could make out the letter inside, but I was able to note four capital letters at the bottom of the page which, from their placement and style, I would deduce R.S.V.P. thus, an invitation.

"The postmark is from Gretna Green, just over the Scottish border. Unusually there is a return address of Falgreen indicating some manor estate or castle, worthy enough to be known by a name rather than an address. Again, this would lend credence to the sender being someone of a moderate station. Well-off, but not necessarily nobility, as is indicated by the lack of title, since he refers to himself merely as Alex Sinclair.

"The envelope bears no smudges and is not wrinkled, so it was likely posted the same day it was written. It does retain a musty smell, typical of old castles either near a river or surrounded by a moat. I believe the River Sark flows into the River Esk channel just south of the town. Kirtle water is also close by.

"The name Falgreen is also a clue, as it could be indicative of a castle surrounded by a green hedge or set upon a green mound, similar to Carlisle Castle, just a few miles south of there."

"This is fascinating, Holmes," I commented as I wrote. "Anything else?"

"I would deduce that your connection to him is from your military days by his addressing you as Captain, Dr. John Watson. Referring to himself as Alex rather than Alexander indicates to me that you and he were close friends, likely in the same regiment. His station in life suggests he was an officer, but his reference to you as Captain *and* Doctor tells me he did not outrank you, for someone who did would refer to you as a one or the other, not both. Therefore, I would surmise that he was likely a Lieutenant.

"The handwriting is very revealing. He is obviously intelligent. There are also indications of strength from someone whom I would expect to be about your age, yet there is also a sense of overcompensation. A little too much flourish, attempting a conceit that really doesn't ring true. Hmmm ..."

Holmes stared thoughtfully at the inked address and even felt along the line for the depth of impression.

"Was he ever wounded?"

I dropped my hands into my lap, dumbfounded. "That is amazing, Holmes!" I went on to explain Alex's injury and how our friendship grew out of my treatment of him. I included the fact that he called me Captain Doctor because I had to pull rank on him to get him to obey my recommendations regarding his convalescence.

Holmes nodded in satisfaction and spoke once more. "I would suggest then, that something has occurred in his life which he wishes to share with you. Something rather significant, I should think, judging by the excitement evident in his writing. So by all means, open it up and share your friend's good news."

He tossed the envelope back to me. I missed it, due to having the pencil in my hand, but it fell in my lap and I quickly took up my penknife again and slit it open.

It was indeed, an invitation to come celebrate the New Year with him at Falgreen, where he promised a fine feast, a cosy room and an adventure that could prove most advantageous to both of us. His wording was rather cryptic and gave no clue as to what this adventure might be. I handed the message over to Holmes and asked his opinion.

A brief glance was all he took and declared, "I should say that this adventure he speaks of involves something quite valuable, Watson. He obviously did not wish to name details, as he could not be sure this letter wouldn't fall into false hands. It is probably something spiritual in nature, physical enjoyment or material enrichment, most likely the latter as I do not think he would be quite so secretive if it were a new religion or a meeting of a pair of eligible ladies. I would recommend that you accept and remove yourself from the dreariness of London's soot-smoked atmosphere for a time. A spirited romp in the country will do you good."

"What of you, Holmes?" I enquired. "Have you any plans?"

He puffed away at the pipe he had lit while I was reading my invitation and announced, "I am determined to catch up on my indexes and old case files in these next few days, unless a new client comes along, of course. In any event, I shall be quite busy and not very good company."

I should note that at this time, being the first year of our living together, my accompanying Holmes on his cases was not as frequent an experience as it would later become. Thus, I felt unencumbered and penned a telegram to Alex, accepting his invitation and expecting to arrive on the 29th of December per his request.

Chapter Two

The journey by train was a long one. I left Euston Station in London at nine in the morning and arrived at Carlisle, just south of the Scottish border, at four o'clock

The scenery along the way was pleasant enough, being primarily rolling hills at first. Being the middle of winter I had naturally dressed for the climate, but the travelling rugs provided by the railway company were welcome all the same, especially in view of the snow flurries that accompanied the train the closer it got to Carlisle.

I had spent much of the journey reading a new work of Jules Verne, *Eight Hundred Leagues on the Amazon*. I found it to be an exciting tale and was impressed by Verne's attention to detail and ability to convey action with the written word. It was a skill I much admired and a secret desire of mine to be able to write in such a manner.

Needing to change trains, I was forced to wait until half past five to catch the next departure from Carlisle to Gretna Green. The train was crowded with several young couples, apparently seeking to start the New Year as newlyweds. Gretna Green was still a very popular spot for weddings, even though the laws which had made it so had changed. In the middle of the 18th century English lords approved new laws to tighten marriage arrangements. Couples had to reach the age of twenty-one before they could marry without their parents' consent and their marriage had to take place in a church.

Scottish law, however, was different. You could marry on the spot, in a simple marriage by declaration, or handfasting ceremony, only requiring two witnesses and assurances from the couple that they were both free to marry.

With such a relaxed arrangement within reach of England, it soon led to the inevitable influx of countless thousands of young couples running away to marry over the border. Gretna Green is a long way from London and you could approach Scotland from several directions.

With Gretna Green perfectly placed to take advantage of the differences in the two country's marriage laws and with an angry father-of-the-bride usually in hot pursuit, the runaway couple could not waste time. Therefore as soon as they reached Scottish soil in Gretna Green, they would find a place of security where they could marry in haste. Back then, that spot was the blacksmith's shop, the first building couples reached in Gretna Green and even now, a century later, it was a popular wedding location.

I finally arrived at ten to seven and was met by Alex himself, who welcomed me in that gregarious fashion I remembered so well. He had put on weight since the last time I saw him, yet retained an athletic build, the addition being more muscle than fat. He no longer wore his deep red hair in a close cropped military fashion, but rather long, though he retained his cavalryman's moustache, to which he had added a neat beard. His Scots burr was thick and hearty as he greeted me.

"Cap'n, Doctor!" he exclaimed, upon wrapping both his hands around the one I extended in friendship. "It's so good to see ye again."

I had seen upon his approach that he still favoured the leg I had set nearly three years ago. He noticed my observation and commented. "The leg stiffens up a bit on me durin' the cold winter months, but I can sit a horse with any man in the county, thanks to ye, Doctor. But I see you walking with a fair limp yourself, Johnny. A war wound I take it?"

I explained about my taking a bullet in the shoulder at the Battle of Maiwand and how Murray, my orderly, had found me to a horse, only to be struck in the leg by a second Jezail bullet during our retreat.

"Aye, a bloody business in Afghanistan. This leg o' mine kept me out of it, but at least ye saved it for me and now it's time to repay ye."

"Whatever are you talking about?" I asked. "And how did you find me?"

"Let's get out o' the cold first," he replied. "I've got a carriage to take us home just over here."

He led the way to a fine enclosed carriage with a driver in full livery. We stowed my luggage and climbed inside. Once we were off he continued.

"To answer your second question first, about a month ago I began m'search by contacting a friend at the war office to see about your current billet. It took a bit o' time, but I finally found that ye had mustered out and were on a pension which was directed to Baker Street.

"Now as to yer first question," he said, lowering his voice conspiratorially, "I believe I'm on the verge o' discovering an old cache o' money that could be a considerable sum. As I owe ye m'life, I felt it only fair that ye should share in it."

I felt a bit overwhelmed, "Alex, I was only doing my duty. Any army doctor would have done the same."

"Aye, but ye pulled that Captain rank on me and took a lot more time than a doctor jest doin' 'is duty. Besides I need a man o' yer intellect to confirm m'findings and make sure I deciphered the clues correctly."

"Clues?" I asked.

He slapped my good knee with a meaty paw and announced, "We're goin' to find that secret cache, Johnny me lad!"

I peppered him with questions, but he put me off, saying he would explain all when we got to the privacy of Falgreen. We drove less than a mile south on the Glasgow Road, crossing over the River Sark and entered into the walled courtyard of Falgreen Castle. The landscape in the area around Gretna Green was primarily flat which gradually tapered away toward the Solway Firth at the northern tip of the Irish Sea. The area is quite green and makes for excellent farming and pasture for sheep and cattle. I did note that Holmes was correct in his deduction regarding the etymology of the name, for surrounding the castle walls was an incline greater than forty five degrees reaching high up the wall from the adjacent fields. It was thick with green vegetation and would have been nearly impossible for soldiers to attempt to climb and breach the massive sandstone walls.

Alex had my luggage taken to my room and offered me a brief tour. "We've about an hour 'til dinner," he suggested. "Let me show ye 'round a bit."

As we walked he gave me a short history lesson. The castle itself dated back to 1140 when it was completed in response to the English castle at Carlisle across the border. Carlisle had originally been built as a stronghold against Scottish invaders. Seeing the usefulness of such a fortress, the Scots built Falgreen for defence against both Anglo forces and as a staging ground for its own southern-bound troops.

For such an ancient structure, I noted that it had been kept in remarkably good repair. The red and green tartan of this branch of the ancient Saint Clair clan was prominent among banners and tapestries and there were various suits of armour and weapons displayed. Each of these was designated by a plaque giving the name of the bearer.

We stopped before one of these suits and Alex could barely contain himself. "This could be the key to our upcoming adventure," he proclaimed as he ran his hand along an arm. "This suit of armour." Turning to me he asked, "Are ye familiar with the history o' the Battle of Solway Moss?"

"I also am of Scottish descent," I reminded him, "We are all aware of that prelude of events just prior to the birth of Mary, Queen of Scots. Though I'm certainly not up on details since my school days."

Alex smiled, "Aye, I was a bit rusty meself until recently. Let me read this for ye." He picked up a large book on a nearby table, the title of which was *A History of Scottish Wars* and read out loud.

24

"On 24th November 1542, an army of 15,000 Scots advanced into England from Dunfries. Lord Maxwell, though never officially designated commander of the force, declared he would lead the attack in person. A later report says that in the absence of Maxwell, Oliver Sinclair, a favourite courtier of King James the Fifth, declared himself to be James's chosen commander. According to this account of the battle, the other commanders refused to accept his leadership and the command structure disintegrated. The Scots advance into England was met near Solway Moss by Lord Wharton and his 3,000 men. The battle was uncoordinated and may be described as a rout. Sir Thomas Wharton described the battle as the overthrow of the Scots between the rivers Esk and Lyne. The Scots, after the first encounter of a cavalry chase at Akeshawsill, moved down towards Arthuret Howes. They found themselves penned in south of the Esk, on English territory between the river and the Moss and after intense fighting surrendered themselves and their ten field guns to the English cavalry. Wharton said the Scots were halted at the Sandy Ford by Arthuret mill dam. Several hundred of the Scots may have drowned in the marshes and river.

"James, who was not present at the battle, withdrew to Falkland Palace humiliated and ill with fever. The news that his wife had given birth to a daughter, Mary, instead of a son, further crushed his will to live and he is reported to have stated that the House of Stewart 'came with a lass and will go with a lass'. He died at Falkland two weeks later at the age of thirty. It is reported that in his delirium he lamented the capture of his banner and Oliver Sinclair at Solway Moss more than his other losses."

"Yes," I agreed. "Now I recall. So this Oliver Sinclair was one of your ancestors?"

"Aye, and this castle was his to command and retain after being ransomed from England. He charged a cousin, Roderick to keep it staffed and ready to use as a staging ground for Scottish troops, which it would later become. Which brings us to the reason I've sent for ye.

"In order to maintain the castle and be ready to raise and supply an army, Oliver was constantly procuring funds and sending the money here. Roderick always feared an attack from the English and so kept that treasury well-hidden. Legend goes that he left secret instructions for his cousin should anything happen to him. But then he died in 1576, at about the same time as Oliver, and the treasury was never discovered."

Alex clapped me on the shoulder, smiled broadly and said, "That's why I've invited ye here, Johnny. It's believed that no one else knew where it was hidden, for there's no record of its use. The story has come down through my family for generations."

Here he pointed to his broad chest with his thumb and announced, "But I've found the message Roderick left Oliver with the clues to its whereabouts. On New Year's Day we're goin' on a treasure hunt!"

Chapter Three

"A treasure hunt?" I asked, sceptically. "You mean to say no one has found this cache in over 300 years?

"If they did, there's no record of it and I doubt the instructions I found have been touched since they were written and hidden away."

"Where did you find them?" I asked with great curiosity, for Alex's excitement was becoming infectious.

"Come along I'll show ye," he replied and led the way to a small reading room that was lined with bookshelves containing a wide variety of books of all ages. He went to a particular shelf, pulled out a large leather-bound tome and set it upon a table. I leaned over his shoulder and saw that it was an old Bible.

"I was re-arranging the books in here last summer and accidently dropped this old Latin Bible. When King James had the English translation published for the public in 1611 these went out o' style and I doubt anyone had occasion to look through it carefully any more. But I noticed a loose page and opened it up to try and straighten it. Turns out, it weren't one o' the book pages but a handwritten note, also in Latin."

Just then we were interrupted by a servant who announced that 'dinner was served'. Alex put a finger to his lips to indicate that our conversation needed privacy and ushered me to the dining room where we enjoyed a fine meal of lamb, potatoes and assorted vegetables. We discussed army days and old comrades. I told him of my current circumstances and about my fellow lodger, who was an amateur detective of sorts. I even explained how he was able to deduce so much merely from the letter I had received inviting me to Falgreen.

"Och! The man is a warlock, to be sure! Two centuries ago he'd have been burned at the stake! Ye say he does this for a livin'?"

"Oh yes," I assured him. "He's quite good at it and makes a decent income helping private clients. Even the police occasionally call upon him for assistance."

"Tis a marvel indeed. If I'd known of him, he might have been able to help decipher the clues a lot faster than the weeks it took me."

"I'm sure your confidence in yourself will be rewarded, old friend. I'll certainly help in any way I can."

"I knew I could count on ye, Johnny. Let's take our brandy and cigars into the study and I'll show ye my discovery and my interpretation."

He led me to a roll top desk where he unlocked the top and retrieved an envelope with some papers. Then we sat at a round oak table under a bright chandelier. He carefully unfolded an ancient page, yellowed with age. "What do ye make of this, with all ye'r Latin learnin'?"

He turned the page toward me and it read as follows:

Ad custodem custos fide et de mammonae
Ortu solis exortu ad finem victoriae strenae
Dum se nobis pastorem, sustentare eum qui pecuniam ovium
Ex visibilibus in ostium quod aperit caelum, ita faciet ad dextram
Arma inter valle umbrae mortis et in mensam ex adverso hostium meorum
Mitte tuam solem et oculum a note, ubi umbra cadit in capitis mei

> *Ad simul et convertam te et auferetur regnum ad Septentrionalis*
> *Et cum iter fecit gradus prophetia Isaiae: umbra in horologio Ahaz*
> *Habens cubitum sub tutela sancti Andreae in vobis quaerite et invenietis in via turn enim circulo recta medium*
> *Rursus bello oriri pretium*
> *Et animam tuam: Deus misereatur*

I was able to make out some phrases, but was at a loss to the overall meaning and confessed as much to my friend. "I can discern some of this, but since my school days my Latin has been pretty confined to medical terms. I hope you weren't counting on me to translate this for you."

He smiled brightly through his whiskers and slid another paper across to me. "Not to fear, Johnny lad. My pastor translated it and I swore him to secrecy," he winked. "Figured that'd be safer than some busybody scholar. Now does *that* make any sense to ye?" he said, handing me another piece of paper. I took it and read in much plainer English:

> To the keeper of the faith and the guardian of mammon
> The full risen sun of a new year dawns on the means to victory
> While the Lord is our Shepherd, the treasure sustains the sheep
> From the door that opens to the sights of the heavens, make way to the right
> Between the battlements shadow of the valley of death and the table in the presence of mine enemies
> Cast thine eye away from the sun and note where my helmet's shadow falls

Go at once and turn thyself away toward the kingdom
of the North
And march as did Isaiah's shadow on the steps of the
stairway of Ahaz
A cubit beneath St. Andrew's protection ye shall find
the way - turn a circle half right
To arise again with the wages of war
And may God have mercy upon your soul

"Well, it's certainly readable now," I commented. "But do you understand what it means?"

"I believe so, but I need someone I can trust to help me. That's where *you* come in."

His full pronunciation of *you* told me how serious he was, so I answered in kind. "Anything I can do to help, Alex. You can count on me."

"I knew it. Cap'n, Doctor," he said, slapping his hand on the table and holding it out. "And here's my hand on it. We'll share whatever we find, fifty-fifty."

I took his hand and replied, "That's terribly generous of you, are you sure?"

He grew serious momentarily and said in solemn tones, "Ye saved my life, Johnny. If not for that, the treasure may have gone undiscovered for another hundred years, or maybe never. 'Tis only fair, I say." Then his smile broadened again, "Now let me tell ye what I think this means and ye can give me your thoughts."

He went through his reasoning, first of all stating that he found the page inserted at Psalm 23 in the Old Testament, which he felt was significant. He went on to explain that he believed the 'keeper of the faith and the guardian of mammon' was Roderick and that his suit of armour in the castle indicated the key. The 'treasure sustains the sheep and the wages of war', both referred to the money collected to raise up an army against the British. He was sure the 'door' and the 'battlements' referred to the high tower which was the closest point in the castle with 'sights to the heavens'. Standing Roderick's armour in the proper place at dawn on New Year's Day would cast a shadow pointing to the starting point of the directions which followed.

Finally stopping his explanation to take a fresh sip of brandy, my old comrade asked, "Well, Johnny what do ye think?"

I removed the cigar from my lips, collected my thoughts briefly, then answered, "You certainly seemed to have reasoned it out logically and I don't wish to dampen your enthusiasm, but it has been three hundred years and there are likely changes in terrain, the heights of trees or even new trees altogether could affect shadows and steps. The land is also fairly flat, with just a slight rising towards the east, away from the river. A shadow cast at sunrise would be long indeed, likely outside the castle walls. Would this ancestor of yours risk burying the money out in the open like that?"

Alex raised his open palm, his own cigar sending smoke upwards from between his long fingers. "Aye, I know there be objections, but I've explored the area where I expect the shadow to fall on New Year's morning. I think we've got a chance here, Johnny, and certainly nothing to lose. What say ye?"

I grinned, "I'm at your disposal, Alex. If nothing else it will be a fine adventure to remember for this gloomy winter."

We clinked our glasses and toasted to a successful quest.

Chapter Four

Friday, the thirtieth, dawned cold and cloudy. I wandered downstairs and found breakfast was being prepared but wouldn't be ready for half an hour yet. The cook, Mrs. Sheffield, offered me a cup of coffee which I took gratefully. With no sign of Alex about, I decided to do some exploring. I threw on my overcoat, muffler and flat cap and ascended the stairwell of the castle's tower. Stepping out on to the rooftop surrounded by battlements, I found my friend looking out across the fields to the west.

I wrapped both my hands around the still warm cup of coffee and took a sip, then asked, "What will you do if it's overcast and there no sun shining at dawn on the first?"

"I've thought o' that," he answered. "I've been coming up here the last few mornings to get an idea of where the helmet's shadow will fall. It shouldn't make more than a few inches difference this close to the actual date, so we should be close to a starting point."

He leaned back and I saw that behind him, propped up against the wall, was a staff with one of the ancient helmets on it.

"I take it this is the height of Roderick," I commented. "Clever to do it this way and not have to lug his entire set of armour up here. So where do you think the shadow will fall?"

He responded by pointing to some ruins that lay between Falgreen and the River Sark. "Yesterday, the shadow fell just north of the foundation of the old kirk there. It's where the cemetery was. It's quite possible the treasure is buried among the old tombs."

"Won't that present a problem with your local pastor?" I asked.

"We'll have to see where the clues take us," he replied. "If it be an actual gravesite we'll bring in the pastor and see what can be done. But I doubt that someone with Roderick's Bible knowledge would desecrate a grave by burying his war chest in it. We'll find out come Sunday morning."

We left the tower perch and retreated downstairs to a welcoming hot breakfast.

The freezing temperature and intermittent hail kept us inside the rest of the day. Alex had some business to take care of, handling the estate and the local folk who rented lands from him for raising crops and livestock. The impression I received coincided with Holmes's assessment. Falgreen allowed him to be moderately well-off but not extremely wealthy. Expenses were often threatening to overcome income and Alex had mentioned that he may be forced to sell off some his holdings.

I was left to fend for myself in his well-stocked library, where I made myself comfortable in front of the fire with the Jules Verne book I had brought along. After a brief respite for lunch, we each returned to our activities. This time, however, I chose to experiment with some writing of my own. I took up pencil and paper and began making notes for a tale of my current circumstances. I allowed my imagination to run with the situation as it existed in the late fourteenth century with the cousins Sinclair attempting to do their patriotic duty for Scotland. I imagined scenes of intrigue, clandestine meetings and passionate debates. It was all speculation, of course, and I would certainly seek my host's permission to use his family for a fictional account. By dinner time, I had put down several ideas which gave me confidence that there was enough to start writing a story and I resolved to begin doing so at the next opportunity.

Over our evening meal, Alex asked what I had found to read in the library. I recommended to him the Jules Verne adventure. The mood was congenial and so I broached the possibility of writing a fictional account of his ancestors and their adventures during those ancient days in Scotland's history as background to our modern day treasure hunt.

He contemplated that as he sipped his wine, a fine vintage of the Graham clan. Finally he responded, "T'would make a grand tale, I'll admit, especially if we find the treasury. But my cousins, those descendants of Oliver, are very protective of the clan's history. 'Tis doubtful they'd approve." He hesitated a bit and I sensed there was something else bothering him.

"What is it, Alex?" I asked, "If you have an objection please tell me, I'll not take offense, I assure you."

He leaned forward and spoke in a low voice, "It's just that, *if* we find a treasure that makes us rich, I'd just as soon not have the news bandied about. Ye know how differently people treat ye when you're wealthy. Everybody lookin' for an investor, every charity, tax collector and long lost relative will come out o' the woodwork lookin' for a touch."

I confess that this thought had never occurred to me and the look on my face must have revealed my disappointment, for my comrade spoke up again.

"Not that it's a bad idea, Johnny. Perhaps if ye changed the names and location?"

"That's a thought," I conceded, grateful for the suggestion. "Thank you."

"That's better then. Now, how's yer leg up for a ride tomorrow, weather permittin'? 'Tis Hogmanay after all and I'd like to show ye the Sinclair lands as we visit the tenants and neighbours. Might even give ye some ideas for your story."

"The leg kicks up with the cold," I answered, "but if the rain and hail subside I could use a good stretching out."

"Very well, then. I've got a couple o' fine stallions that are particularly gentle but can give us a good run when so inclined. We'll start out right after breakfast."

*****

The next morning dawned cold but clear and we packed up our panniers with various breads, sweetmeats and bottles of Scotch whisky, and cantered off to visit Alex's tenants and neighbours. All were welcoming on this festive day, even those who were paying their monthly rents. There was one stop where we were particularly welcomed. A small shop on the outskirts of Gretna Green where a variety of souvenirs and bric-a-brac were sold to the many tourists. When we walked into the shop, bearing our gifts, a petite young woman of about twenty years with doe-like eyes and chestnut hair that curled round her face and across her shoulders let out a cheery greeting and proceeded to fall into a prolonged hug with my companion, followed by an affectionate kiss that bespoke more than a casual friendship. Slipping his arm around the girl's waist, Alex waved in my direction and announced, "Sarah, me darlin', this would be me good friend, Captain Doctor John Watson, as fine a medical man as her Majesty's army has ever produced. He's the one who saved me leg and me life. Johnny, this would be Miss Sarah Lamont, me fiancée."

I bowed, doffed my cap and reddened slightly at this praise, "Why Alex, you never told me. Congratulations, old man!" I started to offer my felicitations to Miss Lamont but before I could utter another word I found myself in a bear hug that was surprisingly strong for someone so small, for she could not have been more than five feet two inches.

"Oh, thank you, thank you, Doctor! You saved my Alex for me!"

Finally disentangling herself, she explained, "I've loved Alex since I was a young girl, but never told him, he being so much older than I. Then he went off to war and I thought I'd never see him again. When he came back wounded I finally made up my mind that I had to tell him how I felt. I could not risk anything happening to him without letting him now how much he was loved."

"Imagine me surprise, Johnny," Alex chimed in, "when this slip of a girl came to visit me at the castle in my convalescence and confessed her feelings. I had only known her as one of the village girls. I'd never dreamed she had a crush on me. The more she visited, the more I felt such a compatibility that our love became mutual. I proposed to her on her twenty-first birthday in October and we're to be married this Spring."

At this juncture, Miss Lamont held out her hand so I could see her lovely engagement ring and said, "You must promise to come to the wedding, Doctor, please, it would mean so much to us."

"Yes, Johnny ye must come," added my friend. "Ye must stand up with me as I take my bride."

I was flabbergasted by all this news at once, but I answered in the affirmative, "Well, I can hardly deny the request of such a charming young lady, nor that of an old comrade in arms. Of course I'll come."

"Wonderful!" said Sarah, clapping her hands in delight. "Now, sit, sit, sit, there by the stove and take off your coats while I get you both some hot coffee."

After a delightful visit with this bubbly bride-to-be, Alex and I mounted up and returned to Falgreen. The rest of the day was spent receiving visits from others celebrating Hogmanay. When an elderly neighbour and his wife left us just before sunset, Alex turned to me and proclaimed they would be the last visitors we would receive.

"Really?" I asked. "When I was a lad we celebrated through the night and well into the next morning."

"Aye, that's tradition," he replied. "But the local custom here is to limit visits only to daylight hours, unless ye've been invited to dinner. I've not sent such invitations nor accepted any this year, for we've a busy day tomorrow. I've ordered breakfast for seven-thirty and by eight-thirty we'll need to be in position."

After dinner that evening, we retired to his library once again and discussed exactly what each of our tasks would be on the morrow. We worked out a system of flag communication between me on the battlements and Alex, near the kirk where the shadow should fall. Since he had been checking this phenomenon for several days, he already knew approximately where to begin. My signals would guide him to the exact starting point. Then I would sally forth to join him and within the hour we hoped a fortune would lay at our feet.

Chapter Five

After a restless night, being excited about what lay ahead, I arose at seven and looked out the window. To my delight, the early morning stars still shone, meaning clear skies for the task before us.

I enjoyed a hearty breakfast with my friend as scheduled, after which, Alex gave all the servants the rest of the day off to go into town and enjoy the celebrations with family and friends.

In the dawn's twilight, we saddled the horses again with panniers. Hoping this time to fill them with treasure. Alex rode out to the kirk and stood near where he determined the shadow would fall. I took my place on the tower roof between the third and fourth battlements, counting to the right from the door, for Alex had determined these were the verse numbers in the 23rd Psalm to which the, 'valley of the shadow of death' and 'the table in the presence of mine enemies', referred.

I held Roderick's helmet on its shaft and when the full sun cleared the horizon I signalled with a bright red flag to Alex. I moved him slightly to his left and backward a couple of steps. When he was in position I gave him the agreed upon sign and left the tower to mount my steed and gallop out to join him.

Upon arriving I found Alex in the old kirk cemetery, compass in hand, facing due north. "Now," he said, "we're to proceed as Isaiah's shadow, which was backwards ten steps."

He slowly retreated ten steps backwards. Fortunately he was between two ancient grave markers, both of which were marked with a St. Andrew's cross, a name, what appeared to be dates and some ancient Gaelic or Latin script, all nearly worn away after three centuries.

"There doesn't seem to be anything significant about this spot," I mused. "I suppose that's to be expected, given the secrecy behind the treasury, but I would've thought there would be something more telling about the location."

"We've still an instruction to 'turn a circle half right'."

Alex turned to his right and stuck his shovel into the ground "So I propose we start here. Perhaps Roderick meant between the protection of two St. Andrew's crosses. We've only got to dig down eighteen inches or so to find out."

"You're sure that's what a cubit is?"

"According to me pastor, a cubit is the length of a man's arm from the elbow to the fingertips, roughly sixteen to twenty inches. If we've hit nothing by then we'll have to ask about digging up the tops of these old graves."

Thus we began our excavation, starting about four feet apart so as to allow for any variation between the length of Alex's steps and Roderick's. The ground wasn't quite frozen, but rough digging all the same. It took us nearly a half hour to dig out a trench four feet long, three feet wide and two feet deep. Unfortunately, no treasure loomed up to greet us.

As this was Alex's adventure, I kept digging until he made the reluctant decision to halt. Conceding that either there was no treasure, or we were in the wrong spot, my friend agreed to pack up our equipment and return to the warmth of the castle.

The next two days passed quickly. Alex's pastor agreed to his request to search the top layer of the adjoining grave site only if he were present, and that ten percent (a tithe as he put it) of any treasure found, be donated to the church. Late Tuesday afternoon saw the three of us again in the churchyard, but once more our efforts proved fruitless.

After another couple of days I returned to London and Baker Street, none the richer in material goods, but certainly well pleased to have connected with my old comrade and the promise of a continuing friendship.

Holmes appeared to have made some progress in his index filing, as the usual disarray of papers about our sitting room was much depleted. When I returned late afternoon he was not in, but Mrs. Hudson greeted me warmly and assured me that she had received my telegram and was preparing dinner for the both of us.

"He's off with that Inspector fellow from Scotland Yard," she informed me. "But he assured me that he'd be home for supper."

"Lestrade or Gregson?" I enquired.

"The weasel-faced fellow," she answered.

"Ah, Lestrade then. Very well, Mrs. Hudson, thank you. Could I trouble you for some tea and biscuits?"

"Of course, Doctor," and she bustled off to her kitchen while I unpacked, stirred up the fire and settled onto the sofa with the afternoon edition of the newspaper I had picked up at the station.

About an hour later, the world's first consulting detective burst through the door, flung his overcoat and hat at the hat stand and greeted me in high spirits.

"Ah, good old Watson! Welcome back," he said, plopping down in the chair opposite me and warming his hands by the fire as he took in my presence with that sweeping glance of his.

He continued, "How is your friend? Not too disappointed, I hope."

I was rather taken aback by that remark and replied tersely, "On the contrary, Holmes, Alex was quite pleased to see me and we enjoyed our time very much."

"Of which I've no doubt, Doctor, for you are excellent company," he said, smiling. "I was referring to the disappointing results of your little adventure."

I leaned forward, my hands upon my knees. "How could you possibly know that?" I demanded.

He picked up his pipe from the table, filled it methodically as he gazed at me, then began to speak.

"Being a civilian again for over a year now has softened your hands and I see not one, but no less than four blisters. The placement of these indicates you were digging with a D-handled shovel. I also note that, despite the cold weather, your face, now that you've lost your tan of army days, has slightly reddened, indicating considerable time spent outdoors.

"I presume that a friend who owes you his very life would not invite you to his castle to dig fence posts. Ergo, you've been digging outside for something valuable, no doubt the 'advantageous adventure' of which he spoke in his invitation.

"Your manner just now when I arrived was cordial, but only that. Had your enterprise been a success your countenance would have revealed a more joyful expression. In fact, I would have expected you to be bursting with good news to share."

"What if I'd been sworn to secrecy?" I countered.

He shook his head as he puffed away at his clay, "It won't do, Watson. In this past year of our association I have learned to read you as easily as you read your paper. You are not a deceitful man, a most noble quality, but one which severely hampers your abilities as an actor. Should you ever wish to take up the stage, I could instruct you for I have some theatrical background. But in your natural state you are the bane of my existence, an honest man.

"No, my friend. While you no doubt enjoyed your visit, there is an underlying disappointment within you."

I stood, looking down at him and shaking my head, then walked over to the sideboard and poured myself a small whisky.

"I am loathe to admit that you are correct, Holmes. While I was satisfied just seeing my old comrade and meeting his friends and fiancée, I am sorry for his disappointment. As unlikely as the odds were, I believe he had allowed hope to get the better of him."

"Ah, a man in love," replied Holmes in that analytical tone of his. "That would certainly add to his eagerness to believe in something against more reasoned judgement. Tell me, Doctor, what was this high hope of his, if you are able to reveal it now?"

I paused momentarily then answered, "Since it didn't materialise I suppose there can be no harm done sharing it now, although I doubt he would want his dashed dream made public."

"You have my word that your story shall not leave this room," replied the detective. "I am merely curious at what motivated him to his action. Motivation is always instructive to someone in my line of work."

I went to my room, retrieved my notes and rejoined Holmes at the dining table, where Mrs. Hudson was now laying out our supper. After she left us, I began my story as I was buttering bread and cutting meat. Holmes merely soaked it all in as he sipped at his wine, deigning not to interrupt his concentration with something so mundane as eating.

When I had finished, he asked to see the translation of the instructions to the treasury left by Roderick. I handed it over and he studied it carefully, then returned it to me.

"A most interesting tale, Doctor," he offered as he handed it back, then reached for the bread and butter. "I trust you will be keeping your notes to inspire your aspirations to become a writer?"

"Why, yes Holmes," I replied. "That is my intention."

"I believe you will find your little puzzle there to be a key to your story. Keep it in a safe place. By the way, when is your friend getting married?"

This abrupt change of subject caught me off guard momentarily, but since Holmes's mind takes frequent leaps beyond the obvious I had already grown used to his apparent disconnections and recovered to answer, "The Saturday before Easter is their intention. They are to be married in the chapel of the famous Gretna Green blacksmith's shop, since the church will not allow a wedding on that date in the sanctuary."

Holmes walked over to the writing desk to gaze upon the calendar, murmuring to himself in tones I could not make out.

Finally he said "That would make it April the eighth, an excellent date."

As he sat back down I asked, "Why is that such an excellent date?"

He smiled enigmatically and offered, "It is numerically pleasing, old fellow. All those even numbers divisible by each other. It will also be an easy anniversary date to remember through their years of wedded bliss."

He raised his glass as he said this and gave a toast to the happy couple, "I should be honoured to attend such an event if your friend wouldn't mind."

I was a bit taken aback by his attitude, which I at first thought to be sarcastic, but now seemed quite genuine. I told him I would request Alex's permission to bring him along when the date grew closer and we left it at that as we pursued our meal and he told me of his latest assistance offered to Inspector Lestrade.

Chapter Six

The months passed slowly, winter eventually giving way to spring. I was beginning to make some headway in establishing a small list of private patients and picking up an occasional shift at St. Bartholomew's Hospital. Holmes managed to keep busy enough to refrain from stimulating his mind with drugs. As I recall, he assisted Scotland Yard in solving two significant burglaries, helped a widow find her missing adult son and solved the problem of the purloined Panatelas from his tobacconist's shop.

Alex and I had corresponded occasionally during this time and in one of my letters I had requested the company of Sherlock Holmes when I came up for the wedding. My old army comrade readily agreed, saying he was anxious to meet the man who could astound others with the powers I had ascribed to him.

Thus it was that we arrived at Falgreen on Monday the third of April. As per the same train timetable which had brought me up in December, we arrived late in the afternoon but this time were treated to a warm spring afternoon's ride and were better able to take in the landscape.

Alex greeted us with open arms and after we were shown to our rooms and dispensed with our luggage, we reassembled in the library for cigarettes and drinks as we awaited dinner.

My army friend and my civilian friend seemed to hit it off quite well. Their conversation covered many topics of local interest. I was surprised and impressed by the depth of information that Holmes was able to provide on the history of the Dumfries and Galloway region and said as much.

"I must confess, Holmes, that I am astonished at your historical knowledge. All this time I've been under the impression that your brain was reserved for those items which related to your chosen profession."

Holmes smiled indulgently and replied, "And you would not be wrong, my dear Watson. I must admit that I have spent some few hours researching this locality at the British Museum in preparation for our visit."

Alex chimed in, "I appreciate yer efforts, Mr. Holmes, for our conversation has been delightful. But what prompted ye to go to such lengths?"

Holmes was puffing contentedly on his cigarette and blew a smoke ring toward the ceiling before he spoke. "As Watson has told you, I have invented my profession as a consulting private detective. Whereas many of my cases involve the solving of crimes, my *raison d'être* is the solving of puzzles. Intellectual exercise is what stimulates me and this treasury of your ancestor has piqued my interest. Mind, I am seeking no compensation, the work is its own reward."

He leaned forward and entreated earnestly, "With your permission, I would like to spend tomorrow exploring the grounds and perhaps ride into town to gather more local information. I am sure you have many plans to finalise for your wedding day and this endeavour shall relieve you of any obligation you may feel to entertain my presence."

Alex looked at me and I merely nodded to ensure my friend's sincerity. Pointing at Holmes he replied, "If ye can find Roderick's treasure, I would be in your debt, Mr. Holmes. I'll instruct the groom to have a horse at your disposal, and anything else ye desire, for ye are correct, there are actions yet to take in preparation for Saturday. Watson, as one of the wedding party, will be an asset to me in that regard. But if ye are content to entertain yerself in this fashion I shall be happy to leave ye to it."

"Just what are you planning, Holmes?" I enquired. "Have you a new interpretation of the clues left behind?"

He merely waved his cigarette in an offhand fashion and stated, "I only wish to test a few hypotheses. I also believe there is more to consider than just the document's instructions. If I am wrong, no harm done and I will have at least exercised my brain cells."

"And if ye are right ye wish no reward?" asked Alex. "It hardly seems fair, Mr. Holmes."

"Several days of free room and board in the fresh country air and a chance to work a pretty little puzzle are sufficient for me, sir. Any compensation you would have bestowed, you may keep as a wedding present," replied the detective.

He would say no more on the subject and so the conversation steered toward the upcoming nuptials until dinner was announced.

*****

The next morning I arose around seven, dressed and descended to the kitchen where I was given coffee by the seemingly ever present Mrs. Sheffield. "Your friend is an early riser, Doctor," she said. "He was in here at six, had coffee from the first pot of the day and was off with nary a crumb to eat. I hope he will return in time for breakfast, for I've much to do the next few days and can't be changing my schedule to accommodate everyone's whims."

I assured her that Holmes's eating habits were quite irregular and if he missed breakfast it would certainly not be the first time. "He often goes a full day without a meal when he is hot in pursuit of an intellectual problem. He says digestion takes energy away from the thought process," I said with wink and a smile.

She was mollified by that and returned to preparing breakfast, which she informed me would be served precisely at eight o'clock. I chose to visit Alex's library and peruse a book as I awaited the start of the day's activities.

Soon I was joined by Alex and we spoke of the order of things which would begin with a ride into town to see to the preparations for the wedding feast. After breakfast (for which Holmes did not return), we went to the stables. It was a lovely spring day and we chose to ride instead of taking Alex's coach. The groom informed us that Holmes had taken out a gentle old mare just after six, stating that he would be riding around the immediate area before going on into Gretna Green where he would give the old girl a good feed, water and rest before returning in the afternoon.

Having met with bakers, caterers and the local drum major regarding music the pipers would play during various stages before, during and after the ceremony, we found it was nearly lunchtime and so stopped into a local café.

To our great surprise we found Holmes seated by himself at a table in a far corner and went over to join him. He was in an effusive mood and welcomed us warmly.

We ordered and as we awaited our food our host posed a question to the detective, "Have you had a productive morning, Mr. Holmes, or have ye been content to enjoy our spring weather and a brisk ride?"

Holmes leaned his elbows on the table and steepled his fingers beneath his chin before answering.

"I am happy to answer in the affirmative to both your questions, Mr. Sinclair," he said. "Angelus is a fine animal and well suited to my horsemanship, which has its limits. I was able to examine your estate fairly quickly and have spent some time in your local library and a good hour speaking with the Reverend Duncan."

"I cannot imagine he would have revealed anything to ye, Mr. Holmes," declared Alex. "He was sworn to secrecy and I haven't had time to tell him of yer willingness to help my … (he looked around to be sure we weren't overheard) cause."

"Holmes followed suit with his voice low, "He has kept your confidence, sir. But he was of immense help when I questioned him about the old kirk near the castle. He was able to show me records that go a long way toward confirming my hypothesis."

The waitress brought the food at that point and our conversation ceased until she left. I then asked, "Just what is this hypothesis of yours, Holmes? What did we miss?"

Holmes tucked his napkin into his collar and took up his utensils. The fact that he was about to eat a square meal told me he had reached a breakthrough of some sort, but he merely said, "This is neither the time nor place to discuss the matter, gentlemen. Let me just remind you of one salient fact to ponder until we can return to the privacy of Falgreen. Are either of you aware of the origin of the term 'April Fool'?"

My old comrade shook his head but I said, "Something about a calendar change centuries ago ... Oh my God ! We went looking on the wrong date!"

"Precisely, Doctor," replied my friend. "At the time Roderick's instructions were written, New Year's was celebrated by a weeklong celebration that began on New Year's Day, March the twenty-fifth. After King James aligned the Scottish calendar with the Pope's decree of January the first, people who were unaware of the change and celebrated on April the first were known as April Fools because of their ignorance."

Alex slapped his forehead in frustration, "And March the twenty-fifth was last week, so we have to wait another year to try again! 'Tis I who am the fool!"

Holmes finished the bite of food he had just taken and washed it down with a swallow of the local ale before replying with a smile on his face.

"My dear Sinclair, I should not have waited to tell you this news were that so. There is one other bit of calendar adjustment to take into account. In 1752, by act of parliament, eleven days were omitted from the calendar year in order to make up for all the leap years which had previously been unaccounted for. When you add those eleven days back in to get the day that aligns with New Year's Day of 1542 you get ..."

I attempted to do the calculation in my head but Alex, counting them off on his fingers, was quicker and suddenly exclaimed, "April the fifth ... tomorrow!"

Holmes held up his hand to admonish our host's raised voice and replied, "Indeed, sir. There are some other factors I wish to bring to your attention later, but for now content yourself to know that tomorrow, you will have a second chance at your adventure."

Chapter Seven

The three of us rode back to Falgreen together, Alex and I in anxious anticipation of Holmes's revelations, he as calm as any gentleman out for an afternoon ride. Upon arrival, we retired to the library where Holmes lit up his briar and settled into a wingback chair.

Once brandies were poured all around, Holmes once again took on the role of instructor and explained his thought process. Leaning back in his chair, he gestured with his pipe stem to emphasise his points.

"The first thing we must realise," said he, "is the amount of money we are talking about. Surely to raise an army would require several hundred pounds. There was no paper currency in those times so we are talking about possibly thousands of coins I should think. That will amount to a significant weight, so it would likely be split amongst several containers. That would require a fairly large space. Not really something you would want to bury in the ground and not have readily available should war be declared. No, your ancestor would want someplace he could get to without digging and to be able to store the containers away from the elements."

"So instead of a gravesite, we should have found a vault or mausoleum," I stated.

"Aye, that sounds logical, Johnny," said my old comrade in arms. "But there be no vaults or mausoleums in the cemetery of the old kirk. We've a mausoleum here within the castle walls, Mr. Holmes, but I cannot see how Roderick's instructions could have led us to that."

"They would not," agreed Holmes. "Your instincts were correct in your interpretation as far as it went. But with a new date, and thus a new position of the sun at dawn, there is another area of the old kirk much more suitable to your quest."

"But there be nothing there but the old stone steps and foundation walls. There's no place to hide several containers of coins."

"I believe there is, Mr. Sinclair," said Holmes, with an air of confidence. "At any rate, I should like to propose that we arise with the dawn tomorrow and follow the directions as before. We've nothing to lose but an hour or so worth of work, and certainly much to gain if I'm right."

It was agreed and early the next morning found Holmes and I atop the tower and Alex once again near the old kirk, but this time farther to the south. When the sun reached its appropriate spot I signalled our host with the flags as before and then we rode out to meet him.

The shadow had fallen at the top of the old stone steps on the guide rail nearest the castle. It was nearly a foot thick and smoothly worn by the weather of three centuries. But there were faint engravings all along them. Having backed down the steps as did Isaiah's shadow on the steps of Ahaz, we found ourselves looking at an engraving of St. Andrews cross.

"By God, Holmes " cried Alex, "It couldn't be much clearer that we are on the right track this time."

Holmes had waited down at ground level and pointed at the wall below the guide rail. There, roughly eighteen inches below where we stood, was an ancient bronze ring, once used for tying up a horse of a parishioner, no doubt.

"I believe this ring is your circle, Mr. Sinclair. If we dig out the dirt which has piled up against the side, we may find that turning it halfway will open a passageway."

We all put our backs to digging out the windswept dirt which had been deposited by the sea breezes. When we reached what appeared to be the bottom we set our tools down. Alex looked at each of us hesitantly and then said, "Well, here she goes then."

With both hands he grasped the ring and attempted to turn it. It refused to budge and his face reddened dangerously. I was about to order him to stop when Holmes reached out and placed a hand on his shoulder.

"I anticipated something like this. Wait just a moment." He walked to his horse and retrieved what appeared to be a railway engineer's oil can. Methodically he squirted oil all around the shaft holding the ring, then ran his shovel handle through the ring itself, holding it in place until Alex could grasp it. With the added leverage and the advantage of the oil soaking the ancient joint, the ring slowly began to turn. At the halfway point Alex proclaimed he felt a noticeable movement of some mechanism within. Together the three of us put our weight to what we perceived to be a door and it gave way, slowly at first, then suddenly flung itself wide and the former Lieutenant and I found ourselves on the floor. The sun was bearing in brightly from behind us, but our own shadows made it difficult to see into the corners. Holmes brought forth lanterns from his pannier and soon we found ourselves staring at six large iron chests in a room that was the same ten foot depth that the stairway was wide. The ceiling sloped at the same angle as the stairs and all of us had to stoop once inside. Each chest was bound by a heavy padlock but my friend produced a set of lock picks and soon had them all open.

One was completely empty and another only half full. Obviously, these were meant for more funds to come which never arrived. The other four were filled with brass boxes weighing nearly ten pounds each and each box was filled with ancient Scottish coins.

Alex dipped his hands into one of the boxes and ran his fingers through the gold, silver and copper coins. "Ye found it, Mr. Holmes ! Yer a genius of the first water, by God !"

*****

The question now, of course, became what to do with the money chests? The full ones each contained six of those brass boxes, so that was sixty pounds plus the weight of the chest itself. It would take two men to lift each one without risking serious back injury. Then of course where should we take them? Were they safer right here, or should we remove them to somewhere within the castle walls? Eventually they would have to be appraised to have their value redeemed. Would a bank accept such ancient coinage? Were they more valuable as artefacts than their actual monetary designation? Should a university or museum be contacted? Would the government get involved? Would the Church make a claim?

Having raised so many questions within just the few minutes which the three of us pondered there, Alex finally made a decision. He took one box from the half full chest and loaded it upon his horse. We resealed the chamber and shovelled dirt back along the front. Holmes used his canteen to make up a paste of mud to rub into the crack of the door. He also wiped away the excess oil around the ring and splayed dirt around it to make it appear as if it hadn't been moved.

With everything back to its normal appearance, we returned to Falgreen. Having forgone breakfast, Mrs. Sheffield had to be convinced to provide us with tea and biscuits, with the promise that she would not need to prepare lunch, since we would be in town.

Having taken on sustenance, we changed into more suitable attire and took the coach into Gretna Green. Our first stop was the office of Alex's solicitor where my friend laid out his situation. Next was to the local branch of the Royal Bank of Scotland, where Alex emptied the contents of his brass box into a safety deposit box, keeping out a handful of samples to use to make further inquiries.

Finally, he dropped us at the café for lunch, excusing himself to go and visit his fiancée, Miss Lamont, to tell her the exciting news.

As we enjoyed a robust meal, such as can only be found in small, family-run establishments and never duplicated by the fanciest of restaurants, I thanked Holmes profusely for his assistance to my friend.

"It was simplicity itself, Watson," he replied, waving his fork dismissively. "As soon as you told me the date of the document I knew your friend had dug in the wrong place. Logic, of course, dictated that the money would not be buried, but rather secreted in some hideaway where it was easily accessible."

I nodded, then asked, "But if he wanted easy accessibility, why would Roderick not keep the treasury within the castle walls? Wasn't he taking a risk in secreting them outside his fortifications?"

Holmes shook his head, "It was actually quite brilliant. If the castle were ever overrun by the enemy, forcing him to escape, he could get away quickly. He could then retrieve the money from the kirk for the Scottish army that would be raised to retake the castle."

"I imagine his faith was also a factor," I posed. "He was obviously a religious man and probably felt that God would protect his funds for his righteous cause."

"No doubt," responded Holmes, quaffing his ale. "And for three centuries it has been done. Now, at last, the money will be used for a more peaceful purpose."

I raised my glass in salute and agreed, "Amen to that!"

[Editor's note: Since there is no future reference to Watson becoming wealthy, it is speculated that between government claims and legal fees, Alexander Sinclair was either forced to turn over the funds, or left with so little that Watson's share was insignificant.]

The Case of the
Gunsmith of Sherwood

Chapter One

It was the summer of 1895. A year in which my flat mate, the great detective, Sherlock Holmes, had already been involved in numerous adventures, such as investigating an incident at the College of St. Luke's[1], the rescue of Miss Violet Smith[2] and the recent saving of John Hopley Neligan from the hangman's noose[3].

Holmes's fame was spreading, due in no small part, I must admit in all modesty, to my publication of some of his cases in *The Strand Magazine*. Thus, it was that mail and telegram delivery had increased significantly to 221B Baker Street. As Holmes had held me somewhat responsible for this inundation of often banal and mundane pleas for his assistance, I was not only forbidden from publishing his cases for several years, I was drafted to aid him in sorting through the maelstrom of requests.

These were the conditions which led me to read a telegram from Mrs. George Burton of Mansfield in Nottinghamshire on a muggy morning in late July. It read:

> MR SHERLOCK HOLMES. GUNSMITH HUSBAND MISSING THREE DAYS UPON COMPLETION OF SPECIAL PROJECT FOR CLIENT. BELIEVE FOUL PLAY. POLICE NO USE. YOUR TALENTS NEEDED. PLEASE COME SOONEST.

---

[1] *The Adventure of the Three Students.*
[2] *The Adventure of the Solitary Cyclist.*
[3] *The Adventure of Black Peter.*

I set it aside for Holmes's perusal upon his return. He had gone to Scotland Yard that morning to meet with Inspector Stanley Hopkins over some detail in the case against Patrick Cairns for the murder of Captain Peter Carey in the *Black Peter* case.

Within the hour, I heard his familiar tread upon the stairs. He came through the door with an exasperated look and, instead of greeting me, pronounced, "Watson, you have heard me say that Inspector Hopkins is one of the Yard's most promising young detectives, yes?"

"Indeed, I have, more than once."

"I am seriously considering amending that opinion," he growled as he hung his hat and coat upon the rack by the door rather forcefully. He strode to the sideboard and poured himself a soda water and then sank into his basket chair where he could gaze out at the yellow fog of the city as it was burning off in the rising temperature of late morning.

"What has he done?" I asked.

"You are quite aware he is a fanatical note taker."

"Quite so. He is most methodical in that regard."

Holmes harrumphed "Methodical, perhaps, but far from neat. The man can't even read his own handwriting from notes he made less than a fortnight ago. I was required to assist him in preparing his report against Cairn for the Crown prosecutor. These are not the type of puzzles I was born to solve."

I smiled and reminded him, "As you have often said, as has every inspector from Lestrade to Gregson to Jones, 'paperwork is the bane of police work', which is why you have an advantage as a private consulting detective."

He ceased fuming as he pondered my answer and finally smiled and raised his glass to me. "*Touché*, Watson. But I perceive that you have perhaps something more suitable for the exercise of my brain."

"How? ..." I started to ask, then thought better of it and reached for the telegram I had set aside, realising that he must have noticed its separation from the piles of 'rubbish' vs. 'possibilities' which I usually use in my sorting method.

He read it over quickly and furrowed his brow. "Economical, yet descriptive. Perhaps Hopkins may be of some use to me after all. Would you care to return with me to Scotland Yard and we'll see if the good Inspector can wire his colleagues in Mansfield to enlighten us?"

I answered in the affirmative, glad to get out and stretch my legs, in spite of the summer heat. A short cab ride delivered us to where a surprised Hopkins greeted us warily as we invaded his office.

"What is it, now? Did I forget something else? I've already sent my report off."

Holmes waved his question aside and stated our purpose, "I am considering a case in Mansfield and wish to have you contact the police there to get the facts they have ascertained thus far, before I decide whether or not to involve myself. Do you know anyone there?"

Young Hopkins leaned back in his chair and smiled. "I believe I can make up for disappointing you this morning, Mr. Holmes. I don't need to contact anyone to get the facts, for I already have them, if you are referring to the missing gunsmith."

Holmes raised an eyebrow and gave a slight nod of affirmation while I leaned back against the door frame to take in the scene. Hopkins misinterpreted my movement as a favouring of my old war wound and offered us both seats while he lifted a large envelope from his desk.

"This arrived this morning from a cousin on my mother's side, who happens to be the High Sheriff of the district. He sent it along with some evidence of stains, metal filings and fibrous threads in the hope that our people could identify them. He fears some of them may be blood which would not bode well for Mr. Burton. Since you find my handwriting so cryptic, I would be willing to let you take the report for Dr. Watson to make a copy, so long as I have the original back later today. The results of our laboratory tests will be telegraphed to the Sheriff's office in Nottinghamshire and I can advise my cousin to accept your assistance, should you decide to take the case."

Holmes held out his hand for the envelope, which Hopkins gladly handed over. I, however, could not remain silent about the obvious and spoke up. "Are you saying your cousin is the Sheriff of Nottingham?"

Hopkins sighed and replied, "Yes, Doctor and let me make something very clear to both of you. Any references to Robin Hood will be met with a cold shoulder and a total lack of cooperation on his part. He and his predecessors have worked long and hard to establish a trusted and proficient constabulary, and while the tourist trade welcomes those who come to see where the legend supposedly roamed, the county officials take a dim view of anyone who does not take them or their work seriously."

"So they wouldn't be 'merry men'?" I asked, unable to help myself.

Holmes gave me a warning look. Hopkins pointed his finger and said, "Exactly, Doctor. Please keep remarks like that to yourself if you value any sort of working relationship with them."

We said our goodbyes and returned to Baker Street. Holmes glanced through the papers while we were still in the cab. When we arrived at 221B he immediately walked over to the telegraph office to send his reply stating that we would be coming to investigate, while I took the envelope upstairs and began my task of transcribing the information.

Chapter Two

The gunsmith, Burton was confused and fearful. The man who came to him with a special need seemed to be a godsend at first. Business had been slow lately and the gentleman was willing to pay well for this special modification to his shotgun.

He was a middle-aged man who walked with a pronounced limp. As such, hunting had become difficult for him. Traipsing over rough terrain for hours on end was no longer feasible and so he had come up with an idea. If his shotgun could be modified with a noise suppressor to muffle the sound of the shot, then if he missed he wouldn't have scared the game birds so far away and could get another shot without overtaxing his handicap.

The fellow even had some rough sketches as to how he thought it could be done and Burton began working on a prototype in his machine shop.

It had taken quite a bit of experimentation, but at last he had manufactured a working model. Burton's shop was out on the edge of town so it was easy to take a short walk to a shooting range he had set up for customers to test his wares. His client, who called himself Colonel White, seemed well-pleased with the muzzle attachment which the gunsmith had invented. The shotgun blast was reduced to a muffled 'pop', much like striking a pillow with a club.

The Colonel had paid well for his merchandise and Burton gladly accepted this boon to his bank account. He even began to wonder if this could become a profitable new product for him to manufacture and sell to local hunters.

Less than a week later, however, he was locking up his shop after a slow business day and was accosted by two ruffians who gagged him with some chemical which rendered him unconscious. He woke up chained by his ankle to a wrought iron bedframe in a stone walled room with no windows.

There was a washbasin with a pitcher of water within reach of his chain and he stood slowly and shuffled over to it to splash some water on his face. He still felt groggy after the effects of the fumes he was forced to inhale. Who were those men? What did they want from him? Would they let him go when they were finished with whatever they wanted?

These questions occupied his mind while he sat back down on the edge of the bed holding his head in his hands. A sound at the door brought his hands to his sides, ready to push off the thin mattress, though he wouldn't be able to go far.

To his great surprise, the person entering the room was not one of his assailants, but an attractive woman of about thirty years with medium length loose blonde hair and features of an almost Nordic quality. Her tall figure was that of strength, not the frailty of so many upper class women in this day and age. Broad shoulders and muscular arms narrowed down to a waist that was trim but not encumbered by any corsetry. Instead, she wore a white blouse and a brown skirt that was about mid-calf in length, which may have been split for riding, though he could not be certain because of the folds in it. The riding outfit impression was augmented by the high boots she wore. When he stood to face her he found himself level with blue eyes that bespoke intelligence and determination.

When she spoke it was in perfect English, but he thought he caught a trace of an accent on occasional words, though he could not place it for certain.

"How are you feeling, Mr. Burton? Any nausea or dizziness?" she asked, with what seemed genuine concern.

"Not so much dizzy as a little light-headed," he replied. "Who are you and what do you want from me?"

"You may call me Lady Lydia, if you wish," she replied. "As to your purpose here, we were quite pleased with your work for Colonel White. We would like you to produce several more of these devices for us."

"You could have just asked," he said tersely. "Why kidnap me?"

She tilted her head as if in thought, then replied, "I am afraid the quantity we require would have aroused an unhealthy curiosity on your part. We couldn't risk you going to the authorities with any wild suspicions."

He sat back on the bed, still feeling the effects of the drug. "Who is 'we'?" he asked.

She shook her head slowly. "I'm afraid that answer would put your life at risk, Mr. Burton. If you cooperate you will be returned to your home when you have finished your task. But were you to find out our identity, we would have to take some unfortunate steps to keep you from revealing it to anyone."

He narrowed his eyes at her, then nodded in understanding. "How long will you need me?"

"Long enough to produce fifty of these muzzle suppressors for various rifles, shotguns and pistols. That should be sufficient for us."

"Sounds like you're outfitting an army," he stated.

She folded her arms and pierced him with a warning look. "Do not speculate on us or our purpose, Mr. Burton. Your life depends on your ignorance."

He nodded in silence and she continued, "We have telegraphed your wife, saying you were called away on a family emergency to your brother's in Brighton. Our people will intercept any reply she makes and keep her in the dark as to your return.

"We have set up a machine shop in this building where you will be taken under guard each day to perform your tasks. Obviously, the sooner you finish, the sooner you will be freed. But do not forfeit quality for speed. Each of your pieces will be fully inspected and tested until we are satisfied. Understood?"

"Understood," he acquiesced, then asked, "Is there any chance I could get some food? I don't know how long I was unconscious, but I'm famished."

The Viking-like woman flashed a disarmingly pleasant smile and nodded, "I will see that a meal is brought into you shortly. We have no desire to compromise your health."

She turned and left the room leaving the poor gunsmith to ponder his situation.

Chapter Three

Having dispatched Hopkins's original report back to the Yard, Holmes and I caught the one-thirty train from St. Pancras and arrived at Mansfield station some three hours later. We were met by a deputy sheriff, who identified himself as Jeremy Forsythe, in response to one of the telegrams Holmes had sent. He escorted us to the Friar Tuck Inn where we were given adjoining rooms.

We quickly unpacked and Forsythe joined us in a cab ride to see Mrs. Burton. We soon found ourselves at a modest two storey brick house on Crow Hill Drive shaded by elm trees and bordered by green hedges.

Mrs. Burton was a stout lady about five feet and four inches in height, with brown hair done up in braided buns on either side of her round face. I judged her age to be about forty. She wore a simple dress of slate blue with dark blue trim at the cuffs, collar, waist and hem.

"Thank you so much for coming, Mr. Holmes and you too, Dr. Watson," she declared. She invited us all to sit around her dining table, where a photograph of her and her husband lay, tear-stained and covered in fingerprints.

Holmes picked up the photograph, perused it and showed it to me, "Your telegram said your husband had completed a special project for a recent client. Are you aware of the nature of his work?"

"He told me the fellow's name was Colonel White and that he had a game leg. He wanted some sort of device to muffle the noise of his shotgun so he wouldn't scare his prey so far away and have to limp after them."

Holmes looked at Forsythe, who was a young man of military bearing and asked, "Were you aware of this?"

"Sheriff Denison took the initial report, I'm sure it's in the notes he sent to the Yard."

I spoke up, having copied that report, "White's name is noted but there is no mention of any such device."

"An unforgiveable omission," Holmes growled. Then he turned back to the distressed wife. "The sheriff's report indicated that you received a telegram from your husband saying he had gone to Brighton. May I see it?" asked the detective.

"Of course, Mr. Holmes, I have it here," she replied, reaching into a pocket of her dress. "I anticipated that you would like to examine it. It's sure proof that my husband was taken away against his will."

Holmes held it up and read it briefly, then set it down where I could see it. It read simply:

> EMERGENCY IN BRIGHTON. GONE TO WILLIAM. WILL WRITE SOON. GEORGE.

"I see it was sent from the railway station," observed my friend. "It seems unusual that he would not come home to pack a bag first. What other facts can you provide?"

"Three, to be precise. One, he and his brother don't get along and haven't spoken in years. Two, he never calls his brother William, it's always Bill. Finally he wouldn't sign it George, he'd sign Geordi. It's a nickname he picked up in his school days because there were so many Georges in his form, so he combined his first name and middle initial."

"I can add one more reason," interjected Forsythe. "The express train to Brighton leaves in the morning. It would have been better for him to wait overnight than to have to go through the several stopovers and changes he would have to make by taking the night train to London, which is the only one that leaves near the hour he disappeared."

"Did you attempt to contact his brother in Brighton?" enquired Holmes of our hostess.

"I sent a telegram the very next morning when the office opened and have received this sham reply," she answered, pulling out another form and handing it over. This one explained that William was in hospital, having suffered a severe heart attack and that George was going to stay on and get the family affairs in order for William's wife to carry on in his absence.

"This is obviously another forgery, Mr. Holmes. It still refers to William instead of Bill and calls his wife Elizabeth when she goes by Betty. Also, Bill is much younger than Geordi. Only in his late-twenties. A heart attack is highly unlikely, I should think."

I spoke up in agreement, "It's not impossible but you're right, the odds are against it. Did you contact the police in Brighton to check out this story?"

This last point I addressed to Forsythe and Holmes nodded in approval at my question.

Forsythe hesitated and finally admitted, "We did so this morning, Doctor. There's been no reply that I'm aware of, though we could have heard back since I came to meet you at the station."

Mrs. Burton slapped the table and declared forcefully, "Do you see what I have to put up with, Mr. Holmes? Nobody took me seriously until they found out I had requested your help."

Forsythe flushed, whether embarrassed or indignant I could not discern, but his words were defensive. "There was no evidence of foul play and men have been known to leave their wives without notice, if you'll forgive my saying so."

"Highly unlikely in this case," said Holmes, holding up his hand to stop the tirade about to erupt from Mrs. Burton. "I believe our next step should be to examine the shop where he was last seen. If you will excuse us, Mrs. Burton, I promise that I will keep you apprised of any progress we make."

As we stood to go the lady reached out and took both of Holmes's hands in hers and implored him, "Please, Mr. Holmes, I know he's alive. I can feel it. Please bring him back to me!"

Holmes patting her hands replied, "I shall summon all the powers at my command, madam. Be strong."

Our next stop was the gunsmith's shop. Forsythe took us around to the back door and showed us where the items sent to Scotland Yard had been found.

"It is our opinion, Mr. Holmes," said Forsythe, "that Burton was overcome as he was locking up his shop for the day. They probably came in the front door pretending to be customers and took him by surprise. Their confrontation led back here and it is quite likely that they knocked him out and carried him off, out of sight of the main street. He must have put up a struggle for a time, as these stains on the doorframe appear to be blood. The fibres we found were caught on this splintered section down here and the metal filings were on the step."

"If you suspected foul play, why not advise Mrs. Burton?" I asked.

Forsythe folded his arms across his chest and looked down, "That was an unfortunate miscommunication by one of our junior officers, who has been reprimanded, I assure you. But once that tack was taken, we felt it would offer her more hope than to tell her that her husband had been kidnapped and was injured in the process."

"Is the Sheriff aware of this subterfuge?" my friend asked, incredulously.

"Er, ... no, we had hoped to spare him the embarrassment as the investigation is running along proper lines now."

Holmes shook his head as he took in all this information. Then he pulled his lens from his pocket. Forsythe opened the door with a key provided by Mrs. Burton. The detective made a thorough examination of the doorway. Upon completion we stepped inside the shop's back room where there were various machines and spare parts unique to the gunsmith trade.

Holmes made a extensive search of the premises. He found a drawer with sketches of engravings which Burton had apparently applied to certain weapons. There was also a drawer which was in disarray, filled with bespoke weapon designs made to fit specific measurements as to stock length or trigger placement, including some left-handed customised work. What was missing was any sign of the noise suppression device he had recently built.

"Our kidnappers also stole his designs," he observed. "There is only one rough preliminary sketch on the corner of a separate section of notes for another device, which they missed. Otherwise there would be no evidence to even indicate he was working on such an invention. But this," he said, holding up the sketch in question, "corroborates Mrs. Burton's report and implicates this Colonel White."

"You are looking for at least three men, Forsythe. This Colonel with the game leg and two henchmen, one of whom is approximately six feet tall, wears hunting boots and was wearing a red wool shirt and blue woollen trousers at the time of the abduction. The other is smaller, about five foot six and wears gentlemen's boots with an unusual wearing down of the outside of the right heel."

"Couldn't that be this Colonel White?" asked the Deputy.

"No, the footstep pattern in the floor does not indicate a limp. It's more likely a bow-legged, or duck-footed fellow."

"Very well," answered the young man, "I'll add that description to our lookout bulletin. If you're finished here, Mr. Holmes we should report to the Sheriff. He may have answers from Scotland Yard or the Brighton police by now."

Holmes was amenable to this suggestion and we soon found ourselves seated in the office of William Denison, formerly an army captain and member of the House of Commons, who now sat as the High Sheriff of Nottinghamshire.

Denison was a fit man in his early forties who still retained his military bearing. With a square jaw, full moustache and a commanding presence, even though under six feet in height. He welcomed us with an attitude I found refreshing. Often the police would resent the presence of my friend, whom they considered an interfering amateur. Denison, however, exhibited an eagerness for Holmes's assistance.

"My cousin, Stan, speaks highly of you, Mr. Holmes," he began as we sat. "As you know the office of High Sheriff has much more to deal with than simply criminal activity. I was chosen for my political acumen and experience. The deep waters of more intricate crimes is not a common occurrence in this district and I welcome your help to find Mr. Burton."

Holmes nodded in acknowledgement, "Yet, you were astute enough to gather evidence and involve Scotland Yard's laboratories. Have you received their results?"

He handed over a long telegram. "This came in not half an hour ago. They confirmed bloodstains, metal filings of aluminium, and fibres of wool, dyed dark blue."

"I surmised as much from my examination," replied Holmes, a bit impatiently, tossing the form onto the desk. "What of your cohorts in Brighton?"

"I had them make discreet inquiries and they assure me that all is well in the household of William Burton. No illnesses, nor apparent disruptions of any kind."

Holmes leaned back, steepled his fingers under his chin and stared at the ceiling for several moments. This attitude of disengagement is a common occurrence, but for the uninitiated it can be most unsettling. Denison looked at me after the silence stretched on and I merely held up my hand and mouthed the word 'wait'.

Finally, Holmes addressed us once again. "I've given Forsythe a description of two of the men you should be looking for. I think the other option we must put into play will depend upon the cooperation of Mrs. Burton. Watson," he turned to me and requested, "I will need you to escort the lady discreetly to Brighton."

"But there's nothing wrong in Brighton," Denison reminded us.

"Which is precisely why she must go there," answered London's finest detective.

Chapter Four

Geordi Burton's days had fallen into a dull routine. He was awoken, fed a stimulating breakfast, put to work in the makeshift machine shop his captors had set up, given a meal break for lunch and continued his work until the high windows in the shop no longer reflected any sunlight. Then back to what he thought of as his cell, for a decent supper and sleep. No one spoke to him except to answer his requests for tools or materials. What little speech he heard from the men divulged a European inflection of some sort. It was neither German nor French, which were the only foreign accents he'd been exposed to in his life. He had finished producing several suppressors for shotguns, which were relatively easy since he had already built a working model. Now he was having to take some extra time to refine his design for a specific rifle. The manufacturer's name had been removed, but it appeared to be a version of an 1893 bolt action German Mauser, though it was a good foot shorter in length than any he'd seen in the catalogues he remembered.

Lady Lydia occasionally brought his meal herself. He knew better than to ask any probing questions, but he did enquire about his wife.

"Mrs. Burton is quite well," she replied. "She did send a telegram to your brother which we intercepted and responded that William was in the hospital and you were staying on to help Elizabeth with her affairs for the time being."

Hearing the names William and Elizabeth instead of Bill and Betty gave a small glimmer of hope to the gunsmith. He knew his wife would find those odd in any telegram purportedly from him. Whether or not she could convince the authorities to look into it was another matter, though she was a formidable woman.

But the more he thought about it, the more he feared that police interference could put him in danger. As things stood, he believed they would let him go when his task was completed. He was certain they were foreigners and would simply leave him behind with no knowledge of where they were going. However, if the police tracked him to this locale he could be caught in a crossfire, or his captors may kill him as they escaped, so he could not identify them before they got out of the country.

It was just another stress and did nothing to help his fitful sleep.

Chapter Five

Holmes dispatched a messenger to Mrs. Burton with very specific instructions. She was to pack a bag and come to the railway station and purchase a ticket for Brighton the next morning. At least two hours before departure, she would send a telegram to the Burton home in Brighton, advising them that she was on her way. When she boarded the train she would seek out the compartment where I would already be waiting and join me, though not acknowledging that we already knew each other. Upon arrival in Brighton I was to help with her luggage, to find a cab and see her safely boarded. I was then to follow discreetly in a second cab and disembark in time to guard over her from a distance when she arrived at her in-laws' door.

"Keep watch over her, Watson. I suspect she will be accosted at some point. Use your revolver if necessary, but do try to take at least one of her assailants alive and get him to Brighton police station."

"Where will you be, Holmes?" I enquired.

"I have another tactic to try, but I shall join you in Brighton in good time," he answered.

"Wait, Mr. Holmes," piped up Denison. "What makes you so sure that Mr. Burton is still alive? Perhaps their purpose was to silence him for good."

Holmes shook his head, "There was no need to leave the shop to do that. They could have killed him right then and there. No, they needed him for some purpose. Let's just hope that purpose takes some time for him to fulfil. I suggest that you have your men be on the lookout for the assailants I described. If they are still in the area, they will need to buy food and possibly other supplies. You should also search the outlying areas for any old buildings or abandoned farmhouses. Any place where a small group could hide out."

Denison took Holmes's suggestions to heart and told Forsythe to ensure that all officers were on the lookout for the men in question. Holmes and I took our leave with a promise to keep the High Sheriff informed of any progress.

Back at the Friar Tuck Inn, we engaged a quiet table in the dining room and ordered up a splendid meal. I questioned Holmes as to what he thought the kidnappers's purpose might be.

"There are a variety of possibilities, Watson. However, working on the principle that coincidence is a rare commodity, it seems probable that this action is related to the creation of the muzzle suppressor for Colonel White."

"That much seems certain, especially since they stole the drawings as well."

"Precisely. Now, what criminal purpose could this silenced shotgun be used for?"

I washed down a mouthful of boiled potato with a swallow of bitter as I thought this out. "I suppose the most obvious would be to kill someone as quietly and surely as possible so that escape is more easily made. If not murder, then the only other purpose I see for a shotgun would be to blast something open, such as a lock on a door or a strongbox."

"There are several other possibilities," replied my friend. "But let us also consider this; now that this Colonel White has the device, why kidnap the gunsmith?"

I thought about that for a moment and replied, "Perhaps he just didn't want Burton to make any more and kidnapped him and stole the documents so he could file the patent himself."

"Rather drastic, Doctor," replied the detective. "He could have broken in and stolen the drawings and filed the patent himself in London without resorting to kidnapping. No, it's more likely that he wanted Burton to make more of them and in a hurry, to the exclusion of all his other work."

"Why would he want more of them?" I asked.

"Since we've identified at least two other cohorts, I would say he is outfitting a criminal gang or possibly a radical political group, bent on violent tactics."

"An army of silent killers?" I speculated, horrified by the thought.

"It's too soon to test any theories without more data, Watson. Which is why I'm hoping you can capture one of their gang alive tomorrow."

*****

The next morning I arrived at the railway station early. Holmes had already left to pursue his own line of investigation before I awoke so I followed his instructions from the previous day. I engaged a compartment and as I boarded I noted the passengers close by. On one side, there was a group of ladies talking excitedly about what I imagined to be a shopping spree in London. On the other, an old bald sailor with a grey beard had lain across the seat, using his duffel bag as a pillow and sleeping off whatever the previous night had wrought for him.

I carried only my medical bag, having left the rest of my luggage at the inn. I had bought a morning paper at the railway newsstand and proceeded to occupy myself with its contents as I awaited our departure. A few minutes passed and then, in the doorway of the compartment, Mrs. Burton arrived. Playing her part as instructed, she asked me to verify her ticket and compartment number as though we were perfect strangers, in case she was being followed. I stood and examined her ticket, confirming her seat and inviting her to join me. I introduced myself as Dr. Hamish[1], a physician *en route* to visit a colleague in Brighton.

---

[1] Generally accepted as Dr. John H. Watson's middle name.

In keeping with our roles, we chatted amiably, as strangers sharing a train compartment are wont to do. Other passengers boarded and walked by us with nary a glance, except to check the compartment number. Eventually, the train departed on schedule and soon we were bustling through the countryside bound for the seaside town of Brighton on the south coast. The two hundred mile journey would take just over four hours with a change of train in London.

As time passed we eventually turned to our own thoughts. She to a book she had brought along and I back to my newspaper where I read an interesting article about a ladies rifle competition in Browndown.

When we pulled into St. Pancras Station from where we would need to continue our journey via Victoria Station, I stood to fetch my bag. I opened the compartment door and noted that the adjoining compartment doors were already opened. Out of curiosity I stepped over and noted that the lady shoppers had disembarked and their compartment was empty. When I turned back I saw two gentlemen in linen summer suits approaching, checking each compartment as they did so. I quickly moved back to Mrs. Burton, arriving at the same time as these strangers.

One of them addressed the lady, pulling out a business card and identifying himself as 'Inspector Crandall of Scotland Yard'. "Are you Mrs. George Burton?" he asked.

My companion answered in the affirmative and he continued, "You need to come with us, madam, we have found your husband and need to take you to him."

She jumped up in excitement and cried, "You found Geordi? Where is he? Take me to him, please!"

As I was standing in the corridor, one of the officers was blocking my way as the other reached out to take Mrs. Burton's arm. When they turned to walk away from me, I debated whether to identify myself, or simply follow them. My decision was soon made for me when their path was suddenly blocked by the ne'er do well sailor emerging unsteadily from the next compartment, his duffel bag slung across his body in such a way as to make passage impossible.

"Get out of the way, fool!" cried the one doing all the talking. The old sailor looked him up and down in a glassy-eyed fashion. The second officer, who was standing between me and this confrontation, pulled out a truncheon from his back pocket and in that instant I knew something was wrong. I reached into my pocket for my Webley revolver and just as I pulled it free the sailor slammed his duffel bag into the first inspector and pushed Mrs. Burton back into the compartment. As he did so, I heard a familiar voice cry out, "They're imposters, Watson! Stop them!"

As the fellow in front of me raised his weapon to strike at the sailor, I grabbed his wrist with my left hand, pulling him backward and off balance while I stuck the muzzle of my pistol under his chin.

"Drop it, now!" I commanded, as I cocked my gun to emphasise the point.

He did so just as the sailor, which I could now see was Holmes in disguise, landed a blow to the jaw of the other fellow, knocking him cold to the floor.

Two railway officials came along and assisted us in taking these fellows to an office in the station where we awaited the police. Holmes, now without the bald cap and whiskers, sat on the corner of a desk while I stood guard at the door, gun still in hand. Holmes had handcuffed the two culprits together and they sat side by side on a small settee. Mrs. Burton was seated in an upholstered chair behind the desk.

I asked the detective the obvious question, "How did you know they were imposters, Holmes?"

"Elementary, Doctor," he replied. "I may not have worked with all the inspectors at the Yard, but I do know all their names and Crandall isn't one of them. Also, their shoes are not standard issue for policemen, the big, silent fellow is wearing a suit that's too tight and Scotland Yard inspectors always show a warrant card for identification when introducing themselves on official business, not a mere business card."

I looked over at the man whom I had disarmed and saw that Holmes was right. His suit was too small for him and he was wearing military style boots.

Crandall mumbled something to his compatriot in a voice too low for me to hear, but it had the sound of a foreign tongue. The big man merely nodded and sat back in a defiant silence.

It wasn't long before Inspector Hopkins arrived with three burly constables in tow and a Black Maria to transport our prisoners. Using a second set of handcuffs, Hopkins detached the truncheon wielder from Crandall. It was soon apparent that he did not speak English, or at least he refused to acknowledge it. The constables readily made their intent known however, and he was handcuffed and loaded into the police vehicle.

This left us alone with Crandall. Hopkins went through his pockets and came up with a wallet with some paper money but no identification papers. Turning out his pockets yielded a handful of coins which Holmes examined briefly. One stood out among the English shillings and sovereigns.

"A twenty kroner gold piece," said Holmes, holding it to the light of the window. "You are Danish?"

Our prisoner shook his head, though a shadow of fear momentarily crossed his face. "Must have got it in change when I bought breakfast this morning," he said with false bravado.

Holmes flipped the coin to Hopkins and folded his arms across his chest, staring intently at the man. He then stepped over and pulled the back of his coat and shirt collar away from his neck.

Crandall tried to pull away but had nowhere to go. Holmes then grabbed his wrist and turned his palm up. Finally letting go and stepping back he declared, "The coat is English but the shirt is made in Denmark. His hands bear all the marks of a fisherman, though he is better educated so likely owns a fishing business. Perhaps on one of the islands off the coast? Romo or Sylt?"

At the word 'island' Crandall stiffened, but eased off when Holmes mentioned Romo and Sylt. The reaction did not go unnoticed by the detective.

"Now what island would produce a man willing to kidnap a gunsmith?"

Suddenly Mrs. Burton slapped the table, stood and shouted, "Enough guessing games. He knows where my husband is. Force it out of him. Make him tell us!"

She charged at the man in a fury and I rushed to try and stop her, joined by Holmes and Hopkins. Seizing this desperate chance, Crandall leaped forward and tried to pry the gun from my hand. Having his hands cuffed in front of him gave him a fool's courage that proved his undoing. During the struggle my finger tightened on the trigger, the Webley went off and he fell to the floor, deeply wounded.

I handed the gun to Hopkins and attempted to staunch the flow of blood from Crandall's abdomen. I looked up at Holmes and shook my head to let him know that the wound was a mortal one.

My friend knelt next to the man and took one of his manacled hands in his own while supporting the wounded prisoner's head with the other. "It's not good, man. At least tell us your name and where you're from so we can arrange to get you back home where your people can bury you."

The man was shaking from shock and crying in pain, "Johan ... Johan Carlsen. Heligoland. Please, don't stop us. Burton will be returned ... unharmed. Our freedom ..." His eyes shut from the effort to speak.

"Where is he?" cried Mrs. Burton.

Delirious from blood loss and groaning as he tried to catch his breath, Carlsen gasped out one last word, "Sherwood ..." and died.

Chapter Six

Something was wrong. Burton could feel a change in the mood of his captors. The day had started out the same as every other day of his captivity. Having completed the suppressors for the shotguns, he had now finished producing twelve such devices for the rifles. Around mid-morning he was interrupted by Lady Lydia.

"We've a change in plans, Mr. Burton. We need you to switch your focus to designing your device for this weapon immediately."

She held out a revolver to him. This time, no one had made any effort to remove the manufacturer's markings and it was clearly a Russian weapon. A double action gun with a seven round chamber and a four and one half inch barrel. The name Nagant was etched into the chromed steel.

Burton took hold of it and examined the barrel. The front post of the sight extended backward to where there was only one inch between it and the front of the ejection rod beneath the barrel.

"This clearance doesn't leave much room," he informed her. "I can work around the sight as I did with the other guns, but with only about an inch of useful surface and such a small weapon, it will be terribly front heavy and hard to balance."

"I understand," she replied, "and just to make it a little more challenging for you, the suppressor must be something that can be fastened and unfastened quickly."

Burton let out a low whistle. "You are a challenging employer, Lady Lydia. If circumstances were different, I could enjoy working for you. But since I have no choice I'll get to work on it and see what I can come up with."

His captor smiled and replied, "Quickly, if you please, Mr. Burton. Your days with us may be coming to an end sooner than we planned."

"Why, what's happened?"

"Certain persons are taking an unhealthy interest in your disappearance. We wish no harm to any innocent bystanders, but we will not be deterred from our cause."

Burton shook his head, "I know better than to ask what your cause is, Lady Lydia. But I have a feeling that I might be sympathetic if I knew."

She placed a hand on his forearm and nodded, "I would hope so, Mr. Burton. But I cannot take the chance that you would reveal our plans. I can only ask that you trust that we mean no harm to England or any of her subjects."

She left him to his work and he took the gun back to his makeshift desk to see how he could overcome the design challenge she had laid upon him. All the while he was wondering just who it was that was looking for him. She had said 'certain persons', not his wife. This made him pause. Was it a good sign or could it spell disaster?

Chapter Seven

With Carlsen dead only his cohort could answer the questions we still had regarding Burton and his abductors. English still wasn't working on the man and we all drove back to Scotland Yard where interpreters were more readily available.

This time we left Mrs. Burton in the care of a police officer while we placed our prisoner in a secure room. Based on the information we had gleaned from Carlsen, Hopkins sent for an interpreter. About a half hour later, a gentleman arrived named Franz Vestergaard, who spoke most of the languages of northern Europe and worked at a nearby embassy. He seemed a rather meek fellow, extremely thin and likely about thirty-five years of age, fair with thinning light brown hair. He sat across from our prisoner with Hopkins next to him. Holmes stood behind Vestergaard and fed him questions. I took position at the far end of the table making notes. The big fellow sat silently, determined to ignore his captors. Holmes chose to open the interrogation by loudly requesting Vestergaard, "Tell him Carlsen is dead."

Unprepared for that statement, the prisoner could not hide his reaction, but he attempted to recover his poise by asking a question.

"Hvad sagde han?"

Vestergaard spoke, "Well, we know he speaks Danish. He just asked 'What did he say?'"

Before he could tell the man what Holmes said, the detective spoke up, "We know more than that. His reaction tells me he knows at least some English." He leaned over the table and stared at the man, "You heard me. Carlsen is dead. We know he was from the island of Heligoland. Now, my good man, what is your name?"

He looked down to his right at the table top and balled his fists. Holmes stood back up straight, ready for any violent reaction. Finally he opened his fists, closed his eyes and took a deep breath before rattling off some phrase to Vestergaard.

The interpreter translated for us, "My name is Peter Olsen. I also am from Heligoland. I speak very little English. I will not betray our cause."

"What cause?" asked Hopkins.

Holmes held up his hand before Vestergaard could translate that and said instead, "We are not concerned about your cause. We only want the return of the gunsmith Burton to his wife."

Vestergaard went into a long monologue that seemed to take an inordinate amount of time. Finally through the translator, Olsen replied, "The gunsmith is safe as long he doesn't try to escape. We only need to borrow his talents for a short while."

Again Hopkins tried to interject, "Why? What is he doing for you?"

"Inspector, please," said Holmes, "Let us dispense with the obvious. We know they need him to design and possibly manufacture noise suppressors for weapons. The *why* is not our current concern." Turning to Vestergaard he said, "Tell him we already know why they needed the gunsmith. Tell him we want the man back and are willing to trade him for Burton."

Hopkins stood and grabbed Holmes by the arm, pulling him back by the door and whispering harshly, "What are you doing? You know I can't trade a prisoner without the superintendent's authorisation."

I joined the conversation to hear what was going on just as Holmes replied, "Are you aware of the situation in Heligoland, Inspector?"

"I've never heard of the place," replied young Hopkins. "Where is it?"

"It's an island off the western coast of Germany, southwest of Denmark. It came under British control by the Treaty of Paris at the end of the Napoleonic Wars. Five years ago, the Queen traded it to her grandson, Kaiser Wilhelm II, so he could command the western entrance to the militarily important Kiel Canal, and other German naval installations in the area. In return England got the German controlled territory of Zanzibar in Africa."

Hopkins shook his head, "What does any of this have to do with Burton?"

Holmes sighed at the inspector's lack of comprehension. "The fact that we now have two men admitting they are from Heligoland and both have mentioned a 'cause' or 'freedom'. I believe it is safe to assume we have come across a faction that is rebelling against their homeland being used as a pawn in European affairs without their consent."

I asked, "But why the noise suppressors? One can hardly expect to fight a battle without being heard."

"Likely as not," agreed my friend, "but it would give them a distinct advantage were they to engage in a sneak attack upon the local garrison. Or they may have other objectives in mind. But this is not our concern. We have been engaged to rescue Burton and that must be our first priority over foreign politics."

"I still can't sanction a hostage exchange," the Scotland Yarder reminded us.

Holmes drew us both out the door into the hall beyond Olsen's hearing and explained his plan. Once he understood, Hopkins readily agreed and we rejoined our prisoner.

Vestergaard translated Holmes's proposal and Olsen looked sceptically at Hopkins who assured him that we had obtained the Superintendent's permission while we were out of the room.

"Mrs. Burton has also agreed to not press charges for attempting to kidnap her, if you will agree to be traded for her husband," he added. "All you need to do is tell us how to get hold of your leader so we can propose the exchange. Otherwise you are looking at a minimum sentence of five years hard labour, possibly in Australia."

The interpreter explained these options to Olsen, who listened intently and grew wide-eyed at the thought of being shipped off to Australia. He spoke rapidly with broad hand gestures indicating his agitation.

Vestergaard relayed his message: "I am ready to die for my homeland, but I will not be exiled to the other side of the world where my family cannot even visit me. I do not know where the gunsmith is being held, only Carlsen knew that, but I know where to telegraph our leader."

Holmes nodded and dictated a telegram for the translator to write down so that Olsen could see our proposal in his own language.

Carlsen dead, Mrs. Burton in protective custody. I am being held at Scotland Yard. Police willing to trade me for gunsmith at time and place of your choosing within 48 hours. Otherwise I will be tried and sent to Australia penal colony. For the sake of my family please agree. - Peter Olsen.

Olsen read the document and looked at Holmes and the Inspector before speaking in heavily accented broken English, "You give word of honour?"

Holmes answered, "I promise you, Mr. Olsen, if your leader agrees to this exchange you will be reunited with your people, and not sent to Australia. We just need you to write down where to send the telegram."

Olsen nodded solemnly, took the pencil from Vestergaard, wrote an address on the paper and handed it to Hopkins. The Inspector read it with a frown and showed it to Holmes who merely smiled and said, "I suggest you pack a bag, Inspector, and wire your cousin that you're coming up for a visit with a temporary occupant for his gaol."

Chapter Eight

The afternoon train found the five of us bound for Mansfield. Olsen was manacled hands and feet and sat between Hopkins and Vestergaard on one side of the compartment, while Holmes and I sat across from them. We had sent the telegram to Sheriff Denison and implied to our prisoner that we had also sent one to his leader as well. In reality Holmes had a plan to set in motion using that telegram as bait and it would not be dispatched until we were on the scene in Mansfield.

Arriving just after seven o'clock, Forsythe was waiting for us with a police van and we went directly to the police station to deposit our guest. We left Hopkins to visit his cousin and Vestergaard standing by, as needed, at the station.

Holmes and I then proceeded to the telegraph station at the main post office. We carried a note with us from Denison, advising the official to cooperate with us and found the gentleman on duty, Harris by name, quite willing to help. Holmes explained our need and dictated the telegram.

Harris looked at the name as he entered the wording on the form advising us, "We don't deliver post or telegrams to 'Fr. Wyt'. There's a boy who comes by a couple times a day to pick them up. In fact, he should be along any minute now."

Holmes's interest piqued at that, "You don't know where this 'Fr. Wyt' lives?"

"No, Mr. Holmes. The arrangements were made by my colleague, Mr. Brown. He may know, but I've only been told that the boy has permission to pick up the Wyt post."

Holmes reacted to this news quickly. He devised a signal for Harris to give us through the window when the boy came in. We would be waiting across the street and would surreptitiously follow the boy to the leader's lair.

Fortunately, there was a public house directly across from the post office, so that two gentlemen hanging about outside would not arouse suspicion. We stood by, smoking and conversing in a natural sort of way, but our conversation was anything but mundane.

"It seems fairly obvious that this Wyt must be the Colonel White who approached Burton in the first place," I stated with confidence.

"A distinct possibility," Holmes admitted. "The Father designation is interesting, and how often have I reminded you that nothing can be more deceptive than an obvious fact? This Wyt could be another family member, or someone totally unrelated. It may even be a code word from our friend, Olsen, advising his cohorts to flee for their lives, though I doubt he is that clever. No, Watson, we'll not concede this identity to the Colonel just yet. We must remain open-minded."

I had just finished my second cigarette when Holmes pointed at a reflection in the pub window. It gave us a clear view of the post office entrance without turning around and we saw that a young boy of about twelve years was entering.

"Watson, you go across the street and enter the post office as if you were a customer. When the boy leaves wait a few seconds then follow discreetly. I will watch from this side of the street. Keep at least one hundred feet back and never look directly at him. If he turns around or stops just keep walking past him, stop at the next corner and pull your notebook from your pocket as if you were checking for an address."

I did as my friend asked. Just as I was entering the building, Harris was pulling up the blind of the window, his signal to Holmes that this was indeed our quarry. The boy was about twelve years of age, thin with curly blond hair and blue eyes, which I noted when he turned to leave telegram in hand. He was dressed neatly in corduroy trousers and a red plaid shirt.

I stepped up to the clerk and asked if there were any telegrams for Dr. Hamish, just to add authenticity to my presence in case the lad could still hear us. I had noted he turned to the right when he left the building and after about ten seconds I followed suit. I saw that Holmes was casually walking in the same direction on the other side of the street. When the boy was away from the building he stopped to read the telegram.

Suddenly he looked around in alarm and broke into a run. His concentration was such that I didn't feel the need to remain hidden as he was unlikely to look behind him. We hadn't proceeded more than a hundred yards when a hansom pulled up next to me, and Holmes cried, "Get in !"

He instructed the cabby to maintain a pace that would keep up with the boy and soon we saw him turn into a side street and run through the door of a cottage. We had our driver pull over a few houses beyond and waited.

*****

Lady Lydia was anxious for news from London. It was imperative that Mrs. Burton be intercepted. She feared that something had gone wrong and the woman had been missed. Her only hope this late in the day was that her men had caught up to the gunsmith's wife in Brighton before she learned the truth and raised the alarm. She had expected a telegram from London that afternoon. When it failed to arrive her concern increased. Having come this far in the first step of their plans, a setback would hamper them significantly, but getting caught would be disastrous and, with no assurance from her men in London, she sent word that everything must be packed and ready to go at a moment's notice. Escape routes had already been mapped out and a ship was standing by, but she had hoped they would have another week so that Burton could finish his work.

Her own bag was packed, a carpet bag with just the essentials. Most of the her things would be left behind.

Nephew, Freddy, had been invaluable to her. As a mere boy he could go anywhere virtually unnoticed and he was smart as a whip. She only hoped he would return soon with good news.

*****

Freddy thought hard as he ran. He did not know all of his aunt's plans. He just knew that she was part of a group fighting for their freedom from Germany. The wording of the telegram he had retrieved for her indicated that something had gone wrong. He knew she would need to be informed at once, but something nagged at his brain. She had taught him to be observant of his surroundings and when he stopped to wait for traffic at an intersection and catch his breath, he realised what it was. The gentleman who had come into the post office behind him was one of those he had noticed in front of the ale house. Why did he wait until that particular moment to come across the street and check on his mail?

He took a moment to kneel and retie his shoelaces, looking behind him and seeing that same man enter a hansom cab. When the traffic cleared he resumed his run at a less frenetic pace, thinking and planning his best options. Finally, he had an idea and turned down a street and into a modest cottage to put it into action.

*****

Holmes and I watched the cottage, waiting to see who would exit. After a minute we saw some movement at one of the windows and could catch occasional glimpses of the boy's red shirt. After several minutes of waiting, Holmes grew impatient. "Our telegram should have produced more immediate results," he observed. "Either a reply or, more likely, flight, for I imagine Olsen would be considered a sacrificial pawn. I believe it's time for a confrontation."

"Do you think that wise, Holmes?" I queried. "We are sure to be outnumbered."

"I do not propose we confront them on that issue, Watson, and this is hardly the location where they are holding Burton, so I don't believe we will encounter any great number. I merely wish to gain access to reconnoitre the situation. Come along and follow my lead."

We paid the cab driver to wait for us and approached the cottage. Holmes knocked with the head of his cane and the door was answered by gentleman in a suit, sans coat and tie, apparently some sort of office worker.

"Yes, gentlemen, may I be of assistance?"

"I do hope so, sir," replied Holmes in his most disarming manner. "We are looking for a boy in a red plaid shirt who just picked up some mail at the post office. The clerk believes he may have taken some of our mail by mistake, and we are expecting a very important document."

The man shook his head in doubt, "The only boy here is my son, Tom and he's been here all afternoon."

"I see," said Holmes, feigning perplexity. "I wonder if I might speak to him?"

The gentleman shrugged his shoulders, invited us in to the hall and called for his son. Seeing the red shirt on his boy stirred up the man's emotion. "Where did you get that shirt, Thomas? Did you sneak out of the house?"

Seeing three large men looking down upon him brought fear into the boy's eyes and he blurted out, "It's Freddy's shirt! He came by a few minutes ago and asked me to trade with him because some men were following him."

Holmes knelt down so he could look the boy in the eye and in a reassuring voice said, "It's all right, Thomas. My name is Sherlock Holmes and we're working with the police. We think Freddy can help us catch some dangerous people. Can you tell us where he went?"

"I don't know, sir," he said with a shaky voice. "He just left by the back door and climbed the fence."

"All right," replied Holmes. "What is Freddy's last name and where does he live?"

"Freddy Bernard, sir. He lives at number 14 Birchwood Road. It's just a few streets from here."

Holmes stood and thanked the boy and his father, adding "Just one more thing, could I have Freddy's shirt? I'll take it to him and have yours sent back. What colour was the shirt you were wearing?"

"It was dark blue, Mr. Holmes," the boy answered as he took off the red plaid and handed it to the detective.

"I'm sorry about all this, Mr. Holmes," said the boy's father. "I was in my den and unaware that all this was transpiring while I was working."

"It's quite all right, sir," replied my friend. "But if either of you see Freddy before we catch up to him, you should advise him to come to Sheriff Denison's office to answer some questions."

With their promise to do so, we took our leave and advised our cab driver to take us to the Birchwood address.

"Somehow the boy must have spotted us," mused Holmes as the hansom proceeded to this new location. "I doubt this was his usual precaution when picking up the mail."

"A quick thinking lad, if that's true, Holmes," I offered. "He'd be a credit to the Baker Street Irregulars"

"Indeed, Doctor. It also gives us insight into the intelligence of our foe. We would do well not to underestimate them."

"You know, Holmes, the name Bernard doesn't sound like it would lend itself to this Heligoland. I would expect something more German or Danish, like the Carlsen and Olsen we've met thus far."

The detective shook his head, "Remember, Watson, Heligoland was under British control for over half a century and it is a popular port despite its small size. Any number of nationalities may be inhabiting the island. Ah, here we are."

Again we found ourselves in front of a modest cottage where a brown and white Spaniel roamed freely in the small front garden, alert to all passers by of either human or animal variety. As we approached the small gate, it stood its ground and emitted a low growl.

Holmes leaned on the gate and brought his eye level down near the dog's. Speaking gently and smiling, the animal soon ceased its aggressiveness and edged closer, sniffing at my friend's outstretched hand. Finally, the tail began to wag and it came closer to get its ears scratched.

We had just felt confident enough to open the gate when the front door opened and a woman emerged. She was a stout sort of around thirty years with short blonde hair, wearing a grey dress and a flowery apron upon which she was wiping her hands. She frowned at the dog and called it to her side.

"Jasper, come!" she commanded. The dog immediately obeyed and she turned her attention toward us in a most uninviting tone. "What do you want?"

Holmes turned his charms from the savage beast to the wary woman and replied, "We are looking for Freddy Bernard. Is he at home?"

"No, not right now. But I expect he'll be along soon if he wants his supper hot. I'm his mother. What do you want him for?"

"We believe he may have picked up a telegram belonging to my friend here, Dr. White."

At the mention of the word 'White', she blanched but recovered quickly. "I don't know why he would be collecting anyone's telegram. Are you sure it was him?"

Holmes nodded and held out his hands, "He was observed, Mrs. Bernard. We just need to know if he actually picked up the telegram we were expecting."

"Perhaps your husband knows his whereabouts. Is he home?" I asked.

She looked at me warily and replied, "My husband's been out of town on business. Won't be back until next week. Why don't you gents let me know your address and I'll check with Freddy when he gets home. If he has your telegram by mistake, I'll have him bring it over straight away."

I frowned at this obvious subterfuge but Holmes spoke up brightly, "That will be quite satisfactory, madam, as long as we get an answer one way or the other tonight. A patient's treatment hangs in the balance."

He scribbled out the address of the Friar Tuck Inn on a piece of paper pulled from his notebook and handed it over. "We'll either be in our rooms or in the dining room. If we are called upon to go out, please have the boy leave the telegram or an answer with the desk clerk. Thank you. Come, Doctor."

I followed grudgingly, thinking this woman knew more than she was telling. Once back in the cab, I confronted Holmes. "Why didn't you press her harder? She certainly made it obvious she knows something."

"I'm sure she knows quite a bit, Watson," he replied. "I am also sure her husband is not away on business. Very likely both he and the boy are involved with these kidnappers."

"How do you know he's not out of town like she claims?"

"Surely you noticed the quantity of ash in the ashtray by the easy chair next to the sofa? Also the odour was quite strong, not stale from being there for days. No, my friend he's been there today. It would not surprise me if he and the boy left within the hour upon receipt of the telegram."

Once we were away from the house Holmes leaned out and called up to the driver to turn at the next corner and stop. Once he did so, the detective wrote out another note and handed it to the driver with several coins and asked him to deliver the message to Denison's office with all haste.

By now twilight was coming upon us. Holmes hailed another cab, this one a larger brougham where we would be enclosed out of sight. Once aboard, Holmes underwent a remarkable transformation. He pulled a red wig from his inner coat pocket and donned it, a moustache and goatee to change his look completely. He then removed his coat and turned it inside out, changing the colour from black to brown. Finally, he indented his bowler on the top and sides to make it resemble a homburg. He paid this new driver a considerable sum to wait with me at the corner while he went on foot to explore the area around the Bernard family home.

Within a half hour he had returned. A satisfied expression upon his face. We waited until Forsythe had arrived with another officer and Holmes gave them instructions to keep the place under surveillance while we went to the station where Holmes could perform some experiments on the red plaid shirt and other items he had retrieved from around the Bernards' house.

Chapter Nine

Burton was well aware that something was amiss. He had been required to work long into the night instead of being allowed to retire to his 'cell' after dinner. He felt sure the altered timetable indicated something had gone awry with his captor's plans. He wondered if it was his wife's persistence or if the law was closing in on this secret operation.

Unbeknownst to him, Lady Lydia was wrestling with a conundrum of her own. Her nephew had arrived at her rooms in Mansfield with the telegram which confirmed her worst fears. After learning he had been followed and how cleverly he had eluded his pursuers, she made the decision that he should come with her and join his father in their Sherwood hideout that night. Having hired a carriage, she and the boy made their way quickly to Sherwood. Now she had to decide what to do about leaving before they were caught. Her father-in-law, Colonel Wyt, had already returned to the continent to pursue the next part of their plan. Her sister's husband, Charlie, who was never seen by Burton, could remain safely in Mansfield with his wife and Freddy. Clark and Addison, who were the only men Burton had seen, being his kidnappers and guards, would be returning to Heligoland with the shipment of arms aboard a private yacht that was even now, waiting at Bridlington.

She was not surprised that Carlsen was dead. He was hot-tempered and impatient regarding their cause. He would have started a revolution without a second thought, and it would have been crushed in a matter of days due to his impetuousness. Olsen was another matter. He was more brawn than brain and he was family, being her late husband's cousin. How could she explain leaving him behind to be sent off to Australia?

She thought over their long range plan. Burton had finished less than half of what they had hoped for. It was possible they could find someone on the continent to work with, but it would delay matters further and insert another layer of confidentiality that could be breached. The operation may be possible to accomplish with the weapons they had at the ready, but to succeed would cost them dearly. It would likely turn into a suicide mission. Could she ask that much?

That thought was too heavy a burden on her at this moment and she shook it off. That part of the plan was still weeks away. Tonight she had a decision to make and the sooner the better.

She met with Charlie and advised him to take his son, and make their way to Sheffield for a few days. After she had Clark and Addison secure Burton in his quarters she told them of what had happened with Carlsen and Olsen and said it was time to move out with what they had. They would each drive a vehicle with the contraband well hidden amongst other cargo bound for the coastal town of Bridlington via different routes.

Clark protested her decision to stay behind with their prisoner and do what she could to secure Olsen's release. "Don't be a fool! You know it's a trap. They'll capture you and send you off with Olsen."

"That may be so," she admitted. "But I can buy us some time and you two must get what arms we have to the Colonel if our plan has any chance to succeed. Now, go! I have things to discuss with our prisoner before we attempt any exchange."

Chapter Ten

While laboratory conditions in Nottinghamshire were not on a par with those of Scotland Yard, Sherlock Holmes was still able to make several conclusive deductions from experiments he completed.

It was late into the evening when he invaded Denison's office with his findings.

The High Sheriff, politician though he was, took his police work seriously and was still on duty despite the late hour, assuming that the London detective would have need of him. He was sitting in his office with Hopkins when we arrived.

"Ah, Mr. Holmes," he declared. "Have you found anything of significance?"

"I have been able to deduce much from the evidence at hand," Holmes replied. "But I need someone with local geographic knowledge to complete the picture."

"That I can assist you with," he answered. "I'm quite familiar with the area from Nottingham to Sheffield."

"I am particularly interested in Sherwood Forest," replied the detective. "I am aware the subject of Robin Hood can be a bit trying, but even legends have some basis in fact. Are there any hideouts in the forest near both sycamore and birch trees, holly bushes, limestone soil and possibly a structure built with oak planks?"

Hopkins let out a low whistle, "That's pretty specific, Mr. Holmes. You gleaned all that from the shirt and the evidence you found around the house?"

"Traces of all those elements were found in the cloth and among the footprints of both father and son around the buildings and yard," he answered. "We know from Carlsen's dying words that they are in Sherwood. Evidence indicates two men, other than this Colonel White or Father Wyt were involved in the kidnapping, so that makes at least three besides Carlsen and Olsen. They would need to be in some sort of structure that could support the manufacturing of these noise suppressors and also have a place where they could lock up Burton when he wasn't working. This indicates a fairly significant structure or perhaps a cave with oak support beams framing various rooms and doors. Yet it would also need to be inconspicuous to the general public travelling through the woods."

Denison shook a finger at Holmes in appreciation of such thorough information and replied, "I believe I know just such a place." He reached into a filing cabinet behind him, extracted a map of Sherwood Forest and laid it upon his desktop.

"Hmm, actually there are two," recalled the High Sheriff as he stroked the stubble of a day's growth of beard on his square jaw with the back of his fingers. "There is a hidden forge where the outlaws built and repaired their weapons. There's also a hunting lodge that was expanded into a hotel for tourists over here," he pointed. "But it was closed down after a fire destroyed much of the ground floor a couple of years ago."

Holmes considered the two locations. They were about a mile apart but along the same road. The clearing was closer.

He declared, "We need to make our way there tonight. We cannot assume they will fall for our proposed prisoner exchange. It is more likely they will pack up whatever contraband they have and make for the coast immediately."

"Surely we should wait for daylight, Mr. Holmes," answered Denison. "We cannot risk a confrontation in the dark of night."

"There's a full moon out and they will surely not wait for sunrise. If we do not act immediately, we will lose our prey and Burton may be sacrificed because of whatever knowledge he may have gleaned. Or they could take him with them across the sea and that will complicate our rescue ten-fold. No, we must move now. How many men do you have?"

Denison hesitated, weighing the wisdom of Holmes's suggestion, then finally replied, "I need to leave the standard night patrols on duty, but I can gather at least four police constables to assist us. I'll send for them immediately."

While we waited, Holmes paid a visit to Olsen's cell. The big man was fast asleep and so the detective was able to easily accomplish his task. When all the police constables arrived it was still an hour from midnight and we set out for the first location, the clearing in Sherwood. Hopkins drove a police van and I rode along with him. Just in case they were needed, Olsen was locked in the back with Vestergaard.

Ahead of us, Denison, Holmes, Forsythe and three other policemen, all armed with rifles and pistols, led the way on horseback. Forsythe rode point, keeping an eye out for anything suspicious, or any sign of an ambush. They covered the seven miles to the clearing in less than an hour and we were about twenty minutes behind them in the van. When we arrived we found that the buildings had been emptied and there was no sign of recent occupancy. Holmes was anxious to move on, afraid that our quarry had already got a significant head start on us. Denison however, insisted that the horses needed a brief rest and water. He led us to a stream about two hundred yards away and a discussion ensued about best approaches to the old hunting lodge so the time was put to good use.

Having watered the rested the horses, we moved on up the road. I should note that Sherwood Forest is no longer the vast wooded area where Robin Hood and his band could hide out undetected. Over the centuries much of the land had been cleared for farms and only a government action had preserved what little remained of the famous forest.

It was now close to two in the morning as we approached the lodge. We had halted about a hundred yards away while

Forsythe went ahead on foot. He reported to Denison upon his return.

"There's no sign of any guards about, but there is a light burning in a room on the north side on the ground floor. I couldn't see any sign of movement within."

Denison's military background as a former army captain came to the fore. "It could well be a trap, gentlemen. They may be tempting us with the only light source to lure us in."

He, Hopkins and Holmes revised our initial plan of attack. The Sheriff and three of his deputies would scour the woods on the north side, ensuring that no attackers were lying in wait to trap us inside. Holmes, Hopkins and I would enter from the south side after Holmes picked the lock on what appeared to be the main entrance. Forsythe would remain on guard with the van and our prisoner.

We made our way silently inside after the lock gave way to Holmes ministrations. Guns at the ready, we allowed our eyes to adjust to the moonlight that shone brightly through the uncurtained windows. Slowly, we made our way through various rooms, eventually arriving at the lit room without incident. There a lantern stood upon a table with a note addressed to 'Scotland Yard'.

A quick perusal by Holmes led him to take up the lamp, open the door and wave the 'all clear' for the Sheriff and his men to come in.

More lamps were found and the room brightened considerably. Denison posted his deputies as guards outside, just to be safe, and the rest of us gathered round as Holmes had Hopkins read the message aloud:

To Scotland Yard,

I am writing this at the insistence of my captors, who speak English better than they read it.

They are understandably suspicious regarding your proposed exchange of prisoners. They assure me that they wish no harm to me or anyone in England.

However, they are passionate about their cause and loyal to their comrades and will take whatever steps necessary to ensure the safety of both. Please be assured that Carlsen was not authorised to cause any harm to Mrs. Burton, but to merely detain her. Your capture of Olsen has upset their timetable and they feel a need to consider alternate plans and devise a safe method to exchange me for him. They are fearful that you would somehow determine where their messenger was bringing the telegram and are falling back to a secondary hideout tonight.

Sometime tomorrow afternoon, they will send their terms for the exchange to the Sheriff's office.

Geordi Burton

"Well," said Denison, "it appears we must wait for them. We can't track them in the dark, even with a full moon."

Holmes merely shook his head, "We actually could, but it would be such a slow and tedious process that we would likely end up at the end of the trail at the same time as we would by waiting for first light."

He looked around the room and walked over to the fireplace, removing his glove he knelt, reached in and felt the ashes. "Cold, they've been gone at least two hours." He brushed off his hand and stood. "Denison, if I may suggest, you and your men should return to town with your prisoner. If you will leave us two horses, Watson and I will stay here, glean what clues we can from this place and attempt to follow any trail at first light. I believe we shall be able to send word or meet with you again by noon tomorrow."

Denison was agreeable, Hopkins volunteered to stay with us but Holmes waved him off, "Thank you, Inspector, but you need your rest for what lies ahead. Go back and get a few hours sleep so you have your wits about you. Watson and I will be fine."

After all had left us, Holmes turned to me, "You also, my friend, need your rest. I'll have no need of your services until morning and I suggest you take advantage of the sofa in that last room we came through."

"What about you, Holmes? It's been a long day."

"I am on the scent, old friend. Until I explore the myriad of possibilities, my mind cannot rest. I shall continue poking about this place and will awaken you after dawn when I have determined which way to go from here."

Chapter Eleven

Burton had listened intently as Lady Lydia explained their situation to him. It became obvious that her intelligence and passion for her cause made her a natural leader, even among the men in her cadre. The story of how she became involved after the death of her husband at the hands of German sailors, who were never punished, touched his heart and he found himself totally sympathetic to her cause.

"Lady Lydia, I wish you had told me all this before," he said. "We could have worked out some sort of business arrangement. Even now, we could set up a plan for me to continue to ship you what you need."

She put her strong hand on his forearm and smiled, "You are a good man, George Burton, but what we must do is for our homeland and I cannot ask outsiders to risk themselves for us. People are going to die. If we fail, anyone helping us will be subject to arrest and possibly the death penalty. I will not ask such things of a man who has no stake in our freedom."

Burton shook his head. "I cannot remember who said it, but in school I learned that 'the freedom of all is the business of all. If you stand idly by when another's rights are taken, who will stand by you when it's your rights that are threatened?'"

Lydia looked at the gunsmith with a new respect, and nodded, "Well, said, Mr. Burton. But I still cannot allow you to know our plans. However, if you truly wish to help, then you can write a letter for me ..."

Chapter Twelve

I awoke to a whistling noise. The room was barely lit from the first rays of dawn sifting through the trees outside. Sitting up on the sofa and turning toward the sound, I saw a light in a doorway next to the room where we had found Burton's note the night before. I wiped the sleep from my eyes and walked into what appeared to be a large kitchen. Holmes was just taking the kettle off the stove when he saw me standing in the doorway.

"Ah, Watson, just in time. I've prepared a light breakfast for us. There's a water closet down the hall to your left and we can then eat and be on our way."

I scratched my head, attempting to restore some semblance of order to my hair, and asked. "On our way where, Holmes?"

"We've no choice but to return to Mansfield, Doctor. There are van, carriage and horse tracks leading in four separate directions outside. All of which were made last night. It's impossible to know which conveyance was used to spirit Burton away. But I have discovered several facts which may give us the upper hand when it comes time to exchange our prisoner."

We found ourselves back at the Sheriff's office about two hours later. Denison was not in yet, but Forsythe was there, sleepy-eyed but diligent.

Mr. Holmes! Dr. Watson! I'm glad you've come, sirs. This telegram arrived just a few minutes ago." He handed over the missive and Holmes read it aloud.

TO THE HIGH SHERIFF AND SCOTLAND YARD STOP IN CASE WE OVERESTIMATED YOU AND YOU DID NOT FIND OUR NOTE LAST NIGHT LET US REITERATE THAT WE WILL CONTACT YOU THIS AFTERNOON REGARDING YOUR PROPOSAL FOR EXCHANGE STOP WE WISH NO ONE HARM JUST THE SAFE RETURN OF ALL PARTIES STOP COLONEL WHITE STOP

Holmes noted the address of the telegraph station and advised Forsythe to prepare a contingent of deputies for action that afternoon. He and I then proceeded to the railway station from where the telegram had been sent.

The official on duty was cooperative, but not the most observant of fellows. He was an older man with thinning grey hair and thick spectacles. He informed us that a gentleman came to the window about two hours ago with the message already written out. He told the man that the Sheriff's office was only a few streets away and sending a telegram seemed to be a waste of money. The man insisted, so he transcribed it on to a telegraph form and sent it along at nine o'clock, per the man's instructions.

"What did this gentleman look like?" enquired Holmes.

"Just an average sort of fellow, about forty, average size, maybe the same height as your friend here," he answered, nodding in my direction.

"How was he dressed?" Holmes pressed.

"Now that was odd," said the old man, "The signature said 'Colonel' but he was dressed more like a workman. Oh, and he needed a shave."

"What about his hands, did you notice anything unusual about them?"

"Can't say as I did. Never saw his left hand. He just handed me the paper and the money to pay for it. Didn't get more than a second's look."

"Do you still have the paper he gave you?" asked Holmes, bordering on impatience.

The old grey official stepped back from the window and fished through his wastebasket, pulling out one wrinkled paper after another. Finally he found the original message and handed it over.

Holmes snatched it up, startling the fellow. I felt it only polite to step in and mollify the situation, offering the man a half a crown for his assistance, which he grudgingly accepted as he glared at the detective.

Holmes handed the note to me and turned back to ask another question.

"One more thing, was anyone with him?"

"No one I could see," answered the telegrapher. "He did look over toward the tracks a couple of times while he waited. But if someone was there they were out of my view."

"Thank you," Holmes offered, as he turned on his heel and led me back toward the police station.

"Notice anything about that note?" he asked as we walked.

I read through it and saw nothing especially unusual. It was neatly written in pencil on a quarto sized piece of paper. Then I saw it. "It's the same handwriting as the note we found last night. This was written by Burton!"

When we arrived back at the station, Denison and his cousin, Hopkins, were on hand. Holmes explained his findings from the night before, including a most revealing detail that none of us had considered.

We made contingency plans with various options depending on what the kidnappers proposed. Denison had lunch brought in at noon but we ate sparingly, too anxious for the action which would soon occur.

At precisely one o'clock, an attractive blonde woman came through the front door and handed an envelope to the officer at the front desk. As she turned to leave she found her path blocked by the tall angular frame of the world's first consulting detective. He stared down his aquiline nose at the defiant face before him and greeted her, "Good afternoon, Frau Wyt."

To give her credit, she boldly turned back to the man at the desk and demanded, "Officer, this gentleman is in my way and I wish to leave. Please order him to step aside or I shall press charges."

Holmes shook his head, "It won't do, madam. I know who you are and what you've done. You have much to answer for."

"And just who are you, you impertinent fool?"

My friend bowed slightly and replied, "Sherlock Holmes, Frau Wyt. I must admit, until last night I had not anticipated a woman in the midst of this little problem. I should have realised, considering his native language, that the 'Fr.' in Olsen's address stood for 'Frau' instead of the English 'Father'. Finding your boot prints at the lodge and other signs of a woman's presence brought that fact to mind."

"Whatever are you talking about, sir? I was merely asked by a gentleman down the street to deliver that envelope. He was limping with a cane and would have had difficulty walking so far, so I agreed. Now I should like to be on my way, so step aside."

Sheriff Denison appeared from a doorway, "Even if that were true, madam, we would need to hold you for questioning. If you're not involved, then the very least you could do for us is to provide a detailed description of this so-called cripple."

She was trapped and she knew it, but she now played an unexpected card.

"Very well, gentlemen, then let me inform you of the situation as explained in that letter. Mr. Burton is safely sitting on a bench outside Much's Hardware shop. There are two gentlemen with silenced rifles within line of sight. If I am not back in thirty minutes, they will shoot him. If I am followed, they will shoot him. If anyone approaches him with the idea of speaking with him, spiriting him away or shielding him with horses or vehicles, they will shoot him. If anyone attempts to find and stop either of my men, the other will shoot him. All we wish is to take Olsen with us and leave the country without any more bloodshed. Mr. Burton knows nothing of our plans, so there is no need for us to kill him unless you force our hand. We have committed no crime against England, nor do we plan to."

"We only have your word for that, madam," said Denison, "and I'm afraid that's not good enough."

She sat in a convenient chair, leaning on her parasol, pulled a paper from her handbag and held it out to him, "I understand you were a military man, Sheriff. If I give you the word of my father-in-law, Colonel Wyt, on his oath as an officer, will that satisfy you? He wrote this out at the beginning of our task with instructions to give it to any authorities were we captured."

Denison took the note. I could see over his shoulder that it was written on a British military letterhead, but the insignia was faded with age. He read it to himself and replied, "I should like to believe this, madam, but how can I?"

She stood again, "The Colonel was on the command staff of the garrison when we were under British control. He is an officer and a gentleman. I'm asking for your trust, Sheriff and you're running out of time," she emphasised with a nod toward the grandfather clock in the corner.

"When would you desire this exchange?" he enquired.

"Now wait a minute, William," declared Inspector Hopkins. "I can't let you exchange a prisoner without authorisation."

The High Sheriff looked at his cousin with authority, but in an apologetic tone replied, "He is a prisoner in my gaol, Stanley, and the life of one of my constituents is at stake."

He turned and implored Frau Wyt for an answer.

"We had proposed two o'clock in our letter, but since I am here, let Peter come with me now. Just know this, our men will stay on target for an hour once Peter is released, you may not approach Burton until then, by which time Peter and I shall be safely away and one of my messengers will inform the marksmen that they can stand down."

Holmes requested Denison, Hopkins and I to step into Denison's office where he outlined a plan.

Within a minute, we and the Inspector had returned. Thirty seconds later, Denison came out with Olsen and Vestergaard handcuffed together. The big man cried out when he saw Frau Wyt and began jabbering away in his foreign tongue, but she silenced him with a raised hand, then went to his side. She whispered in his ear and he looked at her incredulously. Then she turned to us.

"We will take our leave now, gentlemen. Please remove the handcuffs and remember our instructions. Mr. Burton seems a pleasant fellow and was most cooperative once he accepted his situation. I would be loath to see anything happen to him."

"I'm afraid that's not possible," declared Holmes. "We've allowed you to see Mr. Olsen, but we have not verified your claim as to Burton's whereabouts. Olsen can go with you now, but he will remain handcuffed to Mr. Vestergaard. Inspector Hopkins will release him once Burton's identity has been established by Dr. Watson here. I presume you have a signal to give your men to hold their fire until the Doctor is close enough for that identification to take place?"

She hesitated, then acquiesced. "I can do that. Your terms are acceptable, so long as all your men remain across the street from Burton's position and do not attempt to communicate with him."

"Very well," answered Denison, being the one in authority. "Gentlemen, please escort Frau Wyt and Mr. Olsen out."

While we made our way through the streets of Mansfield, Holmes and Denison went to his house in hopes of putting a plan into action that would allow us to follow our prisoner.

Forsythe, who had remained out of sight during the confrontation at the office, but was able to watch what transpired through a crack in the door, was given Holmes's red wig and goatee beard. Dressed like a an office clerk, he took up a position at the railway station ticket office so he could note if our quarry was headed out of town by train.

It was Holmes's belief that we had all avenues of escape accounted for. But there was one factor even he could not have foreseen.

Chapter Thirteen

As we strolled through the streets of Mansfield, I was next to Frau Wyt in front of Olsen and Vestergaard. Hopkins brought up the rear to ensure we were not attacked from behind. When we reached a point across the street from Much's Mercantile, the lady bid us stop as she stepped out into the street. She opened and closed her parasol twice, waited a few seconds and then opened it again, giving it a twirl over her shoulder as she looked about in all directions. Then she rejoined us and pointed to where Burton sat, reading a newspaper and pausing every few seconds to look around. He saw us and dropped the paper into his lap.

"There is your gunsmith, gentlemen, safe for now," she declared. "Now, will you please release Peter and let us be on our way?"

Hopkins looked around but was unable to spot the marksmen we had been warned against. Reluctantly he unlocked the handcuffs from Olsen and Vestergaard. The big fellow rubbed his wrists and said something which the interpreter translated as 'thank you'.

"Let me add my thanks, gentlemen," said the lady. "Now I have something to tell Mr. Burton, and we will leave you to pick him up in one hour." She pointed to a clock in a nearby tower and continued, "At two-thirty, everyone shall be free of this business."

*****

Geordi Burton watched as Lady Lydia appeared across the street and his concern grew. He became even more confused when she performed several manoeuvres with her parasol. At last he felt some relief when she crossed the street with a man who had been released from handcuffs. She stopped about six feet away from him and told her companion to go on into the shop and wait for her.

"Mr. Burton, as you can see the police and I have come to an understanding. They will collect you in one hour. I appreciate your remaining here until that time."

"I am glad you got your person back. I'll do as you say. But remember my offer."

"I am appreciative, Mr. Burton, but this is our fight. Good bye."

Burton could not explain the feelings that came over him in that instant. Suddenly, he did not want this woman to walk out of his life forever, but he did not know what he could do or say to prevent it. Finally he found his tongue, "I … If you should change your mind, a message addressed to Geordi at my shop will bring you whatever assistance I can offer. God speed, madam."

The woman bowed her head in gratitude and patted Burton's shoulder as she walked past him into the shop. She whispered, "God bless you … Geordi."

*****

Hopkins and I remained stationed across the street and sent Vestergaard back to inform Holmes and Denison how things stood. Within twenty minutes we were joined by them and one other companion.

I knelt and petted the bloodhound that now sat at our feet. Denison introduced him as Galahad, a dog with the keenest nose.

"What will you use to give him the scent?" I queried. "I did not notice you pluck anything from Frau Wyt. Is there some piece of Olsen's clothing he left behind?"

Holmes answered, "I anticipated that it may come to something like this, Watson. You recall I paid a visit to Olsen's cell last night?"

I nodded my head and he continued, as he pulled a small bottle from his coat pocket. "I doused his boots with this chemical which is unique enough for a good hound to follow for quite some distance. Now, which way did Wyt and Olsen go?"

Hopkins answered, "I can't figure it, Holmes. They went into the merchant's shop but have not come out."

Holmes became agitated with concern. "What's behind that shop?

Denison thought a moment and replied. "There's a warehouse and then an alley for deliveries."

Holmes took the leash from Denison and held the bottle under Galahad's nose. "All of you wait here," he commanded. "If I'm not out in five minutes surround the area. If I signal you from the door, Watson, you and Hopkins come and join me while the rest of you stay on guard here."

Before anyone could reply, he was off across the street. As he walked past the gunsmith he stooped to pet the dog about ten feet away from where the man sat. He did not appear to say anything, but did lift his hat and wipe his brow with his sleeve as he gazed into the afternoon sun. Then he went inside.

In less than two minutes, he appeared in the doorway and waved. Hopkins and I split off and each approached the door from the opposite side, arriving about ten seconds apart. Stepping into the shop, we found Holmes in animated conversation with the general manager.

"This is Mr. Thorsen, gentlemen," he said. "Apparently he and Frau Wyt are well acquainted. Only he knows her as Lady Lydia."

Thorsen shook his head, "No, sir! She's just a good customer, that's all I know. She buys goods with cash and rents a space in my warehouse for storage. I told you she went back there a little while ago, I didn't keep track of when she left. I was with other customers."

Holmes shook his head, "She's not there now. What did she store?"

"What business is that of yours?" he demanded.

Hopkins showed his Scotland Yard identification and the man became more cooperative.

"Just surplus goods. Food, clothing, kitchen supplies. Things she bought in bulk to get a lower price and then come in for when she needed them."

Holmes led the way with Galahad in the lead. The dog was soon scratching at the door of a particular cupboard. Holmes found it unlocked. "She left in a hurry," he concluded. There were numerous supplies on the shelves. Extra clothing hung from a rack and there was also a pile on the floor. Holmes knelt and picked up various items. "Her dress, and Olsen's clothes. They've changed, but fortunately for us it appears Olsen retained his shoes."

We walked on through the warehouse to the back alley, a cobbled street wide enough for large vehicles to pass each other. There was no dirt and so no sign of any footprints, but Galahad picked up the scent of Holmes's chemical and proved eager to lead the way. However, Holmes had another task in mind first.

We walked back through the shop and he stopped again about ten feet from Burton. But this time, instead of ignoring him as we had been instructed, he turned to the man and spoke.

"Mr. Burton, I believe it's time you came home."

Hopkins grabbed his sleeve and said, "What are you doing, Holmes. They'll shoot him if he moves!"

Burton refused to look in our direction but raised the paper up to cover his mouth as he spoke, "He's right. The lady told me I couldn't move until two-thirty or I'd be shot."

"She may have told you such a thing, but it's not true. There are no marksmen about," stated the detective with absolute certainty.

Burton lowered his paper and looked directly at us. "If you are so sure, then come stand around me and see who the bullet hits first."

Holmes turned to us and pointed out toward the buildings along the street with his cane. "Note gentlemen, there are no flat roofs nearby for a gunman to stand upon and no open windows for anyone to shoot from. In addition, based upon my observations at the hunting lodge, all of Lady Lydia's cohorts have split up and left in different directions. The only tracks coming back to Mansfield were made by a single carriage and the depth of track indicated no more than two persons. The lady and the gunsmith."

He swivelled on his heel and walked over to stand in front of Burton, "My only question, sir, is why you went along with this ruse?"

By now Denison and Vestergaard had come across the street and we all stood around the gunsmith. He looked up in resignation and declared, "Take me to the Sheriff's office and I will tell you all I know."

Holmes handed Galahad to the Sheriff and asked that he and Hopkins follow the trail left by Olsen's shoes as far as they could. The rest of us escorted Burton back to the office where we sent for his wife, then sat around a table in an interview room to see what the man had to say.

He first of all assured us that he had not been harmed in any way, save for the initial drugging. He then explained what had been required of him and how his days were spent under the watchful eye of two men, whose names he did not know, and an occasional visit from Lady Lydia. He did have the impression that a third man arrived occasionally with supplies, but never saw him. He did not see Colonel White during his captivity, though he knew he was connected to these conspirators.

He described in great detail the various weapons he had modified with the noise suppression devices, but he claimed not to know what purpose his captors had in mind for the weapons, other than they would be used in some foreign country.

At that point his wife arrived and, after a tearful reunion, he asked for some privacy to discuss a matter of importance with her before continuing his report. Holmes granted them the use of the interview room and we retreated to Denison's office. Denison himself returned in the interval, having left Hopkins at the railway station with Galahad where the trail had come to an end at the platform.

"I thought you might wish to examine the scene yourself, Mr. Holmes. I've left Forsythe and Stanley there to answer any questions you may have. You may continue to use Galahad if need be."

"Thank you," replied the detective. "Burton has been regaling us with the story of his captivity. His wife has just arrived. I must caution you though. I believe he is holding something back."

"Well, we'll see about that," huffed Denison as he led the way back down the hall. Just as we arrived, Burton opened the door.

"Ah, Sheriff, just who we need to talk to. Gentlemen, please come in."

When we had all gathered in the room where Mrs. Burton now sat at the table, the gunsmith took up a position behind his wife with his hands on her shoulders. She reached back and patted his left hand as she nodded at him.

"Gentlemen, I have explained the situation and the motives of Lady Lydia and her troupe to my wife and we have both agreed that we do not wish to press charges. You may cease your pursuit."

"What!" bellowed the High Sheriff. "They kidnapped you and attempted to kidnap your wife! You can't possibly be serious! Did they threaten you into this action?"

I noted that Holmes's reaction was subtle and readable only to myself, having been exposed to his various moods for these many years. He was suppressing a smile and there was a nearly imperceptible nod of his head. He finally spoke.

"I do not believe that to be the case," he said, staring at Burton the whole time, then addressing him. "You know more than you're telling. We know about the situation in Heligoland. Are you aware of their specific plans?"

The gunsmith shook his head, "No, Mr. Holmes. Lady Lydia was insistent that I not ask questions, nor even venture a guess as to their purpose. They could not afford their plans to become known."

"Surely though, you must have speculated as to the use of these devices you were making for them."

"No more than any other person might," he answered. "They obviously need to take some action that requires stealth. But as to what or where that might be I have no clue, only the lady's assurance that it will not be in England."

Holmes nodded and turned back to Denison, "I believe that puts your duty at an end, Sheriff. With no complaint you have no jurisdiction to proceed further. We will go on to inform your cousin of what has transpired and let him decide what Scotland Yard's responsibility may be."

The Sheriff, reluctantly, let the Burtons leave. As we also turned to go, Holmes enquired of the interpreter, "Mr. Vestergaard, I believe your services will no longer be required, would you care to accompany us to the station? I believe there is a train for London departing soon"

The meek young fellow answered eagerly, "Indeed, I would, Mr. Holmes. My bag is in the back. Let me retrieve it and I will be right with you."

In a short while we departed our hansom and entered the railway station, quickly finding Hopkins and Galahad by the ticket window.

Holmes called for Forsythe who came to the window immediately.

"I'm told you did not see the lady or Olsen. What have you seen?" enquired Holmes emphatically.

Forsythe shook his head, "Olsen did not come to the window and no woman matching her description bought any tickets."

Holmes tapped the counter with his knuckles, "The dog indicates that they were here. Did any woman buy two tickets?"

"Most of the travellers have been men, or men travelling with wives or families. The only women to buy tickets were a mother and her young daughter, a pair of young ladies off on a shopping spree to London, and a nun."

Holmes's face lit up at that last, "A nun? Who was she travelling with?"

"There was a priest with her, as you would expect. He sat over on that bench, hunched over like he was trying to catch his breath. But it couldn't have been Olsen. What I could see of his hair under his hat was as black as coal and Olsen's hair was fair. The nun also had black hair, not blond."

"How could you see her hair if she wore a nun's habit?" I asked

"There was just a wisp of it hanging down by her right eye. She made an effort to tuck it back up while she waited for her ticket."

"Oh, that clever woman," stated Holmes. "She deliberately called your attention to her black hair so you would not report any blond woman buying a ticket. She and Olsen were likely wearing wigs which they can dispose of easily when they need to change their appearance again. What train did they purchase tickets for?"

"They left about forty-five minutes ago for Sheffield."

"When is the next train to Sheffield?"

"There's another one leaving in twenty minutes."

Holmes wrote out a telegram to be sent to the Sheffield police and then did something surprising. Instead of remaining in pursuit by taking the next train north as I had presumed, we stayed at the station with Vestergaard, sent for our luggage and awaited the next express to London.

Holmes then did another unusual thing. As he knelt to pet the bloodhound, he examined its leg. Shaking his head he spoke with some consternation, "Galahad seems to have strained his leg. I think I shall take him on down to London to have him looked at. I should hate to return him to the Sheriff in less than pristine condition after he performed so well."

When I questioned him regarding our destination, Holmes merely shook his head in resignation, "From Sheffield they could have gone on in any direction by train, coach or on horseback. Our main concern at this point is to return to London and let the Yard send out the alarm for all customs offices to be inspecting all outbound cargo for the weapons."

Hopkins readily agreed. He sent off a telegram to the Yard and then went to retrieve his luggage from his cousin's house. Within an hour, the four of us were southbound for the crowded metropolis.

When we arrived at St. Pancras, Vestergaard immediately left to hail a cab while Holmes kept Hopkins and me on the platform discussing the case. So long as the weapons were on British soil, Hopkins felt England was under obligation to stop their shipment, since they were likely to be used against the Germans who were overseers of Heligoland and considered allies of Great Britain, being ruled by the Queen's grandson.

Holmes pointed out the fact that this case now should fall under the jurisdiction of the Foreign Office and indicated that he would be reporting his findings to his brother, Mycroft.

Checking his watch he announced, "I believe, however, we still have a chance to apprehend Frau Wyt and Olsen."

"What do you mean, Holmes? We are fairly certain that they went up to Sheffield?"

Before the detective could answer, Galahad perked up and began tugging at his leash. Holmes gave him his head and we all followed at a trot. "I don't understand, Holmes," I shouted, trying to keep up, "What scent is he following?"

"As I suspected, Wyt and Olsen doubled back. They're somewhere ahead in that crowd departing the last carriage."

By now the bloodhound was hot on the scent and barking loudly. Suddenly two persons dressed in clerical garb broke into a run and made their way to a waiting cab. At a shouted command the driver whipped up his horse at a gallop.

Holmes whistled for a cab but we had to fight the crowds to engage one and by the time we did so our quarry was out of sight. Still Holmes cried out to the driver, "The Danish Embassy, fast as you can, man!"

Our four-wheeler jolted off and careened through the streets for around a mile and a half. Hopkins asked, "Why there, Holmes?"

"That's where Vestergaard works."

"Vestergaard?"

"No time to explain now, gentlemen. There's the embassy up ahead and there's our prey exiting their cab. Watson, have you your revolver?"

I replied in the affirmative and handed it over to his outstretched palm. He leaned out of the window and took aim, firing a warning shot while we were still fifty yards away. Unfortunately, instead of halting, they dashed for the gate and up the steps. Two soldiers took up positions in front of the door and levelled their rifles at what they thought were armed assassins as we approached after departing our own cab. Hopkins shouted out that we were police while Holmes returned my Webley to me.

One of the guards lowered his weapon while the other kept us covered. As he approached the gate, Hopkins explained to him that the three who had just entered the building were wanted by Scotland Yard. The soldier, a lieutenant, explained that the three were now on Danish soil and any requests for extradition would have to come through official channels.

Unable to take any further action we resigned ourselves to returning to Scotland Yard where Hopkins could make his report. Holmes and I stayed with him to help fill in the final details. Uppermost in my mind, of course, was how he knew to go to the Danish Embassy.

"Simple deduction, old friend," he replied, as Hopkins stopped writing to listen in as well. "Whatever plans Frau Wyt and her band have in mind, there is no possible faction on Heligoland large enough to withstand German military forces. Even if they took over the garrison or did something within the German government to disrupt the oversight of their island, eventually the Germans would take it back. Their only hope was to ally themselves with another foreign power who would allow them self-rule, but under the protection of a nation not beholden to either Germany or England. The most likely candidate in close proximity is Denmark. After the

Schleswig Wars[1] there has certainly been no love lost between the Danes and the Germans."

Hopkins spoke up, "Where does Vestergaard fit in, and how did you come to suspect his involvement?"

Holmes pulled a cigarette from his case and lit it. Staring at the smoke as it curled toward the ceiling he answered, "Pretending to be a Norwegian explorer for nearly three years[2], I naturally had to speak the language. There are several common roots with the Frisian language of Heligoland. Enough for me to realise that Vestergaard's dialog with Olsen was much longer than the questions we were posing. It was also natural that Frau Wyt's group would have some inside, though unofficial, connection with the Embassy of Denmark here in London. As you saw, it was Vestergaard's cab that our prey sprinted for."

Hopkins nodded and resumed writing his report, Holmes, having answered all of the Inspector's questions, suggested that he and I should stop for dinner on the way back to Baker Street and we were soon partaking of stuffed game hens, potatoes and various green vegetables at Simpson's.

As we ate I continued to question my friend about the case. "Tell me, why do you suppose the Burtons refused to press charges against the kidnappers?"

Holmes buttered some bread and replied softly, "I believe that continued exposure to Lady Lydia's charms and promises made Burton sympathetic to her cause. As he said, he was never harmed by them. He was well-treated and fed. Only his freedom was temporarily impeded and she made it seem that it was all for a good cause." He pointed his butter

---

[1] The First Schleswig War was the first round of military conflict in southern Denmark and northern Germany which lasted from 1848–1851. Ultimately, the war resulted in a Danish victory. The Second Schleswig War was the second military conflict as a result of whatbecame known as the 'Schleswig-Holstein Question'. It was fought in 1864 because of a succession disputes concerning the duchies of Holstein and Lauenburg when the Danish king died without an heir acceptable to the German confederation. This war resulted in a German victory.

[2] The Great Hiatus – For three years Holmes travelled under the name of Sigerson, after the Reichenbach Falls incident which required him to go into hiding. See *The Adventure of the Empty House* by Arthur Conan Doyle.

knife at me and continued. "Having been exposed to the Kaiser's minions and travelling through some nations under German control, I cannot blame the lady for her desire to throw off his rule. In spite of his familial ties to Queen Victoria, I might have done the same thing myself, were I in Burton's position."

"So you would put her in the same category as Robin Hood? A freedom fighter attempting to throw off the rule of a despotic relative of his true sovereign?"

He smiled, "Rather poetic, considering the location of this little adventure, don't you think, Doctor?"

I raised my wineglass in a toast and clinked glasses with my wise friend, stating, "To freedom fighters of all generations!"

He replied, rather soberly, "May the lady find peace as well."

*****

In her quarters within the Danish Embassy, Lady Lydia had relaxed with a glass of sherry. She had an hour before dinner downstairs, so she went and sat at an escritoire in the corner of the room and took up pen and paper. She felt a strong desire to explain herself to the tall, forceful man she had met at Nottinghamshire.

My Dear Mr. Sherlock Holmes ...

[Editor's note: There are further notes in Watson's files regarding Lady Lydia and Sherlock Holmes, but he chose to end the case of the gunsmith at this juncture. If the rest of the story proves to be instructive or entertaining, an attempt will be made to bring forth the conclusion of this encounter between the detective and the rebels of Heligoland.]

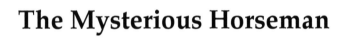

The Mysterious Horseman

Chapter One

One morning in the May of 1894 I decided to visit my old friend, Mr. Sherlock Holmes, with a view to discussing the possibility of moving back to Baker Street now that he had returned to London following his three years abroad. As I ascended the seventeen steps to our formerly shared rooms at number 221B, I heard him playing furiously on his violin.

Having been invited to arrive at this hour, I entered without knocking, not wishing to interrupt his melody. I stood by the sideboard as he continued to finish the piece.

When the final note emanated from his bow, I applauded his performance and remarked, "I've always enjoyed that finale, Holmes. It reminds me of fiery horses with the speed of light in clouds of dust, and hearty cries of cavalrymen charging into the fray across the plains of Afghanistan. It's unfortunate that such glorious sights always end in bloody battle, for they are truly inspiring otherwise."

Holmes answered as he put his violin into its case, "I do not believe that is what Rossini had in mind when he wrote the *March of the Swiss Soldiers*, Doctor. But it is fitting that you should think of horses at this time. I've received an urgent telegram from our once beleaguered client, Colonel Ross."

Holmes and I each sat in our well-worn, familiar chairs before the fireplace as I replied, "What is it this time? Did he misplace Silver Blaze[1] again?"

"No, Silver Blaze has retired to stud and has been quite successful, if the Colonel is to be believed. In fact, one of his fillies, Silver Stockings, is currently with a superior stallion from America in hopes of producing yet another champion. It is this stallion's owner that is causing concern on the Colonel's part."

"He suspects something criminal of this person?" I enquired.

Holmes shook his head as he lit one of his familiar clay pipes filled with shag from the Persian slipper hung by the fireplace. "No, Watson, he reports that they are a victim and he fears for the man's life."

"So we're off to Dartmoor and King's Pyland once again?"

"I should welcome your company, dear chap, if not inconvenient to your patients, especially Mr. Gowers, from whom you've just come. Can he spare you?" he replied.

I had not realised how much I had missed this habit of his, irritating though it could be. So, naturally I had to respond.

"I left my medical bag, and my top hat with the stethoscope secreted within, down in Mrs. Hudson's hallway, Holmes. How could you possibly know I had been to see Mr. Gowers this morning?"

Holmes sat in his chair, apparently stoic as ever, yet I could just detect a slight upturn of a smile. He had missed this little game as much as I.

"The seam of the handle of your medical bag still leaves an impression on your palm, Doctor," he mused. "This not only tells me you've made a medical call this morning, but that you walked from there, carrying your bag instead of taking a cab and letting it rest on the seat next to you. That puts it close by. I know that Gowers lives but a quarter mile away on Knox Street where there is much construction going on and you

---

[1] *The Adventure of Silver Blaze.* Submitted to *The Strand Magazine* by Arthur Conan Doyle 1892 was based on an adventure that took place in 1888.

could hardly make the journey without mud and cement dust clinging to your shoes and turn ups, as I clearly perceive."

I looked down and, though I had wiped my shoes upon entering the house, there were still traces of the offending material clinging to the sides as well as to my trousers. I shook my head, as ever in wonder at his powers of observation and deduction, and answered.

"Gowers actually started out as Dr. Anstruther's patient and in your absence I've had the time to return his favours to me many times over. He would certainly be willing to cover my practice for a week or so. A turn in the country would be a welcome change. When do you propose we leave?"

"I knew I could count on my old campaigner!" He clapped his hand on his knee in delight. "There's a train from Paddington at two o'clock which will have us in Dartmoor in time to join Colonel Ross and his guest for dinner. You go pack and I shall send off a telegram advising him of our coming. I shall meet you at the station at one forty-five. Oh, and do be good enough to bring your revolver. It is best we be prepared for any contingency."

I returned home and did as he asked. All the while I was packing I marvelled at the feelings that had awakened within me at the thought of more adventures with my friend. I had not realised how melancholy I had become in the past year since my poor Mary's death. I'd had a miserable holiday without the company of my wife at my side and I must admit to spending too many evenings in solitary contemplation of a glass of brandy. Yes, fresh country air and the thrill of adventure were just the tonic I needed.

Sitting in the railway compartment across from Holmes as we steamed our way toward Dartmoor, I enjoyed the *déjà vu* of seeing him in his Inverness cape and ear-flapped travelling cap. It was as though we had gone back in time to 1888 and our first journey to King's Pyland to find Colonel Ross's missing thoroughbred.

Chapter Two

After changing trains in Exeter it was just after seven o'clock when we finally arrived in Tavistock. A carriage was at the station to greet us and we were soon winding our way through the green fields and woods to King's Pyland, the estate of the famous sportsman, Colonel Ross.

Upon arrival at our destination, our feet had hardly hit the ground when the gentleman himself burst through the front door and hurried to greet us. He had changed little in the ensuing years since we found his horse and solved the murder of his trainer. His small frame was as erect as ever, his hair and side-burns now completely white and his monocle replaced by silver rimmed eyeglasses.

The dapper retired soldier shook our hands vigorously and led us into the house and his private study where he offered us brandy and cigars. Our welcome was a good more congenial than the condescending attitude he had exhibited at our first encounter. That attitude quickly changed when Silver Blaze was found in time to win the Wessex Cup and a fair fortune for his purse. Now he greeted us like old friends.

He addressed us in low conspiratorial tones, "I wished to see you alone first, gentlemen, before introducing you to my guest, Mr. Reese. He is not sanguine about the idea of bringing in outsiders to assist with this situation. He was emphatic that he wanted no police involved, but I assured him that you are not affiliated with the official force and he reluctantly agreed.

"Unlike you, Mr. Holmes, I am no expert in these things, but I believe he has a secret. I cannot imagine that it is criminal, for he has been as gentlemanly and gracious an American as I have ever met. He is excellent company and is especially knowledgeable about horses. He does seem to drift off into quiet reflection now and again, as if some memory was preoccupying his mind."

Holmes was silent for a moment, watching the smoke from his cigar curl toward the oak panelled ceiling. Then he asked what I thought to be a rather incongruous question.

"Tell me, has he requested a cash payment for his stud services?"

Colonel Ross was momentarily taken aback by this change in subject, then answered, "Why, yes, Mr. Holmes. How could you possibly know that? He said that he had no desire to establish a bank account in England and preferred cash."

"He would not even accept a cheque or a wire transfer to his American bank?" I asked.

The Colonel shook his head, "No, Dr. Watson. He says he doesn't trust these processes and prefers the solidity of cash, gold or silver."

"Is he a horse breeder by trade?" enquired Holmes.

"It's a sideline, he says. He professes to be a lawyer," answered our host.

"Ah," responded the detective.

"What?" requested Ross. "Is that significant?"

"It is an interesting fact, Colonel. Its significance is yet to be determined. May we meet him now?"

Our host rang a bell for his butler and told him to ask Mr. Reese to join us.

The gentleman who came in was strikingly handsome. I estimated his age at roughly fifty years due to the salt and pepper shading of his full head of hair. Though the colour may have been added to by the deep tan and the leathery look of a man who had spent a good deal of time outdoors. His clean-shaven face was framed by a strong square jaw. He was six feet tall in his grey linen suit. A silver watch chain hung across a trim waist and his hands hung loosely at his sides until he stretched out his arm to greet us. His grip was firm and confident.

"Gentlemen, I'm Jim Reese," he announced in a pleasant sonorous voice. "I appreciate your coming. I tried to explain to the Colonel that I wished to put no one else at risk, but your reputation has spread even to Texas, Mr. Holmes. If there is anyone in England that may be able to assist me, I believe you are that man."

Having exchanged greetings, we all sat down again. Mr. Reese facing us in a relaxed manner as he crossed his left boot over his right knee. He declined any brandy or cigars, settling for tea instead.

Holmes sat still, observing the American before speaking. I have seen many people, both clients and criminals, fidget nervously under the scrutiny of those steel-grey eyes. But Reese merely sipped his tea, then set the cup down and folded his hands in his lap awaiting our questions.

Finally the detective spoke, "I appreciate your confidence, sir. "Would you please tell us just what has occurred that you perceive to be a threat?"

The gentleman smiled and I saw his thumbs rise from his clasped hands in what I took to be a gesture of resignation. "It may be coincidence, but in all my years in the legal profession, I have learned not to accept coincidence at face value."

Holmes nodded in agreement and bid him continue.

"When my ship arrived at Plymouth, my luggage was *accidently* diverted. It was discovered after nearly an hour's search and delivered to the Harbour Master's office where I was able to verify that the contents were all in order. There was no way to tell whether or not the locks had been picked but nothing was missing, so it was assumed that someone had mistakenly set it aside for a different passenger."

My friend interrupted and asked, "When did this take place and what was your ship?"

"I came over on the *RMS Majestic* to Liverpool. I had a layover there of a week while my horse was quarantined and then came round to Plymouth on the steamer *Calypso*."

Holmes pressed him for more detail as to the individuals he dealt with in Plymouth, then moved on. "What other incidents have concerned you?"

"When I first arrived in Tavistock, Colonel Ross had been called away, so my first few days were spent at an inn in town while my horse was boarded at the local livery. When I came back to my room after dining out on my second evening, I found that someone had entered while I was out and gone through my bags, but fortunately not my locked trunks. While I was taking inventory of my possessions I received a message from the blacksmith that he'd had to chase away a stranger who was attempting to examine my horse.

"Fortunately, the Colonel returned the next day and I moved out here to be his guest and my horse is now well protected with his other stock by numerous stable boys."

"Yet," pursued Holmes, "there have been further incidents since your arrival at Kings Pyland."

Reese nodded, "Nothing quite so invasive, Mr. Holmes. But on two occasions while out riding I've taken note of a man on horseback observing me from a distance."

"Can you describe him?' asked the detective.

The Texan shook his head, "He was too far away. I could only say that he was wearing brown clothes and seemed to be wearing what you call a flat cap. Judging by the way he sat his horse I would guess he was a little under six feet tall and a bit stocky."

I wrote down this information in my ever present notebook, and asked, "What of his horse's colour?"

Holmes nodded approval at my question and Reese replied, "Unfortunately, Doctor, it was an all too common bay with a black mane and tail, nothing distinctive."

Holmes asked a few more probing questions and found that Reese was from Fort Worth, Texas, but had spent many years 'riding the circuit', offering his services as both defender and prosecutor in various areas of the massive state.

We soon retired to dinner where the Colonel's cook, the widow Straker, served up a sumptuous dinner, including a fine leg of lamb. Afterwards we took a turn about the grounds and wandered under the moonlight down to the stables where Ned Hunter was now head groom. He greeted us heartily and turned up the lamps so that we might view the American horse thought worthy enough to contribute to the Silver Blaze lineage.[1]

Reese stood before a magnificent white stallion, stroking its jaw while the horse nuzzled the Texan's cheek in a clear show of affection

"This is Silver Chief, son of Silver King," he declared. "It seemed destined that he should be mated with Silver Stockings out of Silver Blaze."

"Why come all the way to England, Mr. Reese?" I asked. "Surely there is suitable stock in Texas, or elsewhere in America, for breeding even this stalwart fellow."

Reese let out a small sigh as he stroked the mighty steed's neck, "My law partner recently retired and the firm just isn't the same without him. I needed to get away and contemplate my future. My grandparents always regaled my brother and I with stories of growing up in England and I thought I should like to visit while still young enough to do so. It also gives me some experience at horse breeding, which I may decide to take up full time."

Holmes approached the horse and stroked his muzzle, "Indeed a magnificent animal, sir. Has he won many races?"

"A few," replied the American. Then he laughed, "Though I'd wager we've spent more time outrunning Indians and bandits than running in circles around a track!"

The Colonel spoke up then and announced, "Silver Chief has shown great promise since his arrival. We've been waiting for him to become acclimatised after his long voyage, but we're planning on a private race between him and Silver Blaze in the next few days. In the meantime, we exercise the horses every morning, if you care to join us, gentlemen?"

---

[1] Ned Hunter was the stable boy who had been drugged when Silver Blaze was stolen. Mrs. Straker was the widow of John Straker, the trainer who betrayed both his wife and his employer and met his end in an ironic twist of fate. (*The Adventure of Silver Blaze*, 1892.)

Chapter Three

Thus it was that after breakfast the next morning, we returned to the stables where our mounts awaited us. Colonel Ross's stock now included six thoroughbreds in addition to draft horses for his coach and other vehicles.

The Colonel himself chose Silver Blaze while he had Hunter mount up on Silver Stockings. Holmes took up the reins of a beautiful red and black roan named Red Fire, while I had a gentle bay mare called Sofia, our host remembering my old war-wounded leg.

Reese, dressed in the style of the American West, including a white Stetson hat, black boots and gloves, seated himself on Silver Chief who was wearing a magnificent black leather saddle with silver trimmings.

"That is a beautiful saddle, Mr. Reese," I commented, admiringly.

Reese looked down at it and then smiled at me, "I suppose it is a bit ostentatious, Doctor. The advantages of owning a silver mine."

"Surely you don't use that saddle while racing?" commented Holmes "I should think it much too heavy."

"It's my favourite," declared the big Texan. "It's broken in well after those long rides across the plains of my home state. But I've arranged to borrow one of the Colonel's racing saddles when the time comes to face off with his champion."

We sauntered to the moors at an easy pace, alternating between walks, trots and canters as we traversed the rolling hills and fields. Coming to a large meadow that was fairly flat, Colonel Ross suggested an impromptu race, just to let the horses stretch their muscles. He, Reese and Hunter would ride to the far end, about a quarter mile away, where an old oak tree stood alone. They would circle that and return to where Holmes and I would remain as observers. I was chosen to give the starting cry and they were off.

Hunter had the obvious advantage, being of lighter weight and on a younger horse. He soon took the lead by about two lengths. The Colonel, by no means a large man and riding on his champion, Silver Blaze was making a good show in second place. Silver Chief, weighed down by his heavy saddle and a two hundred pound rider remained within striking distance but seemed to have no hope of overtaking the lead.

Holmes had asked me to bring my field glasses along and I was able to keep a close eye on our companions. I handed them to my friend as they approached the oak.

"Is there anything grander in nature than watching horses gallop across wide open spaces, Holmes?" I observed. "Reese's stallion is putting up a good effort, but the extra weight is too much for him to overcome. Yet that white steed galloping at full stride is a beautiful sight."

He took up the binoculars and watched them make the turn. Smiling, he handed them back. "Frankly, old friend, I think horses unencumbered by riders are the grander sight," he replied. "And the race does not always go to the swift, Doctor. Take a look."

Bringing the glasses back up I was surprised to note that the three riders were now neck and neck, pounding their way back toward us and closing ground quicker than I could have imagined.

"How could Reese have caught up so quickly?" I asked. "He must have been a good four lengths behind Hunter when they approached the turn."

"A horse bred in the cattle country of Texas is bound to be primarily of quarter-horse stock, Watson," answered the detective. "Their ability to make sharp turns at high speed is legendary. The Colonel's horses are used to the wide turns of a race track and as they rounded that oak, Silver Chief cut the turn far more quickly."

Still, the distance left to go gave the lighter riders ample opportunity to sprint for the lead and they were slowly pulling away again when suddenly Reese pulled sharply to his left, galloping toward a copse of trees on the low hill bordering the meadow.

"Where's he going?" I cried, turning my field glasses in that direction. Looking ahead of his track I saw a lone rider among the trees quickly wheel his horse and gallop away.

"There's someone up there, Holmes!" I shouted.

My companion spurred his horse to action towards the hilltop yelling back, "Have the others follow us, Watson!"

Red Fire was a spirited animal, but meant for the flat ground of the racetrack and unable to traverse the hill as quickly as Silver Chief. Yet even that gallant white steed could not close the ground quickly enough after the race he had just gone through. By the time we had caught up to Holmes and Reese they were at a stream contemplating in which direction the observer had gone. Meanwhile their horses were busy drinking the cool moorland water.

Once we were all together, Reese informed us that he had spotted the rider on the hill as they raced back from the oak and thought it was the same man he had noted previously. The fact that the man had run away when approached did not bode well for his intentions.

The Colonel spoke up, "We've always had trouble with touts lurking about, attempting to spy on either my horses or Lord Backwater's, next door at Capleton."

"Under normal circumstances I would agree," responded Holmes. "But added to the other events I believe this requires further inquiry. I suggest we split up and check upstream and down to see where he leaves the estate. Perhaps we can track him back to his lair, or determine where he hired the horse, which could enhance our search."

As Ross and Hunter knew the lie of the land, they would lead each search team. I accompanied Hunter upstream while Holmes, the Colonel and Reese followed the water's path down through the valley.

The groom and I worked our way slowly up the meandering stream, carefully examining the banks for any signs of a horse. After about a half mile of this, the stream narrowed to where smaller creeks, too narrow for a horse's track to remain hidden, branched off. Convinced that our spy had not come this way, we turned our horses back and made good speed in attempting to catch up to our party.

By the time we reached them, we found they had quit the streambed and were now above us on a road where a bridge crossed over. Holmes and Reese were checking the ground closely for fresh tracks. Colonel Ross remained mounted and was looking about in all directions for any sign of our intruder.

Convinced that they had found the trail of the mysterious rider, they did not even bother to ask us how our own journey had fared. Instead, Ross enquired if he could borrow my field glasses and I handed them over for him to peruse the countryside.

Holmes and Reese conferred like two old trackers comparing signs in the dirt, finally agreeing that the rider had turned his horse in circles, either deliberately to obscure his track, or in hesitation of which way to go. In either case there seemed no clear cut trail to follow.

The detective at last looked up to our host, "Colonel Ross, assuming our observer is not a local man, where is the nearest livery stable where he could rent a horse?"

"There are two in Tavistock, Mr. Holmes," answered the wizened old soldier. "One near the railway station and another at the south end of town, on the road to Whitchurch. But many of the locals also have horses for hire."

That seemed to strike a chord with my friend, but he chose to pursue the livery stable angle first and we rode into town together. I must admit that, with Reese in his western garb riding up ahead with Ross, I almost felt as if we were a posse on the American frontier. Although as far as I knew, I was the only one who was armed.

Chapter Four

The first stable we visited was the one near the station. It was a fairly large facility with a good sized barn and pens. An adjacent building housed several carriages and vehicles for rent. The proprietor was a big fellow who also did the blacksmith work. His barrel chest and muscular arms dominated a form that must have weighed at least two hundred and fifty pounds. A bushy black beard and moustache surrounded his full-lipped mouth and he greeted us with a bellowing 'Halloa'.

Well known to Colonel Ross, who introduced the fellow as Conner Jackson, he proved amiable and cooperative. In answer to Holmes's questions he informed us that he had, in fact, rented a bay horse to an American recently. The fellow had paid a week in advance and he hadn't seen him for several days. When the transaction first took place the fellow said he was staying at the Black Lion Inn, but had since moved on to other accommodations, though Jackson did not know where. He had a significant deposit and the first week's rental fee and was not concerned about the fellow not returning.

"What was his name? What did he look like?" enquired the detective. "Any distinguishing features?"

Jackson thought a moment, then replied, "He called himself Bob Castle. Pretty much an average fellow. Stocky but not fat. About five foot ten, with brown hair, brown eyes and clean shaven. There was about a one inch scar at the back of his left cheek, below his ear. Too wide to have been a knife cut."

Reese, who was standing to Holmes's right with his thumbs hitched in his wide western belt, cocked his head slightly at that remark, but did not speak. Holmes chose to ignore the gesture for the time being and continued to question the stable master as to the clothing he had observed the fellow wearing and which direction he noted the man riding off.

"The only time I saw him leave town he was heading north, but that was three days ago. I haven't seen him since."

We took our leave and proceeded to the Black Lion Inn to see what else could be learned about this Castle fellow. On the way we were hailed by the operator at the window of the telegraph office.

"Colonel Ross!" cried out the middle-aged, bespectacled gentleman. "I've a message for your guest!"

Reese dismounted and took the message in hand, tipping the fellow in the process. He read over the message quickly, folded it and tapped it on his left fist as his eyes raised skyward."

"Anything wrong, sir?" asked the Colonel with concern.

Reese looked down and slid the paper into his back pocket. Forcing a smile he replied. "Oh, it's nothing, Colonel. Just my foreman at the mine writing to inform me of a new discovery. But it's in a dangerous section. If you'll excuse me gentlemen I should reply to this. I'll join you momentarily."

We continued on while he stayed behind to write out a return message. At the Black Lion, a rustic old place whose ancient walls and sagging beams could not be ignored, despite the attempts at decorating with historic banners, tapestries and coats of arms, we questioned the desk clerk about Bob Castle.

The skinny, middle-aged desk clerk with a high pitched voice was well-acquainted with Colonel Ross. Thus, when we described who we were looking for, he responded to our questions readily enough.

"Oh, yes, the American fellow. He arrived last week. Let me see," he paused to flip the pages of his register. "Here it is. He arrived last Tuesday and left on Friday."

Holmes studied the signature, then asked, "Did he state his business?"

"No, sir. He was very private like. Took his meals in his room and didn't appear to socialise with any of the other guests. Didn't have much luggage. Just a pair of suitcases. He did buy some clothes while he was here. Something less American in style. Wanted to fit in, I suppose."

"Would that have been a brown suit and flat cap?" enquired the detective.

"Right enough, sir. That'd be him."

"Did he give any indication of where he was going when he checked out?"

"Not a word. Just came down with his suitcases, paid his bill and walked out the door without so much as a 'by your leave'. I haven't seen him since."

"Did he pay his bill, by cheque?

The clerk shook his head, "All cash."

We left the inn and decided to stop at a public house across the street to consider the situation. Reese, having finished his business, rode up and joined us at that point and we entered the establishment together.

Once seated, and having placed our orders, the big Texan asked what we had learned.

"It appears obvious that Castle is our man," replied Holmes. "Although that is not his real last name."

Colonel Ross set down his pint glass and looked up sharply. "How could you possibly know that, Holmes?"

Patiently, my friend explained, "The signature reveals much about an individual, Colonel. In this case the first name, Bob, was written in a smooth flow, but Castle, was written with an obvious hesitation after the 'Ca'. Also, the 'stle' did not have the flourish of the rest of his signature. He is not a very creative fellow, but he does show determination as well as deviousness."

Turning to Reese he continued, "Does that name seem suggestive to you, Mr. Reese, perhaps in conjunction with his description and scar?"

Reese held his coffee cup in both hands below his chin, with elbows on the table. Gazing through the rising steam at the detective he replied, "I've been racking my brain, Mr. Holmes. I've pursued cases against hundreds of men over the years and there are scores that fit his general description. The scar is interesting, but as you can imagine, scars are common among those who work the cattle ranches and mines or fight off hostile Indians. Even the inevitable bar scrapes among those blowing off steam on a Saturday night leave men with souvenirs of their mishaps. If I were home, I could go through my files, but with Bob being such a common name there's no one popping to mind."

He took a gulp of coffee and set it down as the waiter arrived with our food. It may have been my imagination at the time, but I thought I detected a welcoming of this distraction from our client.

After our meal we chose to ride back to King's Pyland, keeping a sharp eye out for any signs of this mysterious rider or evidence of his track. Being fairly certain he had not gone into town, Holmes questioned Colonel Ross on the possibility of any of the local folk taking in boarders.

"If the scoundrel came north, there are precious few places he could board both himself and a horse. Most of the lands here in Dartmoor are owned by breeders who would be very wary of strangers around their thoroughbreds. Some of the smaller farms might be open to taking someone in. Up around Willsworthy, perhaps. It's about four miles north of Tavistock."

"What of your immediate neighbours, Lord Backwater or Colonel Wardlaw?" asked Holmes.

"Impossible!" pronounced our host. "Backwater's trainer, Silas Brown, is a mean old cove who wouldn't allow a stranger within a hundred yards of Capleton Stables. And Colonel Wardlaw has retained three of his former officers to set up a private guard around his land. It's like a fortress. No chance anyone could gain access there."

"Brown is still in Backwater's employ?" I asked.

"Why, yes, Doctor," answered Ross. "Oh, he's a bit long in the tooth and drinks more than he should, but he's a long time and loyal fellow to Lord Backwater."

We spent the rest of the afternoon in separate activities. Ross had the business of the estate to tend to and Reese retired to this room, stating that he had decisions to ponder based on the telegram he had received.

Holmes and I took advantage of the quiet of our host's study where my friend settled into a comfortable chair and grasped his old briarwood and tobacco pouch for what he deemed would be a prolonged pipe session. At his request, I ensconced myself in a chair by a reading lamp and began perusing a book Holmes had noted upon the Colonel's shelves about the history of southwest England and Dartmoor in particular.

The hours drifted by slowly. At one point the windows grew dark with the passing of storm clouds but the threatening rains never came. One of the servants did come by to stoke the fireplace, as the temperature had dropped considerably, but Holmes, in his trance-like state took no notice of him and I merely nodded my thanks.

My eyes were growing heavy from the history lesson before me. I could draw no conclusions from the political history of the area that would affect our case. Geographically I learned that there were over one hundred and sixty hills or tors, twenty-two rivers and numerous tin mines and abandoned farmhouses from its ancient past. These last two items caught my attention as those of greatest interest, as they could provide hiding places for Reese's persecutor.

When we were informed that dinner would be served in half an hour, I closed the book and set it on the table next to the lamp. As I stood I noted that Holmes still sat, staring into the fire in a near hypnotic state. I gently laid my hand upon his shoulder and merely stated, "Time to dress for dinner, old friend."

He blinked and sat up straight, setting his now cold pipe into his pocket with his tobacco pouch.

"Dinner. Yes, that would be a necessity," he mumbled. He stood and clapped me on the arm. "Yes, Doctor, by all means let us dine."

That odd statement was followed by his striding purposefully out of the room. I merely followed, shaking my head at the peculiar workings of the great detective's mind.

At dinner once again with our host and his guest, our conversation naturally turned toward ideas of our next course of action. I informed the gathering of my discoveries regarding abandoned mines and farmhouses. The Colonel agreed.

"That would make sense. There's certainly no shortage for him to choose from."

Holmes, however, looked askance, pursed his lips and finally shook his head.

"While it may be possible, I find it unlikely," he stated. "It has been a cold spring season and he has only rented a horse, not a vehicle in which he could carry supplies. His food and bedding would be limited to his saddlebag and blanket. What could he cook? In addition, how could he dare to light a fire against the chill of night time on the moor? Even if the fire's glow could be hidden, there is no disguising smoke from a chimney or a mine shaft. How does he keep his horse out of sight? No, there are too many objections, gentlemen. He must be boarding with someone in the area and likely paying a high price to keep his presence secret."

"What do you suggest?" asked Reese, with great concern.

Holmes steepled his fingers above his plate, "That will depend upon you, good sir. I believe we can draw him out using you as bait while the rest of us keep a discreet distance. When he approaches we charge in and surround him. It will depend upon your bravery, but I do not believe his intention is to kill. At least not from a distance, for he has never levelled a rifle toward you. He may have murder on his mind, but I believe he wants you to know who he is before he commits such an act. That should give us an advantage."

"I've been in far more dangerous scrapes with fewer brave men at my side, Mr. Holmes," answered the Texan in that melodious baritone voice of his. "I'll not shirk at a chance to put this matter to rest once and for all. What do you propose?"

Chapter Five

We agreed to a plan of action for the next day and after dinner retired to Ross's study. The Colonel and I enjoyed brandy and cigars while Holmes settled for his pipe and coffee. Reese, as was his habit, declined tobacco or alcohol and shared a pot of coffee with the detective.

When it came time to retire for the evening we bid each other good night, but Holmes hung back with our host as Reese and I made our way up the stairs. I was later informed of their discussion:

"Colonel," asked Holmes, "do you have any correspondence or documents from Mr. Reese that includes his signature?"

"I believe I do, Mr. Holmes," he answered, checking his desk drawer and pulling out the requested paperwork. Handing it to the detective he enquired, "Does this tell you anything?"

Holmes examined the document, a hand-written letter, which Reese originally sent from America. It was a full two pages.

"This will do nicely, Colonel. May I take this to my room to evaluate? Having this amount to work with will allow me to create a much more accurate picture of your guest."

"By all means, Mr. Holmes. But can you at least tell me if he is playing a deceitful game?"

Holmes gazed at the paper and replied, "I'd prefer not to rush to judgement on this one, sir. Compared to Castle, Mr. Reese is a much more complex and highly intelligent individual. I could only venture at a glance that Jim is not the name he normally uses, but that could be just because he goes by James when practicing law. I'll be able to give you a much fuller report in the morning."

"Well then," the former soldier replied, "I'll leave you to it. I hope he is as legitimate as he appears, because I do care for his company."

"As do I, Colonel," answered Holmes.

What neither man knew was that the next day would reveal more than any of us had expected.

*****

We had planned an early start, hoping to gain position on our observer before he realised our deception. Holmes had proposed that we arise at six o'clock to be in position by sunrise at six forty-five. By six-fifteen however, there was no sign of Reese. Colonel Ross sent one of his servants up to see if the Texan was awake yet and he soon returned, holding out a handwritten note addressed to our host.

"Mr. Reese is not in his room sir. His bed has been made and this was laying in the middle of it."

Ross unfolded the paper, scanned it and muttered to himself, "The bloody fool!" For our edification he read it aloud:

Gentlemen,

I cannot, in good conscience, allow you all to risk your lives for a problem which must ultimately be settled by me. I am fairly certain of Bob Castle's identity and his purpose is to avenge his father, whom I put in prison over twenty years ago and was hung for his crimes.

The telegram from my mine foreman suggests that he knows my true identity, which means that both I and my family may be in danger. Should I not survive this encounter, please inform the same gentleman I telegraphed yesterday. The telegraph operator has the name and address.

Colonel, forgive me but I am leaving Silver Chief in your care and borrowing Red Fire so as to be better camouflaged in hopes of catching him unawares. Mr. Holmes, your skills surpass your reputation and I've no doubt you will uncover my identity. I just ask that you keep it secret for my family's sake.

Godspeed gentlemen. I hope to enjoy your company at dinner this evening.

Jim Reese

After a quick perusal Holmes declared, "It is as I determined from the letter you gave me last night, Colonel. He is intelligent, methodical, patient and stubborn. I suggest you have your stable lad saddle our horses. I need to do something which you, as a good host, should not be a part of, therefore I beg you not to enquire of my actions for the next fifteen minutes."

Ross started to protest but the look on Holmes's face made him think better of it and he left us to see to preparations for our journey. Holmes indicated that I should follow him and we went upstairs to Reese's room.

It was as neat and tidy as if the maid had just departed. Holmes went straight to the wardrobe and opened the door. There on the top shelf sat the bright white Stetson. Holmes pulled it off the shelf and threw it on to the bed. Then he pulled out the Texan's trunk and I helped him lift that onto the bed as well.

The detective made quick work of the lock and the discoveries inside were unique, indeed. Among the papers was a sealed envelope on top labelled 'In the event of my death'. Also a law degree, properly dated but with a name other than Reese. The telegram he received the previous day was there and it read:

SIX GRAVES DISTURBED STOP BELIEVE TRUTH KNOWN STOP BC REPORTED SAILING FOR ENGLAND STOP BEWARE STOP BLAINE STOP

"A rather disturbing missive, Holmes," I said, reading over his shoulder. "What do you make of it?"

"It's open to interpretation, Watson," he replied. "For now we need data in order to act."

As he continued to move objects about he revealed a double holster for a pair of .45 calibre pistols neatly wrapped, but one of the ivory handled Colts was missing, as were several rounds of bullets from the belt. Two other objects he found seemed in juxtaposition as to their purpose; a round metal disk and a black strip of leather. At the time I was totally at a loss as to their meaning.

Holmes, however, understood their significance immediately and threw them down, grabbed the other revolver and a handful of bullets, slammed the trunk shut and re-locked it.

"Come, Watson. We must hurry!"

Putting the pistol in his pocket, he snatched the Stetson off the bed, rushed out of the door and down the stairs. Breathlessly I followed, trying to ask him what the meaning was behind what he had found.

"No time, Watson," he called back over his shoulder. "But he is a man whom many would wish to capture and I fear he may have underestimated his opponent."

Catching up with the Colonel in the stables we found Hunter just finishing saddling up our mounts. Ross explained how Reese had tricked the young man into letting him ride off on Red Fire. He had borrowed an old black flat cap, explaining that his Stetson would be too recognisable from a distance. He was also wearing a black overcoat, making his appearance totally unlike his usual riding garb.

Holmes, in his grey Ulster, was only slightly taller than the Texan and when he put on the white Stetson it would have been hard to distinguish them from a distance, especially when he mounted the big white stallion.

Hunter indicated the direction in which Reese had headed. The three of us took off at a gallop to lend our assistance, unwelcome as it may have been. When we crested one of the hills on the moor, Holmes reigned in Silver Chief. Requesting my field glasses he pointed them to the west, scanning the fields and the tree line on the hill opposite.

"Why are you looking that way, Holmes?" asked our host. "Reese's trail leads south."

"I confess I am acting on an hypothesis, Colonel, he replied. "But with the data at hand it appears to be better than even odds."

Suddenly he stood tall in the saddle and peered eagerly through the lenses. Handing them to Ross he pointed, "And we seem to have a winning hand. Look there, just along the tree line above that group of boulders."

Even with my naked eye I could see movement where Holmes pointed. The Colonel, with the assistance of the binoculars, exclaimed, "That looks like our stranger all right, and that appears to be Silas Brown with him!"

"Silas Brown?" I queried, "The trainer at Capleton?"

"A long shot, Watson," declared Holmes. "But based upon our past dealings, a reasonable theory."

We formed a plan and then Holmes rode off at a canter across the field below the tree line, following the trail of our client. All the while imitating Reese's riding posture as well as he could. Colonel Ross and I circled around so as to come up behind the two interlopers.

The hill fell down to the level of the moor and Holmes noted that the riders, instead of coming down the southern slope, turned to the west and disappeared. Realising that

Reese must have rounded the hill and was now riding up the vale on the opposite side, Holmes dug his heels in and encouraged the big stallion to a full gallop.

Emerging on the other side of a small tor, Holmes was suddenly confronted by the two men, now wearing masks to cover their faces and with guns drawn. Reigning his horse in, Holmes studied his surroundings and chose to comply with their demand to step down rather than make a run for it. Before he could dismount, however, the thinner of the two cried out, "That's not your man! That's Sherlock Holmes! We've been tricked!"

The stockier fellow, apparently Bob Castle, raised his pistol and pointed it at Holmes's head, "Where is he? Where's that American calling himself Jim Reese?"

From the top of a large rock behind the two villains, a deep voice called out, "Right here, mister! Now drop those weapons!"

When Castle and Brown turned at the sound, Holmes drew his own gun and exclaimed, "I suggest you listen to him, gentlemen."

Brown, a sensible, if avaricious man, put his gun away and raised his hands. Castle reacted like an enraged, cornered animal and fired at Reese. The big Texan ducked and the explosion of his gun rang out simultaneously with that of Holmes's. Castle screamed in pain and fell off his horse, clutching his right shoulder, now ruined by the impact of bullets entering both front and back. Still, he desperately lunged for his fallen weapon with his left hand, but it was knocked away and out of reach by a second shot from Reese.

The Colonel and I had been riding toward the sound of gunfire and that was the first sight I had of the encounter, which was described to me later by Holmes.

Castle then collapsed from shock. Not having my medical bag, I did what I could to treat his wound, but Holmes's bullet, which he had meant to throw off the culprit's aim by striking the shooting arm, had severed the subclavian artery. I managed to fashion a tourniquet of sorts from Castle's belt and shirt, which I tore into the required shape and size.

Having lost consciousness there was no way to transport him on horseback. Reese and Holmes gathered branches, blankets and ropes to create a travois and we loaded Castle on to it behind his horse.

Travel was slow and it took nearly an hour to return to King's Pyland. By then, Castle had suffered severe blood loss and his pulse was thready at best. We turned Colonel Ross's drawing room into a temporary operating theatre now that I had access to my instruments. However, the severity of the wound was too great and he passed beyond mortality before I could even attempt to repair the artery.

We had some of the stable lads wrap the body and remove it to an outbuilding while one of them rode into town for the police surgeon and Inspector Gregory, who was still the local law, as he had been during our previous visit.

Retiring to the Colonel's study where Holmes had handcuffed Silas Brown to a chair, the detective began an interrogation of our prisoner.

"How did Castle come to stay at Capleton? Surely Lord Backwater was unaware of his presence."

Brown, who was once a defiant and surly fellow, had withered over the years and now he meekly replied to Holmes's questions.

"I met him riding out on the moor a few days ago. We got to talking and he told me he was on the trail of a notorious American outlaw and needed a place nearby to operate in secret until he was sure this Reese fellow was the man he was looking for.

"He offered me a considerable sum of money to let him put up at our stable and take his meals with the lads. Said it shouldn't be for more than a few days."

"What made you come out with him this morning?" demanded Holmes.

"He said he was convinced that he had the right fellow and he wanted me to help capture him because he was known to be a fierce fighter when cornered. He told me there was a large reward and I could have a percentage of it."

Reese spoke up, "If that were true, why the masks?"

Brown looked up into those piercing brown eyes and cleared his throat, realising how weak his answer was going to sound.

"Because he didn't have jurisdiction, he didn't want to cause no trouble in case we got the wrong man. We would've let anyone we stopped by mistake be on their way without being able to identify us."

"Humbug!" declared Colonel Ross. "You're nothing but a highwayman!"

Brown shrank under the older man's accusation and cried, "No, sir, Colonel, sir. I swear I thought I was bringing a criminal to justice!"

"Then you're a bigger fool than I always thought you were," spat the Colonel in disgust as he turned away. He slung the cigar butt he was smoking into the fireplace, then went and sat behind his desk.

Holmes gave Reese a look that I was not sure how to interpret. It was either an appeal for permission, or a request that he be trusted. Reese, apparently, recognised it for what it was and gave a brief nod.

The detective, who had been standing over the frightened trainer, now retreated to the fireplace mantel and lit a cigarette. Blowing a long trail of smoke toward the ceiling, he at last spoke to all of us, though his eyes were fixed on our prisoner.

"Your *guest*, Brown, was not a lawman, or even a bounty hunter. He was an outlaw and the son of an outlaw who Mr. Reese here put in prison twenty years ago. That man was hung for his murderous crimes and the son was seeking revenge. His name was not Castle though it is not important for you to know his true identity.

"Six years ago, I advised Colonel Ross that a little amnesty be granted in the case of Silver Blaze, when it was, in fact, you who would have kept the horse hidden and not found in time to win the Wessex Cup. I see now that my leniency was misplaced and only a just punishment may correct your flawed moral compass. You will be turned over to Inspector Gregory to answer for your part in this misadventure."

The butler stepped in at that juncture and enquired of the Colonel as to what he should tell the cook about lunch. With a slap of his hand on his desk he responded, "Gentlemen, I don't know about you, but I always enjoyed a hearty meal after a military campaign and none of us had breakfast this morning, so I'm all for it. What say you?"

We all agreed that, while it may not have been tempting considering the death we just witnessed, physical sustenance was quite necessary after some sixteen hours without food. We left Silas Brown handcuffed to his chair and went to our rooms to clean up for lunch.

Arriving in the hallway where our guest rooms were all situated, Holmes and I caught up to Reese and he invited us in. The detective turned over the Stetson and the Colt .45 to his client. Reese looked at the pistol and then to Holmes.

"Obviously you've been in my trunk and learned my identity," he stated, without accusation.

"A necessary precaution to ensure your safety as my client," replied Holmes. "Colonel Ross was not aware of my actions, nor is he privy to the information I discovered."

Reese withdrew the trunk from the wardrobe and threw it onto the bed. Opening it up he replaced the Colt Holmes had handed him, as well as the one from his pocket, into their holsters. Picking up the framed law degree he ran his fingers across the name.

Waving us to the guest chairs he sat on the bed and asked, "How much have you ascertained?"

My old friend folded one leg over the other and interlaced his fingers in his lap, tapping his thumbs together as he looked over at the American. After a moments pause he responded.

"I was well aware that you were more than you seemed from the first time I laid eyes upon you. Your tanned complexion indicates considerable time spent outdoors, and your walk was that of a man who spent many hours in the saddle. That, of course, could be explained by your 'riding the circuit' of courts throughout Texas. What puzzled me was the difference in your skin texture around your eyes and temples.

I must admit that took me some time to arrive at a suitable explanation and I was still unsure of my hypothesis until I looked into your trunk and found the leather strip.

"What I was sure of, was that your references to practicing law were along the lines of enforcement rather than judicial. The way you hold your hands close to your hip when you walk indicated a man ready to go for his gun at a moment's notice. Even when not wearing your holster it is ingrained in your muscles to retain such a stance. When I saw your gloves, I recognised that the wear pattern was not only typical for a horseman's reins, but the peculiar smoothing of the grain of the thumb and forefinger was that of a man who used a revolver quite frequently."

Reese nodded in appreciation of my friend's deductive reasoning and asked, "What made you so sure I was not some outlaw hiding out in England?"

"That was a consideration for a time," Holmes replied with a smile. "The fact that you insisted on cash and no wire transfers leaned heavily toward you not wanting your identity known. When I asked the Colonel for a sample of your handwriting I became aware that, while J.R. are your real initials, your name is not Jim Reese.

"However, the rest of your handwriting, your manners, your intelligence, especially regarding the law, and the fact that you were willing to have me investigate, indicated that you did not fear exposure from either the Colonel or myself. The explanations you offered were reasonable, if not complete. As I began to correlate all this information, it triggered a memory of someone I had read about many years ago. Taking that into account with your current age, all the pieces fell into place. Therefore, I saw my only consideration need be to protect you, not judge you."

Reese, having put down his degree, now picked up the metal disk, a circle surrounding a star, a lawman's badge.

As he gazed upon it he told us his story of how his life had changed and his career path chosen on one fateful day when Castle's father and his gang ambushed the posse Reese was riding in. The details are not for public knowledge, but the man we knew as Reese became a symbol of justice on the American frontier.

"But that was nigh on to twenty years ago now," he continued. "The man who rescued me and rode by my side in my quest for law and order has suffered from deteriorating health. He has returned to his people to live out his remaining days. I believe I once read something the Doctor wrote, quoting you saying 'I would be lost without my Boswell'.

"I don't think I want to go on without someone to share the quest, someone I can count on to have my back. Civilisation has made mass inroads into the American West and my services are not as vital as they once were. To try to continue on my own at my age ..." he shook his head. "No, I may still pursue justice as a lawyer in the courts, but the rough and tumble life of a lawman isn't for me any more. The appeal of a quiet life beckons and if I can avoid the likes of Castle and his ilk, I think it's time to retire."

His soliloquy was quite moving and I realised that he could well be speaking for Holmes and myself in the not so distant future.

The detective stood to leave. Reaching out to shake Reese's hand he spoke softly, "Sir, I assure you that everything we have discovered will remain a secret. Make whatever explanation you see fit to the Colonel and to Inspector Gregory. As far as we are concerned," he continued, nodding in my direction as he spoke for both of us, "you were pursued by Castle as a result of mistaken identity.

"I wish you good fortune in whatever endeavour you choose to pursue. But I do not know if the call to arms in a righteous cause can be silenced in your heart. In some ways I believe we are alike. Your thirst for justice is akin to my thirst for solving crimes. I cannot believe it will be easily slaked."

We then retired to our rooms to dress for lunch. As we walked down the hall I asked my friend, "I saw the name on the law degree, Holmes, but who is he? What's the real story behind a masked lawman?"

Holmes shook his head, "This is one adventure your readers will have to do without, Watson. He hides his identity to shield his dead brother's family from being used against him. This secret is one we must keep. Not even your frequent tactic of changing the client's name will be protection enough in this case."

Inspector Gregory arrived just as we finished eating and our explanations trumped the poor excuses Silas Brown attempted to make. The Capleton trainer was arrested and taken away. Gregory wrote up his report as a misadventure due to mistaken identity as we had suggested.

We stayed on at King's Pyland for two more days, enjoying the fresh country air and Colonel Ross's hospitality. When at last we parted company, Reese promised to keep in touch and let us know what path he would choose.

At the railway station, we found our train was running a half hour late and so we walked down the street to a nearby bookstore. As Holmes perused the latest editions of newspapers, I wandered among the shelves in idle curiosity. Suddenly, next to the Penny Dreadfuls, I saw a display of American Dime Novels and one in particular caught my eye. On the cover was a masked rider wearing a white Stetson on a rearing white stallion with an ivory handled pistol in hand. The title told me all I needed to know and answered the questions which Holmes would not: *The Lone Ranger and the Hunt for Butch Cavendish.*

The Rest of the Story

The preceding is the story Watson prepared, but his notes go much further. Attempting to honour his promise of secrecy, he left certain facts out or without detail. Eventually he felt he could not publish the tale without revealing too much and left it among his un-submitted manuscripts. However, his notes go on to reveal what was later brought to light in the annals of the American West.

The world now knows the full story of the Lone Ranger, John Reid and his Indian companion, Tonto, who roamed the West enforcing law and order in those wild and violent times of the late nineteenth century.

Reid was a lawyer who had just graduated from law school in the East when he joined his older brother, Captain Dan Reid and a posse of Rangers, in pursuit of the infamous Butch Cavendish gang. (Obviously the father of Bob Castle in Watson's tale). Betrayed by their scout, the Rangers were ambushed and massacred near Wild Horse Canyon. The younger Reid, seriously wounded but alive, was found by the Indian, Tonto and nursed back to health. He vowed to uphold the law and bring Cavendish to justice. But to do so, he felt it necessary to adopt a secret identity and chose to wear the black mask to hide his features. In burying the posse members he had Tonto dig an extra grave so that the world would think all had perished. This would leave his brother's widow and young son protected from threats of outlaws seeking an advantage.

169

The Reid brothers did, in fact, own a small silver mine and John took their old partner and retired Ranger, Jim Blaine, into his confidence. Blaine worked the mine and prepared silver bullets as a symbol of pure justice for the Lone Ranger, who swore never to kill and always shot to wound, so that villains could be turned over to the courts for just punishment.

Watson's notes do not reveal whether or not the white stallion was actually the famous Silver, known to be the Lone Ranger's horse. Chronologically it is possible for Silver to still be alive and capable of stud service in 1894.

A letter from Reid to Holmes and Watson was found attached to Watson's manuscript. Dated 1904, it indicates that the American was now working as a corporate lawyer for Thomas Edison's movie production company in Manhattan, New York, and was a Western lore advisor on the 1903 film *The Great Train Robbery*.

Fun Facts

Unlike the 2013 movie, which shows the Lone Ranger beginning his career in 1869, it is more likely that the events of his beginnings took place at least five years later. This is based upon two historical facts:

The Texas Rangers were disbanded in 1860 and not re-organised until 1874. They also did not start wearing badges until around 1875.

The Lone Ranger is always pictured using Colt model 1873 revolvers.

Silver King and Silver Chief were the actual names of the horses used to play the role of Silver in the 1938-39 *Lone Ranger* movie serials.

March of the Swiss Soldiers is the finale of *The William Tell Overture* by the Italian composer Gioachino Rossini, written in 1829. It became the theme music for *The Lone Ranger* radio program from 1933-1956, as well as *The Lone Ranger* television show, which ran from 1949 to 1957, and all the *Lone Ranger* movies.

Crime fighting apparently runs in the Reid family. The Lone Ranger's nephew, Dan Reid Jr., was the father of Britt Reid, later known as 'The Green Hornet'.

Credit for information about The Lone Ranger, is due to George W. Trendle and Fran Striker, who brought the facts to light in their 1933 radio program.

The Adventure of the
Italian Gourmet

Chapter One

The smells of herbs and spices assailed us as we walked into Rivano's Ristorante. I had experienced my share of Indian food and Middle-eastern dishes during my army days in India and Afghanistan, but this was a new experience for me. My new friend, the amateur detective Mr. Sherlock Holmes, had invited me to dine with him at this establishment and it was my first experience of Italian cuisine.

We were shown to our table by a young waitress with raven hair and dark brown eyes that sparked with intensity. Her accent was charming as she welcomed Holmes and introduced herself as Carmen. She handed us menus that were filled with the names of exotic-sounding dishes. Holmes advised her that we would need a few minutes to decide, but to please bring us a bottle of Chianti and she left us for the kitchen.

As I studied the menu I found it impossible to choose. Finally, I turned to Holmes and asked for a recommendation.

"First of all, Doctor, I should warn you that most of these dishes have varying degrees of spiciness and you may wish to indulge in moderation and be prepared to take some bicarbonate of soda later on. They are likely not on a scale with some of the curry dishes you experienced overseas, but they are a different blend which may affect you in unknown ways."

"Thank you, Holmes," I replied. "But the aroma in here has whetted my appetite and I am eager to explore the possibilities."

My new friend smiled, gazed down at his menu, then spoke, "Very well. Then I would recommend you try the pesto Genovese. It's a specialty of Chef Rivano and should not overly excite your digestive system."

When Carmen returned with the wine and a basket of freshly baked bread, which smelled of butter and garlic, we placed our orders. Holmes opted for something called lasagne and we sipped our wine as we awaited our food.

"So, Watson," he casually stated, "when will you be picking up your new walking stick?"

I set down my wine glass and sat up straight, "I do not recall telling you I'd ordered a new stick, Holmes. How did you know? Did I leave the receipt lying about?" I automatically started to reach for my wallet, where I thought I had secreted the order, when he stopped me.

"Nothing quite so easy as that, dear fellow. But it was no small matter to deduce through casual observation," he replied, as he lounged easily in his chair.

I was still getting used to this habit of his, where he made statements of fact, seemingly out of thin air, yet entirely accurate. Although he had yet to be wrong, I still challenged his method.

"Come now, man. Surely you must have followed me, or spoken to my merchant."

"Please, Watson," he sighed. "You are a remarkably easy fellow to read. Don't take that harshly, most people are. It has been obvious since I met you that you have been unable to become comfortable with your army-issued cane. The combination of your war wounds to your shoulder and leg have left you quite out of balance. I am no doctor, but I perceive that your present stick is too long, thus putting pressure on your bad shoulder. Anyone could notice your occasional wince, especially when you take the stairs. I have also observed blisters from time to time, where the skin has not toughened into calluses quite yet. The fact that these appear on the palm of your hand indicates to me that you should switch from a 'J' handle to a Derby style, where the pressure shifts to the more padded part of your hand below the thumb. As a medical man yourself, you would naturally realise this and therefore take the proper steps to alleviate your discomfort.

"Being on an army pension leaves you little surplus income for luxuries and so you have been saving up. I often hear you dropping your daily change into a jar in your room each night. While there are versions available, you would naturally prefer something more indicative of your station as a medical man. Not having an exact knowledge of your income, and only an estimate of your expenditure, leaves me insufficient data to determine how long it would take you to reach the full amount. However, I would estimate that you will have sufficient funds by Thursday next."

I sat there looking at this magician to whom I had connected myself. Every observation and deduction was alarmingly accurate. Still I wouldn't give in just yet.

"You think yourself very clever, Holmes," I stated, leaning forward to look him in the eye. "But, don't you also need to know the cost of the stick I have ordered in order to complete your formula?"

He gave that irritating little smirk with which I was becoming all too familiar, just prior to his more showy revelations, before he answered with the exact amount of my purchase price.

"Dash it all, Holmes!" I cried, pounding my fist on the arm of my chair as I leaned back. "How could you possibly know that?"

Carmen arrived just then and set down our orders. Looking at me with concern she asked, "Is anything wrong, *signore*? I brought the food as quickly as I could."

I looked up into those eyes and immediately regretted my outburst.

"No, no, my dear. Everything is quite all right. You have been an excellent hostess. It's just my friend here can be most exasperating."

She looked at me in disbelief and pleaded, "Oh, no, no. *Signore* Holmes is a good man, *un buon amico!*"

Holmes responded, "It's all right, *Carmenita*. The Doctor was just surprised by something I said. Thank you for bringing our food so quickly."

The young lady curtsied with a shy smile for my friend and left us to our meal.

I began eating what turned out to be a tasty combination of pasta, potatoes, garlic, green beans, pine nuts, red pepper flakes, basil, some type of cheese and a few other spices I was not familiar with, all mixed in what Holmes told me was olive oil. In combination with the garlic flavoured bread and the Chianti, it was a delightful meal. I asked my friend how he come across this place.

"I met Giuseppe Rivano last year when I was still living on Montague Street" he replied. "There was a case involving an intrigue regarding his daughter and some claim of a childhood marriage arrangement with a man from their old village near Genoa."

"Carmen is his daughter I take it?" I offered.

"Is that a guess or an observation?" he queried.

It was my turn to impress my friend. "My studies of medical Latin were enough to allow me to recognise that she had called you 'a good friend' and you referred to her in the diminutive, *Carmenita*, which tells me you have some personal familiarity with her. As you keep telling me, 'observation and deduction' reveals the truth."

"Very good, Doctor," he smiled, which gave me no little pleasure at his praise. "At any rate, the man arrived in London to claim his bride when she was due to turn sixteen. Giuseppe argued that the arrangement he had with the man's father was to settle an old family dispute, but that his leaving his village and coming to England put an end to that and the arrangement should be voided."

"But the gentleman from Genoa did not agree?" I deduced.

"He was no gentleman, Watson. I was able to prove that he was in fact an imposter. The groom-to-be had died as a boy. This fellow was a cousin who saw a chance to take advantage of the situation and not only gain a bride, but also a foothold into Rivano's restaurant business. Once exposed, the Italian community was quick to rally to Giuseppe's aid and the cad was forced to flee back to Italy."

"No wonder she stood up for you so vigorously when I became agitated."

"Yes, she and her father are quite passionate about the debt they feel they owe me. So much so that I am able to assist you toward the purchase of your new cane by virtue of the fact that our meal tonight is, as Chef Rivano puts it, *gratuito*. A courtesy which they have extended to me for life, but which I am loathe to take advantage of too often."

The proprietor came out from the kitchen to see how our meal was and Holmes introduced me. He was a stout fellow, as befits his occupation. The olive skin crinkled with joy around his eyes and a thin moustache topped his infectious smile. I complimented the man on my meal and he beamed with delight.

"I am glad to hear you say so, Dr. Watson. Do you see that man over there?" He whispered conspiratorially, as he pointed to a large fellow in a dark suit, sitting a few tables away from us. I answered in the affirmative and he continued.

"That is the restaurant reviewer and food critic, John Valentine. He has ordered the same dish as you and I pray he agrees with your compliments. A good word from him is worth more than a year's *pubblicitá*."

We wished the cheery Italian well and completed our dinner as he went back to the kitchen. When we finished our after-dinner wine, we walked out past Valentine's table. He was about halfway through the same meal I had just devoured and seemed to be enjoying it quite well. As we stood out on the pavement hailing a cab I commented to Holmes, "From the looks of Valentine's appetite at gobbling up Rivano's cooking, I'd say there will be an excellent review for your friend in *The Times* tomorrow."

"A logical deduction, old chap," he replied with a smile and a pat to his full stomach.

But who says newspapermen are logical ...

Chapter Two

Holmes had been right, the exposure to a new combination of spices had affected my digestion somewhat later that night, but some mineral water and a small dose of bicarbonate took care of it. By no means was I discouraged from desiring to go back to try more dishes in the future.

I arose the next morning to find that Holmes was not up yet, so stepped out for some morning papers. When I returned our landlady, Mrs. Hudson was in the hall.

"Good morning, Dr. Watson. I was just about to come up and see if you gentlemen were ready for some breakfast."

I assured her that I was quite famished and would ring down twice if Holmes was of a similar mind. Stepping up to our rooms I noted that the fire I had started before leaving was going quite well. The warmth of the room was welcome after being out in the morning chill of an early spring day. My friend had arisen and a cloud of tobacco smoke had accumulated above his chemistry table near the window, where he was mixing some new concoction.

"Good morning, Holmes," I said cheerily. "Mrs. Hudson would like to know if you are ready for breakfast."

The man was concentrating so hard that, at first, I thought he hadn't heard me. Then a poof of smoke jumped from the retort he was heating and he let out a 'Ha!' of satisfaction. He began to make some notes and finally said, "Watson, do be good enough to ring down for some breakfast."

As we awaited our morning fare, I sat on the sofa and opened *The Times*, after setting down the other publications by my friend's chair. I had learned that the newspapers were a constant source of information for Holmes who had a shelf containing index books filled with tidbits of information he used in his work.

For myself, I was curious as to the review of the restaurant we had enjoyed the previous evening and flipped through the pages seeking out Valentine's column. Holmes returned to join me after washing his hands of the chemicals with which he had been experimenting. He picked up the top paper from the stack I'd laid out for him. Whilst he indulged in the agony columns, I found what I was looking for and began reading the reviewer's thoughts on Rivano's Ristorante.

As I made my way down the column I was stunned by one disparaging remark after another. Valentine had criticised everything from the décor, to the staff, to the food. He described the establishment as '... a smelly grease pot where one fights not to choke on the smells emanating from the kitchen or the reeking odour of the serving staff. The wall paintings were crude and certainly not indicative of the great Italian masters. The garish lamps cast insufficient light, ostensibly to create a romantic ambiance, but more likely to hide the unsanitary conditions and poorly cooked food. The dishes served showed artistry in neither presentation nor taste. I was served a *Pesto Genovese* which was of a rubbery texture and over-spiced with fennel, giving it a liquorice flavour which did not mix well with the garlic. The spices and vegetables were of the poorest quality and the wine smelled and tasted like vinegar'.

I could not believe my eyes. I know that each man has his own tastes, but these remarks were blatantly untrue. I cried out to my friend and handed him the offending column to read for himself.

Holmes perused the article quickly, then set the paper down. "Something is afoul here, Watson, and you and I are witnesses that it was not the food."

"It certainly was not. That remark about fennel is ridiculous. I am quite familiar with that herb from my days in Afghanistan and there was no trace of it. Nor was the pasta rubbery at all."

We discussed what was to be done as we pored over the breakfast delivered by Mrs. Hudson. Finally, we agreed that we should call upon Giuseppe Rivano to learn if anything untoward had happened after we had gone.

We left our Baker Street lodgings and arrived at Rivano's at just after ten o'clock. We walked around to the rear entrance, since he would not be opening for business for another hour. There we found the distraught proprietor chopping up meat in preparation for the lunch crowd. The violence of his butcher's knife striking the chopping block told us that he had also seen the bad review. The other staff members were giving him a wide berth. As soon as he noticed our presence he buried his knife deeply into the block and came over to greet us.

"*Signore* Holmes, Dr. Watson, did you read what that *porco* wrote about my business? So help me, if he ever sets foot over my doorstep again I will gut him like *un maiale grasso!*"

Holmes spoke gently, hoping to calm the agitated chef, "Did something happen after we left last night? He seemed to be enjoying his meal as we walked by him on the way out."

"I tell you it was *perfecto*. I prepared it exactly as I did for Dr. Watson and as I do dozens of times each day. I don't even have fennel in my kitchen. It has no place in any of my dishes. He ate with gusto and no complaints at the time. He also had the finest wine of the house. Let me show you."

He strode back to his wine closet and pulled out a half bottle of a red burgundy. He poured a soupcon for both Holmes and myself and we agreed it was superb.

"Aha! You see? He is a lying *bastardo* out to ruin my business!"

At that moment the back door to the kitchen opened again and a fellow I had met a few times at our Baker Street rooms came in. He stopped in surprise as he saw us, then walked over to where we stood.

"Holmes, Doctor, what brings you here?" He asked, suspiciously.

"Good morning, Lestrade," answered my friend. "We are just visiting our old friend, Chef Rivano. *Signore,*" he said, turning to the proprietor, "this is Inspector Lestrade of Scotland Yard."

The Italian gentleman bowed to the Inspector, indicating his hands were covered with the results of food preparation so he could not shake hands.

Lestrade took on his most official tone and responded, "Giuseppe Rivano, I am here to bring you in for questioning regarding the death of John Valentine."

"Valentine's dead?" I asked in surprise.

"Yes, Doctor. Not more than an hour after *The Times* hit the streets this morning, with the unfavourable review of Mr. Rivano's restaurant."

"How was he killed?" asked Holmes.

Lestrade called for two officers from the alley to come in and ordered them to search the premises. Then he answered my friend.

"He was stabbed with a large knife." He looked over the kitchen area and walked to a block of knives on the counter. "One which matches this set and would fit nicely into that empty slot."

Rivano protested that he was innocent of course, but could not account for the missing knife. He thought it was somewhere in the kitchen.

"My men will look for it," answered the weasel-faced Inspector. "In the meantime you'll need to come with me."

"One question first, if I may, Lestrade?" asked Holmes.

Reluctantly, he agreed and Holmes faced Rivano, "*Signore,* what time did you arrive this morning and was the door locked?"

After moment's thought he replied, "I come in about nine o'clock and no, the door was not locked. I was going to speak to my headwaiter, Lorenzo, about it. He was supposed to lock up last night."

Holmes advised the man to take heart and that he would look into it. Lestrade lead him away and I stood by for a time, waiting for the two officers to complete their search. Unfortunately they did not find the missing knife. Holmes, however, leaped into action. First, he examined the lock on the back door with his magnifying lens, then went over the ground out in the alley. Returning inside he made an examination of the floor, mumbling complaints to himself about all the foot traffic of the morning. Then, he closely examined the block of knives. He put a handkerchief over his fingers and slowly pulled each knife partially out of its slot. He seemed extremely interested in this activity and was almost oblivious to the two officers, who announced they had completed their search and were leaving.

With them gone, the detective suddenly turned to another man in the kitchen, "Pietro, you will be taking over cooking duties until *Signore* Rivano returns, correct?"

A young man of average build with wild curly black hair and an unruly moustache answered in the affirmative.

"You have your own set of cooking utensils, I see," continued Holmes. "I should like to take this knife block with me for further examination. I believe it may help prove your master innocent."

Pietro readily agreed and other staff members nodded in approval. They were certain their maestro was no cold-blooded killer and knew Holmes had helped him and his daughter previously. My companion bundled up the block of knives in a burlap sack and we returned to Baker Street.

In our rooms, he cleared space on his laboratory table and put the knife set upon it. He seemed to be highly focused, yet I could not understand his purpose.

"I say, Holmes, what is it you expect to find among the knives that are still here? Shouldn't you be asking the Inspector if you can examine the actual murder weapon?"

Holmes sat at his stool, rubbing his palms back and forth before proceeding as he answered. "Indeed, Watson, and I intend to request just such permission. However, there may be valuable evidence among these pieces as well."

"What makes you think so?" I enquired.

"While you were watching the constables bumbling about haphazardly, I found scratches on the door lock, indicating it may have been picked. I also noted some unusual footprints in the alley and traces of the same on the kitchen floor. They were not those of Rivano or any of his staff, for they were much too large.

"Now, note these knives as I pull them out. See how these two have the blades facing the opposite direction of all the others? I believe our killer was pulling out each large knife until he found just the one he wanted for his purpose. These two he put back in the opposite direction without thinking."

I looked on in agreement but then asked, sceptically, "I see what you're saying, but how can you prove it has anything to do with Valentine's murder?"

"Have you read of Sir William Herschel's work with fingerprints in India?"

"I was aware of the practice while I was stationed there. It was used for proof of signature regarding contracts I believe."

"Very good, Doctor. The British legal system has not yet accepted fingerprint evidence as proof enough for convictions, but if I can obtain prints from these knives that were mishandled, as well as matching prints from the murder weapon, and prove that there is a set that does not belong to Chef Rivano or his staff, then we can plant a seed of doubt. That should encourage Inspector Lestrade to at least consider the possibility of another assassin and continue to investigate."

He set about his work and I left him to it. I spent the next few hours checking in with local hospitals. My first stop was St Bartholomew's, the famous Bart's where I had met Holmes just a few months before. They were able to schedule me for a few hours work in the following week. At the recommendation of the Administrator, I went up to Hoxton to call in at Moorfield's Eye Hospital. In their Administrator's waiting room, I struck up a conversation with a visiting medical student from Edinburgh named Arthur Doyle. We hit it off quite famously and promised to keep in touch

186

afterwards. The Administrator took my information and promised to contact me should they need my services.

I returned to 221B Baker Street in time for tea, but discovered Holmes had gone out. Mrs. Hudson informed me that he had left for Scotland Yard about an hour before and promised to be home for dinner. She brought me tea and biscuits and I settled down with an evening paper I had purchased on the way home.

I read, with great interest, the details of the murder of the food critic, John Valentine. His employer had last seen him the night before, when he filed his story on Rivano's Ristorante. Early this morning he was on his way to Finsbury to review a newly established bakery. He had apparently arrived before it opened to the public and had stepped around to the side entrance to see if he could gain access to the kitchen. In the early morning twilight there were few pedestrians about, and thus no witnesses to the fatal event. Valentine was stabbed in the stomach first, and then the knife was thrust into his heart and left behind when the attacker fled the scene. One of the baker's assistants found the body when he came out to empty some rubbish.

It went on to report that the case was under investigation by Inspector Lestrade of Scotland Yard, who had taken a keen interest in one Giuseppe Rivano as a prime suspect and was holding him for questioning.

It gave further particulars of Valentine's career and brief biographical information. I was a little surprised that the paper did not know more about one of its own employee's personal life. There was no mention of anything about the man before he started working for them, some six years ago, only that he had studied on the continent at the *Academia Culinaria* in Milan.

Chapter Three

Just as the lamplighters were attending to the street lamps on Baker Street, the detective returned home. As he was hanging up his hat a thought occurred to me. He had often caught me off guard by telling me where I'd been, or where I was off too, without my having said a word. I decided to give him back a piece of his own and greeted him in that same off-handed manner he had used with me.

"Greetings, Holmes! I see that you been to Finsbury."

He looked at me quizzically, as I pretended to study him up and down.

"I also percieve that you've been exposed to the rubbish of an alley ..." I sniffed the air, "behind a bakery."

"A logical deduction, Watson," he replied, his eyes falling on the evening paper I had just set down. "I'm sure that *The Times* was quite valuable in making that deduction. By the way, what were you doing up in Hoxton? The hospital there is for ocular specialists, as I recall."

He had done it again and I demanded to know how.

"Doctor, if you don't want me to know where you've been, don't leave your restaurant receipts lying about on your writing table. It's quite obvious that you had lunch at the Hare's Lair which is just down the street from Moorfields. Have they need of your services?"

I sighed at his explanation and replied, "They occasionally have patients who have other injuries in addition to their eye problem. I have applied to be on their call list if needed."

"Excellent," replied my new friend. "What about Bart's? I'm sure they can use you."

"Yes, Bart's has me scheduled for some rounds next week. But tell me, how is your investigation going? Are you able to prove Rivano's innocence?"

"I have convinced Lestrade to keep looking into the matter after I pointed out that the kitchen lock had been picked. Unfortunately, Rivano has no alibi other than his own family, who claim he was home at the time Valentine met his end. I did verify that there were footprints in the alley near the body which matched those outside Rivano's door. He was less impressed that I proved there were fingerprints other than Rivano's on both the murder weapon and the other two knives. Also the fact that only those three knives were out of order."

"It's a new science, Holmes," I observed in the Inspector's defence. "It often takes time for such things to become accepted fact."

"Hmmpf!" he snorted. "At any rate, the Inspector is at least looking at other possibilities. He has invited me to search Valentine's rooms with him this evening. Would you like to come along, Doctor?"

"Certainly, if I can be of assistance. I would be most curious to see how a detective conducts such a search."

"Then we shall be off momentarily. I just stopped by to snatch my overcoat and check my indexes before joining the Inspector."

He went to his shelves and pulled out a volume while I retrieved my hat, coat and stick. Within three minutes we were bounding down the stairs with a word called out to Mrs. Hudson that we would not be home for dinner.

Outside the evening chill had settled in, now that the sun was down. A light fog had arisen as the sun-heated pavements cooled. Holmes hailed a passing hansom cab and we were soon on our way to a house near Piccadilly.

Inspector Lestrade was standing on the front steps under the porch light, which threw a dark shadow across his face. I thought it odd, then realised that the trees along the road cast the front of this house into darkness unimpeded by the lamps on the street.

The Inspector greeted the detective cordially, then looked at me curiously. "What brings you here, Doctor?"

Before I could answer, Holmes spoke up. "I thought his presence as a medical man might come into play, Lestrade. He has also expressed an interest in my methods and I felt this would make an ideal demonstration. I assure you he will not interfere."

The sceptical Scotland Yard man frowned, then acquiesced, "Very well, Doctor, you may join us, but don't touch anything."

I put on my best army bearing and replied, "I shall merely observe, Inspector. Thank you."

Having procured the key from the dead man's effects, we entered and locked the door behind us. It was a modest habitat, consisting of a kitchen, dining room and parlour downstairs and two bedrooms above, one of which Valentine appeared to have used as an office and storage space. Lestrade had learned that he was a bachelor with no servants, save for a maid who came in to clean and do laundry once a week.

A quick walk-through the lower floor revealed nothing significant, although my friend took notes of the contents of the kitchen cabinets and also checked the back door lock for signs of tampering. Upstairs, I watched as the Inspector and the detective went through the closets and drawers of the food critic's bedroom. Holmes seemed quite interested in Valentine's clothing, but said nothing. They were very thorough, even checking under the bed and behind the paintings on the wall.

Moving on to the office we found a more daunting task. There were several boxes on the floor and piles of folders with stacks of papers lying about his desk.

"Well, this'll take a bit o' time," sighed the Inspector. "Perhaps we could use an extra pair of eyes after all, if you care to help, Doctor?"

I was eager to do more than stand around watching, fascinating though it was. I readily agreed and asked what I should look for. Holmes overrode the official gentleman's answer with his own.

"Anything that seems out of the ordinary, Watson," he declared. "Receipts, patterns of places he'd go, letters or notes, anything indicating who his acquaintances were. Photographs, trinkets or mementoes indicating places he's travelled to, anything to do with his medical history such as prescriptions. Try to put yourself in his place and see how each item you see would fit into his life."

I took all this instruction in and glanced at the Inspector who merely shrugged and nodded in acquiescence. I stepped over to the opposite corner of the room from my companions. The first place I examined was a shelf containing several books. I began picking them up and fanning the pages, looking for anything hidden in them, such as notes or photographs. I was about to search my third volume when I realised it wasn't written in English, but rather Italian. This revelation caused me to peruse the titles of the other books on the shelf where I found two others in that romantic language. I turned to Holmes just as he was opening the bottom drawer of the desk.

"Holmes three of these volumes are written in Italian. Valentine also went to cooking school in Milan. Could that mean anything?"

He had stopped and was staring down into the open drawer. Without looking he asked me to read the titles aloud and I complied.

He had lifted out a strong box while I did so and was examining it, without so much as a glance in my direction, until I read the third title.

His head swivelled up and he asked that I bring that one over to him as he set the strong box on his lap. I took it from the far right end of the shelf and walked it over. He looked at it like a bookseller appreciating its binding and gilt edges. He brought it up close to his face and peered along its surface. Finally he beckoned Lestrade.

The Inspector was holding a handful of restaurant receipts when he joined us at the desk. Holmes had pulled out his magnifying lens and was examining the edges. At last he spoke.

"Gentlemen, observe. The cover of this volume shows that it is handled quite frequently as you can see where the man's grip has worn down the leather on the lettering. The gilt along the edges is particularly faded as fingers flipped pages rapidly, but only to this point."

He pointed at a place where the wear pattern had stopped and the gilt was like new from that point on. Then he opened the book to that spot and there, close by the spine, was a paper pocket glued in and holding a small key. He took it out, placed it into the lock of the strongbox on his lap and it turned easily.

Lestrade let out a low whistle upon seeing the contents and I confess the sight took me aback as well. The first items that drew our attention were bundled stacks of paper currency. A quick glance showed the amount to be close to seven hundred pounds. Some were still in bank wrappings and others were loose. There was also a stack of Italian lira of indeterminate value.

Holmes set the money on the desktop and then sifted through the rest of the contents. There were two passports, one British, the other Italian, which proved most revealing. The Italian passport was in the name of Giovanni Valentino.

Lestrade then remembered the receipts in his hand. "Wait, Holmes, these receipts show that he frequents Italian restaurants at least twice as often as all other kinds put together. Does this mean Valentine was actually an Italian passing himself off as an Englishman?"

"I believe that is more likely than him being an Englishman who Italianised his name to attend a cookery school in Milan. It also aligns with the fact that all his finer suits are from Italian clothiers in Genoa and Milan," replied the detective as he pulled out more paperwork. "Look, there are more documents here with the Giovanni name."

Further study indicated that the food critic was, indeed, an Italian immigrant. He appeared to have been from Genoa, which seemed too coincidental to the circumstances.

Lestrade posited a theory, "Perhaps he was a member of the Mafia, sent here to intimidate the Italian community."

Holmes shook his head, "Unlikely, Lestrade. The Mafia operate out of Sicily, not northern Italy where Genoa is located. But there could well be something criminal, or at least unethical, about our victim's life. He may have had more enemies than merely the restaurant owners he criticised."

Holmes set the strongbox on the table and ordered, "We must keep looking for anything that could identify his friends or acquaintances. Set aside anything you find that has a name, especially an Italian name."

The three of us kept up our search, setting aside such documents as might assist our quest. We were about twenty minutes into this activity when Holmes suddenly raised his hands and let out a 'shuush!"

Lestrade whispered, "What is it, Holmes?"

The detective held his finger to his lips and whispered back, "Someone has just entered the house downstairs."

Chapter Four

We all sat perfectly still for several seconds in utter silence. Then, at last, we heard the opening and closing of kitchen cabinets directly below. Lestrade stood up straight and started for the door, but Holmes waved him to stop and whispered, "Best let him come to us and not give away our presence. Lestrade, you stand behind the door, Watson, if you would take this side, behind these boxes? I'll take up a position around the end of the desk. When he comes in, shut the door behind him, I'll turn up the lamp and we'll surround him. He may be armed so be careful. Lestrade, do you have your darbies with you?

The Scotland Yarder nodded and pulled the handcuffs from his coat pocket in reply. We took up our places and Holmes lowered the lamp to a mere flicker as he held it behind the desk. In the deep silence of the night only the muffled sound of passing horse-drawn wagons filtered through the walls. Then we heard footsteps coming up the staircase. Instead of turning toward the bedroom first, as we had done, the intruder came across to the room where we lay in wait.

Assuming that the house was empty, he opened the door quickly. It was to our misfortune that he did not just open it enough to step in, but flung it wide until it came around and pinned Lestrade to the wall. The Inspector could not help but let out a noise and tip off the culprit. The man cried something, turned and ran. I dove for him as if I were in my old rugby days but Lestrade, forcing the door off himself, crashed into me and we both went down without laying hands on our man. Holmes sprang from his spot and leaped over us in time to observe the fellow slide down the banister and spring out the door into the street. We caught up outside, as he stared off into the darkness between streetlamps.

Lestrade panted, "Where is he, Holmes?"

My friend waved his hand off down the street, "He rode off on horseback around the corner."

"Did you see his face?" I asked.

"No, but the next best thing," he answered cryptically. "Let's return to our task. We may find the link we need, since he is obviously an Italian compatriot."

"You're sure about that, Holmes?" asked Lestrade.

"He cried out *'maledire!'* when you surprised him, Inspector, Italian for 'damn'. We must determine if he was after the money or to dispose of evidence linking him as the murderer."

We resumed our search of Valentine's office. His Italian connection became obvious as we found more documents and photographs. His appointment journal was in a cryptic shorthand and Holmes obtained Lestrade's permission to take it home for further study. I had returned to my study of the books on the shelves. The first and third Italian titles I had found were cookery books. When I went back to searching them in order I came to that second title again, which actually was a Latin Bible. When I thumbed the pages I noticed some handwritten notes flip by. I went back and found the page again. It was in the division between the Old and New Testaments and appeared to be a chart of names. At the end of one branch was the name Giovanni Benito Valentino and the date 1850.

"Holmes, I think I've found Valentino's family tree."

Both he and the Inspector came over. I handed the book to Holmes as we read over his shoulder.

"Well, that seals it," declared Lestrade. "You were right, Holmes. There's an Italian connection that we must consider."

Holmes nodded and pointed to an entry, "See here, Inspector. There's a Rivano branch off this Valentino line and here's Giuseppe's name."

"Were they cousins?" I asked.

"Distant ones, but yes. This puzzle may be more complex than we thought."

Holmes pondered a moment. I could almost see a myriad of thoughts pass over his face. Then he spoke, "Inspector, it is getting late and you must be hungry. I should like to explore these documents and run some of these names past my contacts in the Italian community. I shall return them to you at the Yard before noon tomorrow and will wish to see Chef Rivano as well."

"It's a bit unorthodox, Holmes. But you have been of some assistance with your theories in the past." He hesitated then agreed. "Very well, I'll give you some leeway. Is there any direction you care to point me to in the meantime?"

Holmes answered in a confident tone, "I would recommend that you check for any Italian ships in port and when they are scheduled to depart."

"You think he'll be booking passage to get out of the country?"

Holmes pursed his lips and shook his head, "Not necessarily a passenger ship, Inspector. The man who eluded us tonight was a sailor and could be on any Italian vessel. You might pay special attention to any whose home port is Genoa. A list of those crew members could prove most useful."

That evening, in our Baker Street rooms, Holmes drew a copy of the family tree from Valentino's Bible. Then he went on to pore over the man's journal, attempting to understand the abbreviations and apparent code words. There was little I could do to assist, so I sat by the fire and reviewed the latest medical journals, hoping to be ready for any situation, were I called upon by the hospitals where I'd registered.

The next morning I arose early, but Holmes was already gone. My enquiries of Mrs. Hudson only revealed that he'd left with no word of when he'd return. I requested breakfast from the kind lady and sat by the fire, where there was a copy of a newspaper which Holmes must have purchased earlier and left behind. I proceeded to read the morning news.

The headlines spouted stories of Robert Cecil, Marquess of Salisbury, assuming leadership of the Conservative Party in the House of Lords. The Natural History Museum was reporting huge crowds at its grand opening. But no one reported any progress in the case of the murdered food critic. I read for a while until my breakfast arrived, then enjoyed the view out the window as I ate. It was a lovely spring day. The morning fog burned off early and, with nothing pending at the moment, I decided to take a walk. I had no sooner informed Mrs. Hudson that I was leaving and opened the front door when Holmes burst in upon me.

"Watson, dear chap, just the man I need. I see you're not off to see a patient. Would you kindly join me for a trip down to the docks?"

"Has this something to do with your case, Holmes?" I asked hopefully.

"I am closing in old boy, but I mustn't dawdle. Our killer will sail on tomorrow's tide if we don't act quickly. Are you with me?"

"At your service," I responded with excitement.

"Excellent! I have observed that you have retained your army revolver. Would you be so kind as to bring it along? I should not like to put you in harm's way unarmed."

We returned upstairs where Holmes retreated into his rooms while I found my Webley gun and made sure it was loaded. He was out shortly, dressed like an old sailor in flared trousers and open pea coat. He had darkened his face and hands to reflect the tan of many years at sea. He also sported chin whiskers and a stubby pipe clenched between his teeth. He advised me to bring my medical bag, assuring me it was more for disguise and hopeful that it would not be needed for its usual purpose.

Outside we hailed a cab that sped us off to the dock Holmes had directed. Along the way I asked, "How did you know the man was a sailor?"

"Did you notice how he slid down the banister? Very few professions indulge in that sort of feat. Sailors do something similar when descending between decks. He also seemed familiar to me, which led me to investigate whether or not he might be that same fellow who bothered the Rivanos before. Once I deciphered Valentino's journal it was only a matter of time before I found him"

He had the driver stop a few streets short of our destination so we could proceed on foot. When I enquired why, he replied, "It would not do for you and I to be seen arriving together by cab, Doctor. The part I play would have little cause for such an expenditure, nor to be in the presence of a fine gentleman such as yourself."

He handed me a slip of paper, "This is the address where we are going. If anyone stops you and demands to know your reason for being here, tell them you received a message that a doctor was needed at that location. It's less than half a mile from here. Go down that side of the street and I'll make my way along this side. No matter what I do, keep a steady pace and I will cross over to you just before we reach our destination. Let me lead you in and do all the talking."

I did as he instructed. As I walked, the smell of the nearby Thames wafted through the cluster of buildings. It was an eclectic neighbourhood with rows of wood framed structures broken up by an occasional brick building. There were houses, small stores, warehouses, more than one tattoo parlour, and a number of inns. Except for few colourful shop signs, it was a grey and brown area. The street sweepers could not keep up with the manure deposited by the numerous drays pulling wagons carrying freight from the nearby docks. It made me all the more appreciative of our Baker Street home and nearby Regent's Park, where one could walk and enjoy the sweet fragrance of flowers instead of fish markets, opium dens and horse dung.

The cacophony of noise emanating from the various structures included workmen shouting, merchants hawking their wares, children playing, and even music of sorts. In that half mile walk, I was also approached by two different women offering me 'comfort' from my journey, assuming by my tweed suit that I was not from the vicinity. I extricated myself from their company on both occasions and finally arrived at the address Holmes had provided.

The place was called Sea Horse House and advertised rooms to let by the day, week or month. My friend had crossed the street just ahead of me and led me inside. Stepping up to the front desk, he spoke to the clerk in a strange accent.

"'Ere, young fellow, what room be that o' Carlo Tedesco? I've brought the doctor for 'im."

The young man behind the counter was taken aback. "I didn't know he was sick. That must be why he's been spending so much time in his room except to go out for meals. He's up in 302."

Holmes thanked him and led the way up the stairs. As pre-arranged, I had a cloth soaked with ether at the ready when we heard Tedesco coming to answer the door. As soon as he cracked it to peek out at us, Holmes burst through the door and tackled him to the floor. I covered his mouth with the cloth and he went still quickly. Behind closed doors, Holmes searched the room. He threw several items into the man's sea bag and together we carried him under his shoulders down the stairs. I told the desk clerk that we were taking him to hospital and paid off his bill. We bustled him into a cab and off to Scotland Yard.

Chapter Five

As we entered the headquarters of the Metropolitan Police Force, our prisoner began to regain consciousness and started shouting in Italian. Fortunately, two officers came to our aid and when Holmes advised them he was making a citizen's arrest, took Tedesco to a cell for questioning. Inspector Lestrade was summoned at Holmes's request. Soon he appeared with a frown on his face.

"What are you up to, Holmes? What is all this costume and makeup about? And who is this fellow you claim to be arresting?"

Holmes, in his strong baritone voice, replied, "I have been about *incognito*, Lestrade, following up on the data I told you I'd found this morning in Valentino's journal."

"Yes, yes, that Carlo fellow you spoke of. I've been having my people check the ships outbound for Italy. We are going to arrest him when he reports for duty tomorrow."

"With a squad of officers positioned at the dock of his ship, I suppose?" responded Holmes.

"Of course. That's how we do things, Holmes. A show of force to limit their resistance."

Holmes shook his head, "He likely would have spotted your men and not report at all. Or, if he did, he might have put up more of a struggle that you supposed. See here."

Holmes reached into the sea bag, pulled out a handgun and gave it to the Inspector.

"That, my dear Lestrade, is a *Pistola Rotazione*. Tedesco could have taken out several of your unarmed constables and gotten away. Watson and I have safely delivered him into your hands with no bloodshed."

Lestrade examined the pistol, turning it over in his hands and noting how many rounds the cylinder held. "Well, I suppose thanks are in order, Holmes. But what about evidence? Can you prove that the code name in the critic's journal is really Tedesco?"

"Let us retire to your office, Inspector and I will lay out the evidence for you," my friend replied, holding up the sea bag with a smile.

After we sat down with the Scotland Yard official in his cluttered office, Holmes proceeded to tell the tale.

"First of all," began the detective, as he crossed his legs leisurely and leaned back in his chair, "I have determined that Giovanni Valentino is a distant cousin of Rivano, from a branch which holds a long-standing grudge amongst the elders of the clan.

"This is not something my client was aware of, being three generations removed from the original offense. However, the journal of the food critic and some papers in Tedesco's possession indicate that the obligation to continue this vendetta, was brought to bear by Tedesco upon Valentino as an honour debt. The journalist was reluctant to continue an old grudge of which he had no part, nor interest. He was not a violent man, but the money offered by Tedesco for merely writing a bad review was too tempting for him to refuse."

"Wait," interrupted Lestrade. "How do we know it was Tedesco who offered the money?"

Holmes smiled and replied, "Valentino's journal kept referring to 'the German'. Tedesco is Italian for German. Likely a family name dating back to when the Germanic tribes invaded Italy centuries ago. Also, there are papers here in Tedesco's sea bag which indicate his contact with Valentino and the story of the old grudge which he used to pressure the man. In addition he also has several hundred lira, which I suspect he was going to use to further his plans here in England."

"But what were his plans, Holmes?" I asked before Lestrade could. "Why go to all this trouble to avenge an ancient grudge which was between two families of which he was not even a member? And why kill Valentino after he did what was asked?"

Holmes steepled his fingers under his chin for a moment, then replied. "To answer your second question, Doctor, once the deed was done, Tedesco wanted no witnesses. He also wanted to take back the down payment he had made."

"Down payment?" queried Lestrade.

"Yes, the journal indicates that Valentino had only received half of the funds promised. The rest would be paid upon publication of the critical review."

"So that's why he came by the house while we were there," declared the Inspector. "He was going to take his money back."

"Yes," replied Holmes with a nod, "as well as any documentation that might have connected the two of them. Obviously, he waited all day until he could break in under the cover of darkness. It's fortunate that we got there before him."

Turning back to me he continued, "Now as to your first question, Watson. Carlo Tedesco is the man who attempted to force himself on Carmen in the false marriage scheme last year."

"What's this?" Lestrade demanded. "You knew this Tedesco fellow before? Why didn't you mention him as a suspect?"

"I didn't know him as Carlo Tedesco during my previous investigation, Inspector. I only discovered that he was a cousin of the man to whom Carmen had been promised in childhood. The name he was using then was Luigi Bianchi. But when he fled the house with us on his heels last night, I thought I recognised him. My reconnoitring at the docks this morning, among the inns favoured by Italian sailors, confirmed my suspicions when I saw him exit his rooming house for breakfast. When I enquired of the desk clerk the man's name, I discovered that he was now calling himself Carlo Tedesco."

Lestrade seemed mollified by that, then asked for the contents of the sea bag so he could examine the evidence.

Holmes pulled several articles and papers out and explained their significance to the Inspector. Among the items were a set of lock picks which Holmes proffered might well have been used at both the restaurant and Valentino's house.

"Also, Lestrade, if you examine his shoes you will note their similarity to those prints found at the scene of the murder and outside Rivano's back door."

"You seem to have wrapped things up quite neatly, Holmes," observed the Inspector. "Have you given any further consideration to applying for a position on the official force?"

The detective smiled and shook his head. "My interests are far too varied to limit myself in such a fashion. However, I would like you to grant me one little indulgence, if I may?"

"Within reason," answered Lestrade, warily.

Holmes made his request and the Inspector shrugged his shoulders and replied "Why not? It certainly couldn't hurt us since it's not admissible."

Holmes was allowed to conduct one final experiment and sent his findings to the Inspector the following day. Tedesco's fingerprints matched the unidentified ones found on the murder weapon.

Chapter Six

One month later, we were again being served by the charming young Carmen. Rivano's was crowded since the full story came out and a new review was written, extolling the cuisine and atmosphere in the highest terms.

This time I decided to try something a little more bold, (making sure I had some bicarbonate with me). I joined Holmes in ordering spaghetti and meatballs and again we were served garlic bread and a nice Chianti before our meal.

I raised my glass to my friend, "To you, Holmes. Your investigation and capture of Tedesco has saved us this bastion of cuisine for many meals to come."

Holmes raised his glass in turn and nodded in acknowledgement of my praise. Setting his wine down again after a healthy sip, he commented, "I was pleased at yesterday's verdict. The gallows shall finally put an end to the man's notorious schemes and leave our dear little *Carmenita* at peace." This last he spoke as he nodded to our waitress, just as she delivered our meals. Once the plates were on the table she threw her arms around Holmes's shoulders in an appreciative hug.

"Bless you, *Signore* Holmes! You have saved me and my Papa from that horrible man!"

"Quite all right, my dear," he responded, awkwardly extricating himself from that tangle of arms. "I was happy to be of service. By the way, could you ask your father to come out when he has a moment? I need to speak with him."

She readily agreed and returned to her duties. While we waited for the Chef to have a moment between meal preparations, I asked my friend, "What do you have to tell Rivano?"

He flashed that quick smile which broadens his face and lights his eyes for but a single moment, then lapsed back to a mere look of satisfaction as he took a bite of food. Before he could swallow and reply to my query, the owner of the restaurant crossed the room in quick little steps from the kitchen.

"*Signore* Holmes!" he cried leaning over and giving the detective a quick kiss on both cheeks as Italians are wont to do. "You have saved my *ristorante* and my daughter! How can I ever repay you?"

Holmes laid his hands on the table on either side of his plate and nodded in my direction, "I could not have done so without the capable assistance of my friend, Dr. Watson, *Signore*. If you could extend your courtesy of meals *gratuito* to him, that would be payment enough. As you can see, he is a rather lean fellow and would highly benefit from your cooking."

I bowed my head in embarrassment, only to be accosted by the Chef with that same affectionate greeting he had planted on Holmes. "*Assolutamente!*" he cried in his native tongue, "Dr. Watson, you are welcome any time, no charge!" he announced as he waggled an index finger in the air. Carmen came by the table to see what was happening and Holmes took the opportunity to retrieve an envelope from his pocket.

"I have one more little surprise for you," he declared as he handed the envelope to the puzzled man. Rivano looked at him, then glanced at me and was met by a shrug of my ignorance. Opening the envelope he cried out at its contents and Carmen quickly aided him into a spare seat at our table as he put a hand to his heart. He could not speak so she took the paper from him and asked Holmes what it was.

"That, my dear child, is what we call a bank cheque. Those numbers represent the amount of pounds sterling which your father may deposit or redeem from the bank in question."

I caught a glimpse of the figures as she had held her hands up in question and could see that it was well over a thousand pounds. I looked across at my friend.

Carmen voiced my thoughts when she said, "Where did this come from?"

Her father, having caught his breath, leaned forward and added his voice, "*Si, Signore* Holmes, what is the meaning of this?"

Holmes sipped his wine and leaned back in his chair with that all-knowing look on his face before replying, "As it so happens, Giovanni Valentino, or John Valentine as you knew him, was a distant cousin of yours. When the police took possession of his personal belongings, he had amassed quite a nest egg. Upon research by a solicitor friend of mine, it was determined that his nearest family members were all deceased and that you are his closest living relative. Therefore the inheritance is yours."

"*Lode alla Beata Vergine Maria!*" he cried

"Mother of God!" I added, not realising I was almost repeating the chef's outburst.

"*Buona fortuna!*" said Holmes, raising his glass to our host and we all toasted the Rivano's good fortune.

The Judgement of
Dr. Watson

Chapter One

It was the summer of 1905 and I was taking a break from publishing chronicles of the adventures of my famous friend, the detective, Sherlock Holmes. I had filled the pages of *The Strand* magazine with nine such stories the year before and did not wish to saturate the public, lest they lose their appetite for my work.

I was soon to celebrate my third anniversary of marriage. My stepdaughter was about to present us with a grandchild and my wife had gone to be with her. My stepson had just graduated from university the year before and was now in a partnership, practicing veterinary medicine at the Royal Windsor Racecourse, just west of London.[1]

Holmes had retired to Sussex and taken up beekeeping, though I suspected he still took on occasional cases if they were interesting enough. I had known for many years that his elder brother, Mycroft, worked for the government. His

---

[1] This information in Watson's notes, though it names no names, seems to confirm the speculation suggested in *Sherlock Holmes and the Case of the Twain Papers*, (Roger Riccard, Baker Street Studios, 2014). In that story Watson began courting Adelaide Savage, the widow of Victor Savage, the victim of Culverton-Smith in *The Dying Detective*, by Arthur Conan Doyle. An adventure which took place in 1890, but was not submitted for publication until 1913. The names of Adelaide and her children were taken from the Granada Television series of *Sherlock Holmes* starring Jeremy Brett and Edward Hardwicke.

position, though not quite defined, was a powerful one with much influence, especially in foreign affairs, and I had no doubt that he would continue to call upon his younger sibling from time to time.

My regular occupation as a doctor with a modest medical practice was going well and all in all we were quite happy with our lives.

Then a knock came to our door.

I was in my consulting room reviewing a patient file, but the maid had gone to the market that morning, so I arose and answered the door myself. As soon as I opened it, my visitor burst in upon me in breathless haste.

"Doctor, you must come with me immediately. It's urgent!" cried out the strident voice of Inspector Lestrade of Scotland Yard as he pushed his way in and caught me up by the elbow.

I balked at this unusual treatment and asked, "What is it Lestrade? What's wrong?"

He yanked my hat, overcoat and cane off the stand by the door, threw them into my arms and rushed me along panting, "No time to explain. We need to go, now!"

"But my bag ..." I started to protest, assuming it would be needed for any medical emergency he was rushing me off to.

"You won't need it, Doctor. Come quick, we must hurry!"

In a thrice we bundled ourselves into a waiting cab and set off at a gallop. The Inspector kept looking out the back window until we turned the corner and were well away from the house. At last he turned and sat back in his seat.

My questions quickly poured forth, "Will you tell me what's going on? Why have you spirited me away in this fashion?"

The Scotland Yarder, who was now nearly sixty and not as physically fit as when he began sharing cases with Holmes some twenty-five years before, was breathing hard. He took off his bowler and wiped his forehead. I noted with surprise how grey his hair had become since I'd last seen him.

Observing his condition, I checked the pocket of my overcoat and found a flask still half full of brandy. I offered it to him and he gratefully took a swig and handed it back. He fanned himself with his hat a few more times, then replaced it upon his crown and replied to my enquiries.

"I'm taking a big risk, Dr. Watson," he spoke softly, not wanting the driver to overhear. "But after all we've been through over the years, I felt I owed you some consideration."

"Well I appreciate your feelings, Inspector. But what would I be needing consideration for?"

Taking a big breath and letting it out slowly, he leaned closer and whispered, "A warrant was just issued for your arrest."

The sounds of the city, with cabs rattling along the cobblestone streets, cries of vendors and shouts of playing children, became muted as this statement penetrated and invaded my thoughts. The unconscionableness of it left me speechless for several moments.

When at last I found my tongue I asked, "Who issued it? What charge are they bringing? This is ridiculous! What about my wife?"

I was peppering the Inspector with questions faster than he could answer. Finally, when I took a breath, he replied, nodding up toward the driver, who, though outside the enclosed cab, would be able to hear if we spoke too loudly. "Not here, Doctor. We'll be at our destination shortly, then I'll tell you all I know."

He must have told the driver where we were going before he hustled me from my home, for I did not recall him giving such instructions. We drove south through Mayfair, circled around Green Park and for a moment I thought he was delivering me to Buckingham Palace to seek mercy from the King. But we passed on by the turn at Constitution Hill. Instead, we were soon disembarking at Westminster Cathedral. As I stepped out onto the pavement I stopped and stared up at the magnificence of the structure. Towers rose to the sky, capped by beautiful domes, the highest rising over two hundred feet above where I stood. Arched windows reflected the morning sun and I stood transfixed until the

Inspector again snatched at my elbow and propelled me through the main doors.

Marble columns, capped by golden Byzantine capitals, lined up along each side of the rows and rows of pews. I noted that scaffolds still stood where workmen were continuing their tasks on the interior decorations, even though we were two years past the official opening.

With a deep sigh, Lestrade announced, "You should be safe here for the time being, Dr. Watson."

"Safe?" I questioned, "Why should I be safe here?"

"The Catholic Church upholds the ancient right of sanctuary. As long as you remain on church property you can't be arrested."

"That's still up for debate," came a deep, yet kindly voice from near the front of the cathedral. The person making that statement slowly walked toward us. He was wearing a red cassock with red buttons down the front, a red sash and a large silver cross. As he approached, Lestrade kneeled and kissed the ring presented by the clergyman. "Your Grace, forgive my intrusion, but my friend here needs your help." Turning to me he introduced us, "Dr. John Watson, this is his Excellency, the Archbishop Francis Bourne."[1]

Not being Catholic myself, I merely gave a slight bow as I held my hat in my hand.

The Archbishop smiled, extended his open hand in welcome and I shook it. It was a firm grasp and I noted he was well built for a man his age, which I judged to be about fifty. His hair was thick and grey and he wore wire-rimmed glasses.

"Welcome, Dr. John Watson. Would I be correct in presuming you to be the friend and colleague of Mr. Sherlock Holmes?"

---

[1] Francis Alphonsus Bourne was an English prelate of the Roman Catholic Church. He served as Archbishop of Westminster from 1903 until his death in 1935, and was elevated to the cardinalate in 1911. As Archbishop of Westminster, he became the spiritual head of the Catholic Church in England and Wales.

"Yes, Archbishop, I have that honour. I'm afraid this situation has been sprung upon me rather suddenly and I am still awaiting for an explanation from our friend here."

"Then let us go to my study, my sons. We'll discuss it over some tea and see what can be done."

The Archbishop's study was more like a small library. It was not ornate, but rather a plain and practical room with sturdy furniture and crowded bookshelves. The large window let in ample daylight and was not of stained glass, though there were markings upon it where it appeared some artist was making preliminary sketches.

After pouring us some tea, the priest settled back in his chair and enquired, "Now, Mr. Lestrade, you mentioned the possibility of sanctuary? Are you not aware that King James I outlawed the practice in England in the early 1600s?"

"No, your Excellency," replied the Inspector, "that's news to me."

"I am surprised you did not know that," chided the cleric gently. "Don't they teach you these things at Scotland Yard?"

Lestrade lowered his eyes and rubbed his forehead with his left hand, "I've never had a criminal claim such an action. I'd only read of it in old stories and files of cases on the continent."

"Well, then, I can see why you would not be aware of the ancient command," replied Bourne. "On the other hand, the King of the British Empire is the titular leader of the Church of England, whereas I answer to His Holiness, the Pope in Rome. Tell me more of what has happened, my son."

With nervous hand gestures and exasperation in his voice, the Scotland Yard Inspector gave out his tale.

"There's a Crown Prosecutor, a young pup named Parsons, out to make a name for himself. He's decided it would be a feather in his cap if he could bring down the great Sherlock Holmes. Unfortunately, his methods would also include Dr. Watson here."

"Why on earth would he wish to do such a thing?" I exclaimed. "Holmes has been a champion of justice for over two decades!"

"This Parsons fellow is ambitious and a stickler for the letter of the law. He's forced several barristers and more than one judge to justify their actions. Some have even been dismissed by their employers or forced to resign. He has some powerful political allies and is looked upon by his party as one of its future leaders. When he takes on a well-known personage he is usually on solid ground and gains political strength when he wins. At the very least he is feared by many and, unfortunately, respected by some influential persons."

"So why Dr. Watson and Mr. Holmes?" asked the Archbishop.

The Inspector wiped his forehead again with his handkerchief and replied in a tone of sad accusation as he turned to me.

"In two of the stories you published in *The Strand Magazine* last year, Doctor, both you and Mr. Holmes appeared to take liberties with the law that were beyond your purview. There was that business at Abbey Grange[2] and also the murder of Charles Milverton[3]. In both cases you let the murderer get away and obstructed justice in doing so."

I sat back and gazed at the ceiling. Thoughts and memories were swirling in my head and I was attempting to organise them into a suitable answer when Lestrade laid a hand on my shoulder and spoke again.

"As an officer of the law, I must warn you, Doctor, that anything you say may be taken down and used in evidence against you. I would imagine that if a solicitor were present, he may advise you to remain silent at this point."

I let out the breath I did not realise I'd been holding and replied, "Thank you, Inspector. I believe I will take that advice. What do we do now?"

Archbishop Bourne spoke up and enquired, "Would it be possible for you to get me copies of these stories, Mr.

---

[2] *The Adventure of the Abbey Grange* – A story in which Lord Brackenstall is found dead and his wife bound and gagged. Holmes was called in to assist Scotland Yard.

[3] *The Adventure of Charles Augustus Milverton* – Tells the tale of a blackmailer whose murder at his home was witnessed by Holmes and Watson.

Lestrade? I should like to judge for myself what the situation entails. In the meantime, we can put Dr. Watson up here while I seek instructions from Rome."

Chapter Two

Lestrade left us with the promise to inform my wife of the circumstances and assured me that Sherlock Holmes was being advised via his brother, Mycroft. Archbishop Bourne took me to the living quarters of the Cathedral staff and assigned me a room. It was actually a very austere little cell with a simple bed, washbasin, writing table, chair, lamp table by the bed and a small wardrobe. The only window was open to let in the summer breezes and I could see the large green trees lining Morpeth Terrace along the back of the grounds. Some few hundred yards away the sounds of trains passing in and out of Victoria Station created a low hum, broken by an occasional steam whistle.

"I'll see that you are also provided with a few changes of clothes," declared Bourne. "They are donated and may not be the highest in fashion, but our nuns ensure that they are clean and in good repair. Of course, we have fresh supplies of undergarments which we purchase, because even priests need clean socks and underwear."

His humour caught me off guard and I looked at him sharply in surprise. His round face had an engaging smile and his eyes twinkled behind his silver spectacles.

"Now, Dr. Watson," he implored, waving his hand toward the bed as he took the chair at the writing table, "have a seat and tell me these stories to which the Inspector referred. My curiosity is far too great to wait for the written account."

I placed my overcoat and hat in the wardrobe and took a seat on the edge of the bed. First I explained that I frequently change the names of those involved and even the locations so as to protect the innocent. Then I began telling the story of Lady Brackenstall of Abbey Grange.

The Archbishop nodded in sympathy at the plight of this poor woman with the abominable husband. She was from Australia and had come to England on a visit where she fell in love and married an English baronet. After their courtship and marriage, the brute showed his true colours and often showed his temper to her. When he was killed one night, Holmes was called in by Scotland Yard. The story told by the widow and her maid was that a well-known gang of burglars had broken in while she was shutting down rooms for the night, her husband having already gone to bed in a drunken stupor. They tied and gagged her and began ransacking the silver plate. When the husband awoke and came down upon the scene, they killed him and stole away with their goods.

Holmes's investigation revealed a different possibility. He noted that she had previous injuries, old bruises and puncture marks, and determined that the number of intruders did not tally with her story based on physical evidence. He confronted her privately, demanding the truth, for he felt she was a much-wronged woman and he could better serve her if the truth were known. She stuck by her story, however.

The woman's testimony had satisfied Scotland Yard, but Holmes, fearing the truth may eventually come out and ruin her, continued to dig into her past. Based on the knots used to tie her up, he believed a sailor was involved. He identified the ship on which she has sailed from Australia and determined that one of its officers was in the vicinity.

Holmes discovered that he was soon to depart on his next voyage on a new ship. Therefore the detective surmised that on that fateful night he had come to say goodbye. Confronted by this hypothesis, however, the widow and her maid still continued with their original story.

Holmes, having speculation but no proof, gave Scotland Yard suggestions that their line of pursuit was in error, but they never did solve the case.

Our conversation was interrupted by the ringing of the church bells which declared the noon hour.

The churchman clapped his hands to his knees and stood, "Duty calls, Doctor. I have a lunch appointment coming in, but I look forward to continuing this discussion this afternoon. Come with me and I will take you to the dining hall. I believe I shall turn you over to Father Hazelbaker. He can see to your needs and be a sounding board for your thoughts."

I rose and went with him to the dining hall where several priests were already seated. We stopped by the entrance as he gazed about the room. Spotting the man whom he sought, he had me follow him to a table where several priests stood upon his arrival. He motioned for them to sit down except one individual, whom he gently took by the elbow and introduced.

"Father Hazelbaker, this is Dr. John Watson, who will be staying with us for a while. I've set him up in quarters, but I'd like you to take charge of his needs during his time among us."

The man who stood before me was skinny as a rail and stood at least six foot two inches. The thin fingers that gripped my handshake were long and seemed fragile. I took care that my grip would not damage them. A shock of wavy brown hair stood out and threatened to fall upon his forehead like a horses's forelock. His lean face was supported by high cheekbones, an aquiline nose, a small mouth that put forth a pleasant smile and somewhat large ears. His eyes were light brown and sparked with an alert curiosity when the Archbishop announced my name.

"Would that be *the* Dr. John Watson, chronicler of Sherlock Holmes?" he enquired as he folded his hands in front of his waist.

"I am happy to say so," I replied with pride.

"And I am honoured to make your acquaintance, sir. Please come with me and we'll get you some food."

"I leave you in good hands, Doctor," said Archbishop Bourne. "But, I'll come and find you later this afternoon, so we may finish our discussion."

Father Hazelbaker led me to the kitchen area where I was presented with a tray that was soon loaded up with a large bowl of potato soup, bread, some carrots and tea. Returning to the table I was introduced around to the other clerics and settled in for a satisfying meal.

Afterwards, Hazelbaker took me for a walk about the grounds. He pointed out the school and the nun's quarters in the distance, emphasising that trespass into that section was forbidden. We walked past a vegetable garden and saw children playing in an open area outside the classrooms beyond the fence. Returning indoors he led me through many of the various rooms where quite a bit of work was still going on.

"I did not realise the church was not completed when it opened back in '03," I commented.

"There's still much to be done, but the needs of the people could be met with what was ready at the time. The rest is primarily ornamentation and some modern conveniences."

"May I ask what your duties are?" I enquired of the young man, as he walked with a gangly gait beside me.

"I assist with mass, hear confessions, provide counsel, help out in the kitchen and play the organ. Of course, all of us are involved in the cleanliness and maintenance of the Cathedral," he stopped and opened yet another door. "As you can see, that in itself is quite the undertaking."

I once again entered the magnificent hall, this time from a side entrance near the front. The priest led me to just below the steps to the altar.

I gazed up in awe at the tremendous height of the archway which rose above red carpeted steps and altar table. Light poured in from several arched windows and an ornate cross with Christ fixed upon it looked down at me.

Touching my sleeve and pointing back toward the entrance, Father Hazelbaker expressed his thoughts.

"There is the true Church, Doctor," he proclaimed as he waved his hand toward the wooden rows of seats extending down either side of the long aisle. "People always say they 'go to church', but in fact, the people are the Church. They are Christ in the world. That figure up there ..." he continued, turning back toward the huge crucifix which dominated the front, "is a mere reminder of their faith and their responsibility in this world to follow His teachings."

I looked up into this intent young man's eyes and saw a fervour there, an intensity that was almost tangible. I replied in a low voice that seemed to fit the solemness of the room.

"You wouldn't be trying out a sermon on me, would you Father?"

A broad grin split that lean face and he nodded in affirmation, "Indeed, Doctor. I'm sure in your professions as both a medical man and a colleague of a crime solver you've seen what faith, or the lack thereof, can do to a person. Every once in a while I like to remind the people that their faith isn't for Sunday mornings only.

"But come, let us finish our tour and you can return to your room to contemplate and pray."

He dropped me back at my room at one-fifteen. While he had shown me a library of sorts where I could read any number of commentaries or philosophical writings regarding the world's religions, I chose a copy of the King James Bible to take back to my quarters. I had noted its presence with surprise in that I am aware of the differences between it and the Catholic version, which includes more books. The young priest assured me that he and his fellows study all the variations of the Christian faith as it is practiced by the Protestant denominations.

"It better prepares us to deal with those who wish to convert to Catholicism or those who question their faith in trying times. We also study the writings of Judaism, Islam, Hinduism, Buddhism, even Confucianism."

"How interesting," I commented.

"Like any endeavour, it's always helpful to be aware of the competition."

I then asked, "Father, I'd like to write to my wife and let her know I'm all right. Can you manage a messenger to deliver a note discreetly to her?"

"Absolutely, Doctor. I'll speak to His Excellency and see what we can arrange." He smiled as he left and bid me good afternoon.

Upon his departure I sat at the desk and began to write to my wife to let her know that I was safe. I realised I needed to be circumspect in how much I told her. Should the status of sanctuary be challenged it would be to my advantage not to let her know exactly where I was. Thus, if she were questioned she could answer truthfully.

I had just finished a carefully worded letter to her, in hopes that a delivery could be arranged quickly, when a knock came to my door.

I opened it to find Archbishop Bourne, whom I immediately invited in. Shuffling along behind him appeared to be one of the workman from the crew still being engaged to complete the interior of the church. He was a stout fellow of about my height, wearing baggy trousers, a collarless work shirt, another garment with multiple pockets, dusty boots and a blue kerchief about his neck which was in much need of a shave.

"Good afternoon, Doctor," Bourne greeted me, "Father Hazelbaker informed me that you wished a messenger to send word to your wife. I have just the man for the task. This is Archie Jones, a most trustworthy fellow."

The workman gave me a knuckles to forehead salute and piped up in a Welsh accent, "Happy to be of service, Cap'n. Whatever you need."

It felt odd to be addressed by my old Army rank, but the idiom was common among the working class and I let it pass. I looked and saw there were no envelopes at the writing desk so, I took up the letter, folded it carefully and handed it to the man, giving him the address and advising him that the house may be watched, so he must be discreet in how he delivered it.

"Not to worry, sir," he replied, stuffing the letter into an inner pocket.

I said, "Thank you, Mr. Jones."

He gave me another salute and turned to leave. Archbishop Bourne waved me to be seated so we could continue our previous discussion. Suddenly, Jones stopped in the doorway and turned back to face us. At first I thought it was because I had sat down that he now looked taller. Then he spoke one more time.

"Actually, Watson, I believe I shall have one of the Irregulars deliver it to your wife at your daughter's home."

I immediately stood from where I had just perched on the bedside.

"Holmes?"

"Indeed, old friend. I felt it was important that we present a united front against this adversary who so values the letter of the law over justice. When I received Mycroft's message I came at once. He informed me of Lestrade's plan, so," he waved a long-fingered hand about the room, "here I am."

Bourne broke out into a pleasant chuckle, then invited Holmes in so he could shut the door.

"All right, gentlemen," he implored. "Now that I am harbouring *two* criminals, I must insist upon the rest of the story. Tell me about this Milverton fellow."

Holmes bid me to be spokesman, saying that storytelling was my forte, not his. Thus, I took up several minutes explaining the activities of the master blackmailer, Charles Augustus Milverton. Holmes chimed in with a few details and soon we had completed our tale.

His Grace sat still upon my finishing. His lips pursed and head nodding slowly. At last, he spoke.

"Is this the way the story was printed up in *The Strand*?"

I thought for a moment, then slapped my knee and exclaimed, "No, by George! Somewhere in the editing process there were details changed."

"Why would anyone change details in a true story?"

Holmes snorted and spoke, "To make it more dramatic for the readers, my dear Archbishop. To sell more copies. I've often complained about romanticising what should have been textbook studies of deductive reasoning."

It was an old argument between Holmes and myself and he had often threatened to write up the cases himself in his retirement years, though that had yet to happen.

Waving aside Holmes's comment, I spoke to the Archbishop. "In the publishing process I submit my manuscript to my agent. He will act as an editor to clean up grammar, punctuation, historical and geographical data and to ensure continuity is maintained in that the story follows a logical sequence and details remain consistent. He then submits it to a publisher who has his editorial staff go over it even further. I've had stories published which may have been as little as 80% of what I originally wrote. I remember now that there was a significant detail that was changed in the Milverton story. One which could easily be fodder for Parson's persecution.

"What was that?" enquired the cleric.

Chapter Three

Having explained the re-written portion of the story and our true role in the Milverton case, the Archbishop was even more sympathetic to our plight.

"Surely you can simply explain what really happened," he said.

"No!" Holmes, who had been leaning against the desk cried out as he stood tall. "Under oath we would be required to give out the true details and the real names of those involved, including the person who we believe may have actually killed him. It will not do!"

I recognised that passion in Holmes's voice and knew it would be useless to argue. But that didn't matter for I agreed with him. Too many people would be hurt.

The Archbishop arose from the chair and spoke quietly, "His Holiness has long ago issued a standing order that the Church is to assist Mr. Sherlock Holmes whenever called upon. 'A debt we owe him', is how I believe he phrased it. I am awaiting instructions regarding your sanctuary status, but do not expect a reply until tomorrow. Until then you are both welcome to stay as our guests."

Holmes thanked the man but shook his head, "I've a letter to deliver to Mrs. Watson and I have developed a sudden interest in this Parsons fellow. I shall remain incognito and conduct my investigations aroud the City of London.

"You, dear Watson, must remain here. No one else knows of your whereabouts and the longer we can maintain that status, the better our chances of defeating this attack. I shall be in touch."

Holmes and Bourne left together and I was again alone to contemplate the situation, wondering who it was in the chain of progression that changed my story in such a dramatically incriminating way.

At the evening meal I again supped with Father Hazelbaker. This time, I turned the conversation around and got him talking about himself.

"As you may gather from my name, Doctor," he responded to my question about his family, "my people come from a long line of bakers and cooks. The legend in my family is that the ancient chef to King Arthur, known as Harmon, was dubbed Hazelbaker by the King himself. It was said that he could take hazelnuts and flavour a wide variety of pastries and other dishes with them. They turned out to be great favourites of the King. The recipes have been added to and passed down for more generations than I can count. My father is a chef to a wealthy household and my brother owns his own patisserie on Baker Street near Portman Square."

I recalled the shop, having been past it many times, as it was just south of 221B where Holmes and I had lived for so long. The smells were delightfully tempting, but I'd never taken the time to stop and walk in. I vowed to do so when this was all over, assuming I still retained my freedom.

We continued our discussion and I discovered how he came to recognise his call to the priesthood, but that is a tale for another time. The evening passed slowly. Though I could hear the evening mass, I chose to return to my room to read and glean what I could from the story of Job.

The next morning, after breakfast, I was brought another visitor by Father Hazelbaker. The stout, short fellow who entered my quarters was familiar to me, for Holmes and I were instrumental in proving him innocent of murdering his father some seven or eight years ago.[1]

"Edgar Mason!" I exclaimed, rising from the writing table where I had been reading a morning paper provided by my host. "You are a welcome sight, sir!"

I shook the beefy hand he had extended and bid the young barrister to take the chair while I sat on the edge of the bed. He set his briefcase on the floor, his hat on the desk and greeted me heartily.

"It is good to see you again, Doctor. Mr. Holmes informs me that the two of you may be in a spot of trouble and suggested I visit you to gather the facts you know, just in case we are required to go to court."

I ordered my thoughts and launched into an explanation of the facts as I knew them, from both my perspective and what Lestrade had told me.

I was explaining the publishing process when Archbishop Bourne entered, a telegram in his hand.

Good morning, Dr. Watson, and Mr. Mason, I believe? I was told you were here."

We both had stood upon his entrance and returned his greeting. Then he held up the telegram and delivered his news.

"I'm afraid we have hit the proverbial snag regarding your sanctuary status, Doctor. Pope Pius X has reminded me that, because the Cathedral is not yet complete and free of debt, it is not consecrated ground. This could be problematical in declaring sanctuary. I am sorry. We will continue to allow you to stay, of course, but should the authorities come to arrest you, they may have a good case to take you away from us."

I sunk onto the bed at this news. Mason rubbed his chin in thought and asked a question.

"Your Excellency, am I correct in assuming you to be the highest ranking official of the Catholic Church in Great Britain?"

---

[1] *A Perpetrator in a Pear Tree* by Roger Riccard ©2016. Published in *The MX Book of New Sherlock Holmes Stories Part V: Christmas Adventures.*

"Yes, that would be correct," answered the Archbishop with a quizzical look.

Mason mulled that over for several seconds and finally spoke.

"I may have another option, but I'll need to do some research. In the meantime, Doctor, I will be meeting with some parties who may be able to shed some light on your case. Mr. Holmes assures me he will advise me of any pertinent information he discovers."

The enthusiastic barrister clapped me on the shoulder and declared, "Chin up, old fellow! I believe we've several avenues to explore that will alleviate this spectre of injustice from you. I'll be back tomorrow with my findings."

He left us in high spirits and the Archbishop turned to me, "Now then, Doctor, since you've had a chance to settle in, I would like to discuss what sort of tasks you might be able to do during your stay with us. As one of my counterparts on the continent put it, 'After all, we are not a hotel. Our sanctuary guests should give us some labour in return for our protection'. I am well aware of your old war wounds and would like to offer you a choice between some sedentary tasks involving your writing skills or more manual labour, such as indoor cleaning or outdoor gardening."

I looked up into that kindly face and smiled, "I should certainly be willing to 'sing for my supper', your Excellency. These warm summer days have little effect on my wounds and I think I shouldn't mind a bit of gardening outdoors."

He led me off to meet Father Scioscia, a rotund Italian of about forty with curly black hair, greying at the temples and calloused hands from his years of tending to the grounds of the many churches he had served.

His accent coloured his speech with charm as he greeted me, "Ah, *Signore* Watson, welcome, welcome! You wish to assist with the *paesaggio,* the landscaping of God's Cathedral, eh? *Bene, bene!* I show you how. Come with me!"

The fellow led me off to a tool shed and had me load up a wheelbarrow with a shovel, hoe and a rake. He handed me a pair of gloves and took me to a specific patch of the vegetable garden.

"This is our *cavoli*, what you would call a cabbage patch. We just planted them last month and we must keep the weeds from choking them out so to have a strong harvest in the autumn."

I looked at the area, which must have been about thirty feet wide and forty feet long, rolled up my sleeves and began my task with enthusiasm. It felt good to be accomplishing something where I could see immediate results in the form of the pile of weeds that accumulated in my wheelbarrow.

As much as I enjoy writing, the sense of accomplishment is always delayed due to the time factor of finishing the story and then waiting for its actual publication. It's the same with my patients. It's a very rare malady, indeed, when my medical ministrations result in instant healing. This manual work resulted in the instant gratification of clean rows of fertile soil awaiting the growth of red cabbage.

After toiling away for a couple of hours, I suddenly became aware of the presence of another individual in the garden. He was a burly fellow with flaming red hair and full bushy beard. He was dressed in overalls with dirt-stained knees and his clothes were damp with sweat on this warm summer day.

The voice, however, was the welcome sound of my friend, Sherlock Holmes.

"Halloa, Watson! I see we've both been getting back to Mother Nature today."

I stopped my raking and invited him to join me on a bench at the garden's edge where there was a pump to provide liquid relief for both man and vegetable. We shared a cup of water and I asked him about his progress.

"I've spent a profitable morning working alongside the landscapers at Parson's home and learned some things about the man and his habits which may prove useful. Last night I wandered among the hangouts of the City's cabmen. As I've told you on many occasions, they are among the most knowledgeable men in all London when it comes to certain types of information. I was fortunate to find two of them who convey our adversary quite often. He has some interesting friends and haunts."

"Anything that can help our cause?" I enquired.

"I have ascertained that he was acquainted to some extent with Milverton," he replied.

"That's very interesting," I responded with raised eyebrows. "If he were a victim of the man's blackmail, he should be glad he's dead. Perhaps he was in league with him?"

"A possibility I intend to explore, old chum. I've also learned that the judge who signed the warrant is Alfred Lyedecker."

"Didn't you have a case involving a Lyedecker some years ago?"

"Yes, it was shortly after your marriage. It was such a rudimentary affair that I did not require your assistance. The judge's brother, Wilfred Lyedecker, was accused by his wife of infidelity. She had come to me to prove her case and, as you know, I do not normally take on such tawdry business and told her so. However, another case brought me into Lyedecker's sphere. I happened to notice his shoelaces and it took little time to put together proof enough for the wife to accuse her husband before both Church and State. It ruined the husband's reputation in certain circles which devastated his business dealings."

"So you believe the judge has a grudge?"

"Most assuredly, Doctor. I presume Mr. Mason has been by to see you?"

"Yes, he was here this morning"

"He has already made some interesting discoveries. Parsons could never have gotten this warrant issued by any other judge with the evidence he claims to have at hand. But he and Lyedecker run in the same political circles."

"So, if this should go to court, you believe no other judge will accept it as a viable case?" I asked, hopefully.

Holmes shook his head, "I do not yet know how deep this conspiracy goes. It is possible that they have other cohorts who could ensure a judge sympathetic to their cause is assigned to this case, perhaps even Lyedecker himself."

"What can we do?"

"I will continue to gather facts. Mycroft is communicating with his own inner circle on our behalf. Do not give up hope, my friend. With any luck, you will be back at your wife's side within a week and playing with your grandchild."

Chapter Four

The following afternoon, I was again visited by Edgar Mason. He had a grin on his face and a spring in his normal lumbering gait. He was brought to my room by Father Hazelbaker, who left us alone while reminding me I was needed by Father Scioscia when I was finished.

Mason was nearly giddy and his broad smile expanded his already puffy cheeks, but he would not invoke his news upon me until we were joined by the Archbishop. When his Excellency arrived, Mason pulled a document from his briefcase and handed it to the elder cleric.

"This, gentlemen, gives us our protected status for Dr. Watson, at least temporarily. We don't need to worry about the legitimacy of sanctuary on non-consecrated ground."

The Archbishop was reading through the document, his head nodding and facial expressions alternating between quizzical and satisfaction. Not having the document in front of me, I questioned the barrister, "What did you do? What is that?"

"That, my friend, is a temporary grant of Embassy status for Westminster Cathedral and all its grounds. As a foreign embassy, the police cannot remove you."

"How did you manage that?" I questioned in puzzlement.

He raised his puffy hand and pointed a finger in the air, "The Vatican is considered a sovereign nation, yet it had no embassy in England. The Archbishop here is the top ranking official of that nation in this country. Ergo, his residence needs to be recognised as an extension of the Vatican, just like any other embassy is an extension of the country they represent."

Archbishop Bourne spoke up, "Can you really do that? Create an embassy, just like that?"

Mason held his hand over his heart, "My father was a judge, sir. Thanks to his connections and my on-going relationships within the court system, I was able to pull in a favour. Even if it is challenged, it could take weeks to overturn. That should give us plenty of time to build our defence, or for Mr. Holmes to convince Parsons to drop the case."

"Would Parsons risk the embarrassment of pulling back now?" I asked.

"It depends on what we find and how we present our case. It would be better for him to drop it now than to risk his reputation by losing such a publicised case in court for all the world to see."

Bourne spoke up again, "What do we do if the police show up to arrest Dr. Watson?"

"You show them that paper and advise them to contact Judge Walter Hargrove. He issued the order. If they attempt to enter forcefully, I've taken steps that should give them pause."

"What steps?" I queried.

"There are reporters from *The Chronicle, The Observer* and other newspapers all stationed nearby. All they've been told is to keep an eye out for any police activity at the Cathedral and be prepared to report exactly what happens, including any violation of Church property by a civil authority. I feel sure that no officer, or even Inspector at Scotland Yard, would dare risk the publicity in a conflict between Church and State under the circumstances of that document's existence."

The Archbishop clapped the young attorney on the shoulder and smiled, "You're a devious man, Edgar Mason, but a true friend to those in need. We shall do our best to keep Dr. Watson safe until you can mount your defence."

"I believe we are making excellent progress in that arena as well," replied Mason, turning to me. "I've spoken to some key witnesses and I think their testimony shall exonerate both you and Mr. Holmes, should it come to that."

I frowned in concern, "What witnesses? The woman I called Lady Brackenstall has returned to Australia and Holmes would never reveal the identity of who we think killed Milverton, nor would I."

"Never fear, Doctor," encouraged Mason. "These are different witnesses entirely and they shall be most convincing, I assure you. Now you go about your business here, for I see by the state of your clothing that the Archbishop has put you to work. My case is nearly complete to present and Holmes is piecing together quite a story of his own regarding this Parsons fellow. I'll check back with you tomorrow."

He turned to leave then stopped and slapped a hand to his forehead, "Oh, my!" he exclaimed, "I almost forgot. Holmes asked me to give this to you."

He pulled an envelope from his inner breast pocket and handed it to me. I recognised the graceful handwriting at once. It was a letter from my wife.

He shook my hand and departed. I peered at the envelope, anxious to open it, but desiring privacy. I set it down on the writing desk and turned to the Archbishop.

Bourne handed me the document Mason had obtained and I read that, indeed, Westminster Cathedral and its environs had been granted status as the Vatican Embassy to Great Britain.

"Quite the lawyer, this Mason fellow," declared Bourne. "I've only thought of myself as an ambassador of Christ, as the Scriptures tell us in *Second Corinthians*. I'd hardly considered my post to be political."

"I am sorry for all this trouble, your Excellency," I apologised. "I had no idea where this would lead."

"Nonsense, my son. We are here to serve and we shall join you in your venture because you are actors on that stage of justice and not mere bystanders. Our Lord's Church could use more men like you."

I bowed in embarrassment at this praise and then was brought back to reality by his next statement.

"Now I believe you have a performance to attend to in the gardens."

I assured him I would join Father Scioscia forthwith, as soon as I read the letter from my wife. As he left me, I quickly sat at the desk and tore open the envelope.

My wife's handwriting exhibited a haste I'd rarely seen, though it was still quite neat. She assured me that no one had confronted her regarding my whereabouts and she was still staying on to assist with the birth of our grandchild, who was due any time now. Holmes had worked out a system of communications with her, in case it became apparent that our daughter's house was being watched, and my stepson had also been appraised of the situation. None of them knew where I was, in case they were ever issued with a writ, but they all trusted Holmes's word that I was safe. Her closing exclamation of everlasting love brought a tear to my eye.

In all the adventures I'd shared with Sherlock Holmes during two marriages, my absence from home had always been voluntary and with the complete blessing of each of my wives. This forced confinement was frustrating, irritating and not a little frightening. I could not wait for this adventure's denouement.

That evening Holmes, back in his Archie Jones disguise, came to visit again. This time he joined me at an out of the way table in a corner of the dining area, where we could discuss things in private.

"Any news, Holmes?" I asked, anxiously. "This situation is intolerable!"

He gave me an appraising look and replied, "Yet I see a healthy touch of the sun has been added to your skin tone, Doctor. This bit of outdoor activity appears to agree with you."

"A side effect I can ill afford at this time. My family and my patients need me. Yet here I am forced into hiding like some common criminal! How can we call this creature off?"

"I have been looking into the life and history of one Colin Parsons," answered my friend. "He is a young fellow of only thirty-one. Graduate of Oxford. Son of Sir Thomas Parsons, former Commander and now arms manufacturer and supplier to His Majesty's Navy. Young Parsons used his father's connections to obtain a post working for the government upon graduation, bypassing more qualified candidates. He has become the fair-haired boy of the Parliament members advocating military build up to protect colonial interests and expansion. His political ambitions are no secret and he is under party consideration for selection to run for the House of Commons, that is, if he can build enough political capital."

"At such a young age?" I queried.

"The government is recognising that the veterans of the Boer War are becoming a significant voting block. They are looking for someone of their age to be their voice."

"Humpf!" I responded. "A voice who fails to conduct thorough research and looks for an easy way to enhance his reputation. That's not the kind of leadership England needs!"

"No, merely that of a politician as opposed to a statesman," replied the detective. "But I have discovered some inconsistencies in Parsons's behaviour that need further investigation. I will be on hand tonight to follow him and see what more I may learn of his activities. Perhaps we can dissuade him from his current course."

"Mason seems to think we can beat these charges," I offered. "He says he has witnesses."

"He does indeed, though they would prefer to avoid testifying unless necessary."

"Who are they?"

Holmes bowed his head, then gulped down the last of his tea and stood to leave, "Mason believes it is better if you are not aware of their identities. That way they can retain their anonymity should their testimony not be required. I must go so as to be in place when our adversary ventures out tonight. I will keep you abreast of new developments."

Thus I was left alone to again ponder my fate for another evening. As I wandered back to my room I heard music from the Cathedral sanctuary. Following the sound, I observed Father Hazelbaker practicing on the organ. The acoustic effects in that empty cavern enhanced his every note as I sat down to listen unobtrusively. He played on for several minutes, not noting my presence. I found him to be a most excellent musician. The long, thin fingers I had been so cautious of proved to be magnificent in their coordination and strength. When he finished his piece he stopped to take out another and finally noticed me.

"Good evening, Doctor. May I help you? Do you wish to pray or are you a music aficionado?"

"Good evening, Father. I do enjoy classical music. An appreciation I developed when I was living with Holmes, who plays an excellent violin. But your performance certainly enhances my prayers and I appreciate your artistry. Please do not let me interrupt your practice."

The thin young face beamed at my praise and he nodded, set up his next sheet music and began a rendition of Beethoven's *Ode to Joy*[1] which allowed my heart to soar at its beauty. For a short while in that time and place, all my cares faded away.

---

[1] Actually Friedrich Schiller's *An die Freude*, popularised by Beethoven who used it in his *Ninth Symphony*.

Chapter Five

While I was lost in thought, Holmes was spending his time in surveillance and observation. He joined me the next day during the mid-day meal.

"I have spent a most productive evening, Watson. However, it did require me to miss both dinner and breakfast, so please pass the bread."

The mere fact of Holmes enjoying a meal was encouraging. He rarely imbibed in anything beyond tea and tobacco when immersed in a case.

"I take it you've made some significant discoveries, Holmes?" I enquired.

Between bites, he told me of his recent activities.

"After our talk I took up a spot outside Parsons's residence. I wore a working man's overcoat over more formal attire so I could go fit in to whatever environment necessary.

"Parsons left his abode early evening and hailed a cab. I was able to overhear the destination he gave the driver and I signalled our old cabbie friend, John,[1] who was standing by. We followed him through various parts of London until we arrived at an establishment of, shall I say, *unique* reputation."

"Unique?" I queried. "How so?"

---

[1] John was the cab driver who provided Holmes's transportation away from the opium den he was investigating during *The Adventure of the Man With the Twisted Lip* by Arthur Conan Doyle.

Holmes took a sip of tea and replied, "Let us just say that the late Oscar Wilde would have felt quite comfortable there."

"What did you do?"

I left my overcoat in the cab and donned an opera cape and top hat instead. I then had John wait for me down the street. As I was wearing a red wig, moustaches and goatee, as well as tinted glasses, I felt I could enter without fear of recognition.

Once inside, I made myself known to the cloakroom attendant, who as it happens is one of my trusted informants. I questioned him regarding Parsons and found that he was a frequent visitor, but he always left alone. His usual routine was to join one or two other men at a table with a view of the stage but at a discreet distance, where their conversation could not be overheard.

I entered the main room where I was assailed by alternating smells of cheap cologne, cheaper cigars and strong beer. I managed to procure a seat at the bar where I had a clear view of Parsons's table from about twenty feet away. I could occasionally catch a snippet of conversation when voices were raised to be heard above the music. Parsons himself sat with his back to the stage, apparently uninterested in the type of entertainment offered. He spent most of his time talking to the one other gentleman who occupied the table at the time. A certain member of parliament whose disguise could not have fooled any trained observer, since the youthful skin tone did not match the grey wig or crooked moustache."

I spoke up at this juncture. "I'm surprised that, given Parsons's conservative politics and crusading personality, he would associate with a person of that stripe."

Holmes waved away my observation, "Politicians will deal with the devil himself to advance their careers or their cause."

The word devil had caused a few heads to turn our way, but Holmes merely put his hand to his heart and bowed in apology. Turning back to me he continued.

"Suffice to say, their conversation went on for quite some time and papers exchanged hands. When he arose to leave, I paid for my drink and followed him to the cloakroom. My informant noticed me lurking at a discreet distance and attempted to elicit some information for me.

"'Leaving so soon, guv'nor?', he asked. Then with a wink added, 'Perhaps I could recommend more suitable entertainment for your fine self?'

"Parsons replied that he had already arranged an engagement for the evening and walked out the door. I retrieved my coat with an extra tip for my man and followed. He hailed a cab, but this time I could not overhear the destination for the horse's whinnying and so signalled John to roust himself quickly, thus we pursued our quarry at a moderate pace.

"About twenty minutes later, he stopped and entered the Janus Men's Club. A popular society for young politicians and businessmen. I myself am a member there, under one of my many guises. Fortunately, I had stowed a trunk of various clothing and makeup in John's cab. In mere minutes I was able to transform myself into that persona, a travelling jewellery merchant, and entered the establishment. The combination of polished furniture, clean carpets and quiet conversation was a welcome respite from our previous stop. I was greeted by one of my fellow members with a hearty 'Hello Henry'.

"Upon being recognised and welcomed, I regaled my fellow members with stories of my travels and included shadier tales of jewellery I had procured for the mistresses of several of my clients on the Continent. One of the lads, a former customer for whom I had furnished a stunning engagement and wedding band set some years ago, introduced me to Parsons.

"'Colin Parsons, this is Henry Fletcher, a long-time member. If ever you need jewellery for an occasion or someone special,' he added with a wink, 'Henry's your man'.

"We shook hands. His grip was strong and he seemed to be appraising me with his eyes, as if wondering how trustworthy I might be.

"'You seem to have your finger on the pulse of European gossip, Mr. Fletcher. Has that improved your business?' he asked.

"I stared right back and replied, 'This *is* the Janus Club, Mr. Parsons. The Roman god of beginnings, endings and doorways. When an open door presents itself, is not one under an obligation to explore the possibilities it affords? As a politician, I'm sure you can appreciate that'.

"Parsons nodded in agreement and invited me over to a serving bar, where he ordered drinks for the two of us. Once we were away from the ears of the others he grew more direct.

"'Might I enquire, have you ever found such information you've gathered to be useful as a source of income?'

"'I am no blackmailer, sir,' I answered, feigning indignance. Then added, 'However, if someone has a need of information I possess and is willing to pay for it, I have no qualms in sharing it. What they do with it afterwards is their business, not mine. I daresay, some of your friends in Parliament have paid handsomely for information on certain persons, both here and abroad'.

"Parsons smiled in understanding, then asked, 'Have you ever read the Sherlock Holmes story about the blackmailer, Charles Augustus Milverton?'

"'I believe I did. Sometime last year I think'.

"'Would you happen to know who Milverton really was?'

"'I assumed that was his real name. Although at the time I thought he bore a striking resemblance to a business acquaintance of mine. A fellow who died some time ago'.

"Parsons then offered a name and it was, indeed, the real name of your fictitious Milverton, Doctor. I replied that it was that particular individual I was thinking of and he became quite intrigued.

"Parsons continued his line of thinking, 'This fellow and I had proven quite useful to each other over the years. I should very much like to stay in touch with his contacts. Would that be of interest to you, Mr. Fletcher?'

"I replied that I would be amenable to continuing the same arrangement I had with our mutual friend, but added a caveat.

"'I am a bit concerned about this Holmes fellow. I'd hate to have my little side business exposed in one of Dr. Watson's stories'.

"A smile spread across his face, 'I am in the process of curtailing the activities of Holmes and Watson. In fact, I have a warrant for their arrest'.

"I put on my best look of surprise and replied, 'Really? When will that happen?'

"Here he frowned a bit but kept a brave face, 'Watson has flown from his home, but I received information tonight that leads me to believe where he is hiding out. Holmes lives in Sussex now, and authorities there are on the lookout for him'.

"'What charges are you bringing? Surely Scotland Yard has welcomed Holmes's assistance over the years. Wasn't he also recognised by the Queen?'

"'Queen Victoria was a sentimentalist,' responded the man with a note of disrespect. 'King Edward is much more practical and I'm sure he will not interfere when the courts prove their case. In their zeal for their version of justice, Holmes and Watson have actually obstructed it by their interference. I'll have them out of the way soon enough!'

"I complimented him on his mission and assured him that, when that occurred, I should be happy to provide what information I could as I conducted my business.

"We rejoined the others for awhile and, after a time I excused myself, claiming that I'd just arrived in London and was still a bit travel-weary. I boarded my cab and had John wait down the street until Parsons left. By the way, I also had John change his appearance by adding a beard and a different hat and coat. As you remember, he is a rather large fellow and tends to stand out. It would certainly not do for our quarry to realise that the same cab driver was following him about town.

"His next stop was in an upper class neighbourhood at the summer home of a prominent businessman. I had John stop within sight of the front door and pretend to be checking his horse's front hoof, as though removing a stone. I stayed well back in the shadows and through a pair of opera glasses, I noted that the door was opened by the wife of said businessman. She greeted Mr. Parsons in a most familiar fashion, indicating that she was either a close relative or someone even closer. It was quite beyond midnight when he left and returned home at last. Surmising that was his destination, I had John hurry on ahead where I disembarked, this time in the guise of a drunken workman. I managed to bump into our 'friend' on the pavement outside his front door and was able to note lip rouge behind his ear, long blonde hairs on his coat and makeup on his collar."

"Well, that seems rather implicit," I said to my old flat mate.

"Indeed," replied the detective. "A nice bit of information to have in our back pocket should things take a turn for the worse."

"So what do we do now?" I asked, hopefully.

"For the moment, old friend, I'm afraid we must bide our time. I will continue to gather data. I've contacted your agent and your publisher to prepare them for what may be coming. Mason is aware of all this and is preparing his case based on facts I have given him regarding the stories in question."

The world's finest detective finished off one last bite, washed it down with a healthy gulp of tea and bid me good day. I returned to the Cathedral garden to continue my work. The breezes carried the fresh smell of mown grass through the air as I ran my hoe back and forth across mulch and dirt that would bring forth a harvest of vegetables. I only hoped I would be long gone before they sprouted.

Chapter Six

Late that afternoon, just as I was washing up for dinner, a knock came upon my door and I opened it with towel in hand. I was met by an agitated Father Hazelbaker. The young priest bid me to sit down as he had news.

I sat on the edge of the bed with the damp towel still wrapped around my left hand in my lap. Hazelbaker paced the room as he informed me that an Inspector Withers of Scotland Yard had arrived with two officers to effect my arrest. I started to rise but he waved me back on to the bed.

"Don't worry, Doctor. The Archbishop told them you had claimed sanctuary and also showed them the papers from your barrister granting the Church temporary embassy status. Withers wasn't happy, but could do nothing in face of these facts. He said he would check on the matter and return tomorrow."

"I don't wish to cause you trouble," I apologised. "Perhaps I should leave tonight."

Father Hazelbaker stopped pacing and held out his palm as though to push me down should I try to stand. "No, Doctor. You're safest with us. Now that they know you are here, it's likely there will be police on the street, just waiting for you to cross the threshold so they can arrest you. We've sent word to Mr. Mason and, unless they wish to start a diplomatic incident, no officer will be allowed through our doors except to worship or pray. I know the Archbishop is already working on a proposal for a compromise. Let's let the night pass and see what the morrow brings."

*****

The next morning I breakfasted with Archbishop Bourne and my barrister. Bereft of appetite, despite the smells of frying bacon and fresh-baked bread, I only sipped at my tea while the others discussed my fate.

"Doctor," said the Archbishop, "I am prepared to convene a confidential tribunal to hear your case, which has the force of law within the Catholic Church. I am hoping that this Parsons fellow can be convinced that this is in his best interests as well."

Mason spoke up at that, "I believe I can sway him in that direction. I am off to see an old friend of my father's this morning who has a bit of influence in government affairs. If I am successful, Parsons will be happy to accept the Archbishop's terms."

"Have you seen Sherlock Holmes in the last twenty-four hours?" I asked Mason. "He has made some discoveries about Parsons which may prove useful, although I would rather not stoop to that level."

"I have not spoken to him directly, but I have sent him word about Withers's attempt to arrest you through a boy he assigned to my office. An *irregular*, I believe he called him."

I smiled at the thought and explained, "The Baker Street Irregulars are a group of young urchins whom Holmes employs from time to time to act as his eyes and ears on the streets of London. They are particularly useful in that they can go anywhere and see everything without anyone taking notice."

"Well, I suspect I'll hear from him soon enough. In the meantime," he rose and bowed to Bourne, "I must be off to my appointment. Do not fear, Dr. Watson. We have a strong case and you have many influential friends"

*****

That evening, Holmes and Mason both joined me for dinner. While the meals at Westminster Cathedral were plain and simple fare, they were quite tasty and plentiful. The aroma emanating from the kitchen and the physical exertion of a day's work overcame my stress and I filled my plate. Mason did likewise, but Holmes ate sparingly.

I asked Holmes to begin the conversation with any new observations he had made.

He looked at me with an impish grin and replied, "I perceive that you have lost about four and one half pounds since you began your new work among the vegetables. The calluses on your hands indicate that you have often been lost in thought and forgotten your gardening gloves. And I do believe …"

"Confound it, Holmes! I meant observations about the case," I cried in exasperation at his attempt at humour.

"Ah, well then. I have had Parsons's comings and goings reported by members of the Irregulars and there is nothing new to report there. I have made various enquiries amongst my contacts in both government and society and there are certain discoveries that may work to our advantage should it become necessary.

"I also observe that friend Mason here has been to Buckingham Palace and by his countenance, I believe he has some positive news from a royal personage."

Mason was almost beaming, but then queried my friend, "How did you know I'd been to the Palace, Holmes? It's true that I was able to gain an audience with King Edward and have good news, but how could you have guessed that?"

Holmes sighed, "I never guess, as Watson here will attest. I observe and deduce and my observations are, that not only do you have pollen from the trees indigenous to the Palace grounds on your coat, but your left boot has a tell-tale scuff mark on its toe that is characteristic of the sixth step of the entrance hall, which is slightly higher than the others, causing many visitors to stub their toe on their way up."

"That's remarkable," replied my barrister.

"Never mind all that!" I demanded, now totally frustrated at this conversation. "What did the King say?"

Mason, looking apologetic, replied, "Ah, yes. Well, I have written instructions, signed by his Majesty, to require Parsons to conduct his preliminary hearing on Church grounds under the tribunal rules set down by Archbishop Bourne. Should the Church find you innocent, Parsons is to cease and desist any further prosecution against either you or Mr. Holmes."

"So there will be a trial?" I asked, somewhat dejectedly.

The barrister put his hand on my shoulder, "His Majesty agreed with me that the best course of action is to let all the facts come out once and for all, so it can be put behind you. Once we prove your innocence, it's done with, forever."

I let out a sigh, "We *are* innocent, but I've witnessed too many trials where legalities override the truth. Remember when you were arrested on circumstantial evidence?"

"Yes, and things looked bleak for awhile," answered the young man. "But then Sherlock Holmes and Dr. John Watson came to my aide. What better chance can you have than that?"

*****

That evening I was summoned to the Archbishop's office. Mason was already there and Bourne waved me to a seat next to my legal representative. In his deep, kindly voice he gave us the news.

"My sons, I have received a reply from Mr. Parsons. He has, reluctantly, by the tone of his message, agreed to King Edward's request. We will convene a tribunal the day after tomorrow at nine in the morning here in the Cathedral refectory. While I am sympathetic to your case, Dr. Watson, I must warn you that our decision will be a final determination on whether or not you go to trial in a criminal court. Once our verdict is reached my hands are tied."

Mason spoke up, "We have the truth on our side, your Excellency."

The Archbishop smiled and pronounced, "… and the truth shall set you free … we pray."

Chapter Seven

The tribunal was set up in the Cathedral's refectory. Dining tables had been rearranged and chairs made available for all the participants. The judge's table was covered in a scarlet cloth with golden borders. A gold embroidered cross was centred on the portion draped down in front of Archbishop Bourne, who was dressed in his most formal *pian* attire. On either side of Bourne were other priests, whom he introduced as Bishop Sebastian and Bishop Slattery. Both of these gentlemen were of an age comparable to his Excellency, thus representing the wisdom of many years of service under Holy Orders.

To each side, at right angles from the judge's table and facing each other, were tables for the prosecution and defence. Parsons sat next to an assistant, who was ready to hand over evidentiary documents etc. I was at the defence table with Mason who also brought an assistant named Oldham, an elderly, balding gentleman with an unruly fringe of grey hair and gold rimmed spectacles.

Beyond them, facing the judge's table, was a gallery of chairs for witnesses and a few observers, who were limited to a handful of priests, including Father Hazelbaker and Father Scioscia. Neither members of the press nor public were allowed, as this hearing was strictly confidential and, should my innocence, as well as Holmes's, be proven, the existence of this proceeding would never be divulged.

His Excellency, Archbishop Bourne, opened the session with a prayer for truth and guidance and then bid the Crown Prosecutor to make his opening statement.

Since this was not a court, neither side were in formal robes. Parsons, dressed in a dark suit that matched his short black hair, stood and grudgingly nodded to the judges. He was not sanguine to this idea, but expediency won out. He grasped the lapels of his coat, cleared his throat and began.

"Gentlemen, it is our intention to prove that this person, Dr. John Watson, along with his accomplice, Mr. Sherlock Holmes, did wilfully, on two separate occasions that we know of, obstruct justice, abetted the cover up of crimes of murder and allow the perpetrators to escape.

"Yes, your Honours, murder. Crimes which broke the sixth commandment of the Church, as well as the laws of England. We shall prove, by Dr. Watson's own words of admission, that he is guilty beyond reasonable doubt. This is a simple case, for not only did the Doctor write out the circumstances in his own hand, he brazenly had the incidents published in a popular magazine for all to see.

"Now one may read these stories with sympathy. It is possible that these murderers may have prevailed in court on the grounds of self-defence. But the court had no chance to make that decision."

He paused for dramatic effect and raised his voice, pointing at me, "This man and Mr. Holmes, appointed themselves judge and jury. They flouted the laws of both the Church and state. When citizens take the law into their own hands, we become a mob of vigilantes, rather than a civilisation of men ruled by law and order. No matter how sympathetic the cause may be, he is, in fact, guilty of duplicity in the murder of two English citizens and we cannot allow him to go unpunished."

Parsons stared at us for several seconds for effect before turning on his heel and striding back to his seat.

Bourne thanked him for his concise statement, then turned to Mason and requested him to state my defence.

Mason placed a hand on my forearm as he rose and gave me an encouraging nod. Then he stepped around the desk and stood before the Bishops. He interlaced the fingers of his hands in front of his ample belly and bowed in respect.

"Your Excellencies, first of all, we wish to thank you for the steps you've taken up to this point to ensure my client's freedom from erroneous prosecution. We are confident that your generosity will be rewarded with the knowledge that you have protected an innocent man."

Mason then turned toward the gallery and waved an arm in my direction, "Yes, I say innocent. This gentle man, this decent man, this courageous man, this doctor of medicine who has lived a life by his Hippocratic Oath to do no harm, this stalwart member of the community, who assists the authorities in the fight for truth and justice more than most men ever will, is innocent.

"We are well aware that the prosecution will produce documents that appear to be an admission of guilt to these charges. We shall deal with those in the course of this hearing. What the prosecution does *not* have and what is most crucial when levelling any charge having to do with murder, are bodies of supposed victims."

A murmur went up from the few seated in the gallery, but a quick raise of the hand of the Archbishop silenced them immediately. Mason turned back toward the judges and continued.

"Yes, your Graces, not only are there no bodies, they do not even have the identities of these supposed victims. They can offer no proof that a crime has been committed other than the words printed in a magazine. It is a spurious action taken by an ambitious politician and we shall be happy to put this matter to rest and restore my client's freedom. Thank you."

Mason returned to his seat next to me and folded his hands atop the papers on the desk in front of him. Parsons glared at him from across the room and was so engrossed in his fury he had to be told twice by the Archbishop to proceed. He shook himself from his distraction and stood once again. He handed issues of *The Strand* magazine to each of the judges, then stood back.

"Gentlemen, you have before you copies of *The Strand* magazine, in which the defendant blatantly describes actions taken by him and Mr. Holmes which resulted in the escape of two murderers. The page numbers are marked and the passages circled for your convenience."

Each Bishop glanced cursorily through the issues before them as Archbishop Bourne replied, "We are well aware of the contents, Mr. Parsons. We have already read them. In fact, we have noted that the author is listed as Sir Arthur Conan Doyle, not Dr. Watson. What other evidence can you produce?"

Nonplussed, the Crown Prosecutor took up more papers from his desk and handed them to Bourne. "The context of the writing makes it obvious that Dr. Watson is the storyteller. These are the typed pages received by the offices of *The Strand Magazine* from which they published his story. You will note that there were no editorial changes to those sections I have highlighted. He is condemned by his own words. I should like to call Mr. Herbert Greenhough Smith to the witness chair to authenticate this fact."

Bourne nodded and Parsons turned and waved a gentleman forward who had stood at the mention of his name. Smith was the editor of the magazine. A graduate of Cambridge, he was now fifty years old but neither his thick brown hair nor full moustache showed any sign of grey. He walked briskly forward and sat in the chair next to the judges table. After being sworn in, he was handed the papers by Parsons.

"Now, Mr. Smith, can you please identify these documents as the ones you received which detailed the murders of Lord Brackenstall and Mr. Charles Augustus Milverton?"

Smith adjusted his glasses and flipped through the pages. Finally, he nodded and handed them back to Parsons.

"Yes, my editing marks are on these documents. They are the ones you had taken by writ from my office."

"Ah, you mentioned editing," smiled Parsons. "Just so there is no doubt that Dr. Watson cannot claim you changed the facts related to the murders, please tell the court that you did not edit that portion of the stories, or revise those facts in any way."

"That's true," replied the editor in a strong voice.

He tried to continue his statement but Parsons cut him off as he turned to Mason and, with a smug smile said, "Your witness."

Mason took up his usual pose with his fingers interlaced across his belly and greeted Smith cordially.

"Good afternoon, Mr. Smith. I appreciate you making yourself available for our proceeding today."

"I'm happy to help, sir. Dr. Watson's stories are important to my publication."

"You hope that he is found innocent then?"

"Indeed."

"But you would not lie under oath to sway the judges?"

Smith looked aghast at such a suggestion, "I am a God-fearing man, sir. My oath is sacred."

"I'm sure it is, sir," smiled Mason. "Now, on your oath, please tell the court, did you receive these documents from Dr. John Watson?"

Smith shook his head, "No, sir."

Parsons snapped his head up from the papers he was reading and frowned.

Mason continued. "Who did you receive them from?"

"They were sent to me by Dr. Doyle. All of Dr. Watson's stories come to me through Sir Arthur."

Mason turned and reiterated this fact to the gallery, "You have NEVER received a story directly from my client. Is that your testimony?"

"Yes, sir."

"Then you cannot affirm whether the typewritten pages you received were written by Dr. Watson or Dr. Doyle?"

Smith looked thoughtful for a moment then replied, "That is true."

I could see Parson's face darkening as his own witness's testimony was being turned against him.

Facing Smith, Mason raised his thumbs as he extended his interlaced hands toward the man.

"Just one more question, Mr. Smith. What sort of stories do you publish in *The Strand Magazine*?"

Smith sat up a little straighter, adjusted his spectacles and began his spiel, "*The Strand Magazine* is a general interest publication. We attempt to appeal to a wide variety of readers. There are interviews with politicians and celebrities. We've done stories about many newsworthy events from new inventions to news from Europe and America. We review theatrical productions and publish fictional stories of various genre."

Mason interrupted him, "Fiction, you say?"

"Yes," replied the Editor, "It is one of our most popular features."

"I see. Did it ever occur to you that the stories of Dr. Watson and Mr. Holmes might be fictional?"

Parsons slammed his hand down on his table and started to rise an objection, but the Archbishop silenced him immediately with a raised hand and a commanding look.

Smith appeared uncertain, "I have met both Mr. Holmes and Dr. Watson on a few occasions. Since they are real persons I had assumed that the stories were real as well. I know that I've read similar accounts of Mr. Holmes's work in the newspapers."

"Were you aware that the names of the clients and victims in these particular stories were not real?"

"Not in these stories especially. However, Dr. Doyle has informed me on occasion that he changes names and locations to protect the innocent."

"Have you ever heard of Lord Brackenstall or Charles Augustus Milverton before?"

"No, sir."

"Then would you concede the possibility that these characters and, in fact, these stories are entirely, or in part, fictional?"

Smith squirmed in his chair. As much as he wanted me acquitted, his reputation was at stake. Finally, he gave a heavy sigh and spoke, "I'm afraid I must admit that it could be possible."

Mason unclenched his hands and spread his arms wide. Turning to the gallery he declared, "Then I believe we have reasonable doubt."

"Objection!" shouted Parsons. "Defence is testifying before all the facts are in evidence."

The Bishops looked on at Parsons in disapproval of his raised voice. Then Bourne spoke, "Your objection is noted, Mr. Parsons. But please maintain your decorum. There is no need to shout."

Turning to my legal representative he requested, "Mr. Mason, please refrain from stating a possible verdict until your closing argument. There are more witnesses to be heard."

Mason bowed, dismissed Greenhough Smith and came back to sit next to me. His assistant shuffled some papers and handed him what he supposed would be a relevant document for the next witness.

As this was not a formal court, the Bishops had decided to let each side alternate at presenting their witnesses and evidence. It was now our turn and Mason called upon his primary witness, Sir Arthur Conan Doyle.

Chapter Eight

"Sir Arthur," began Mason, "We appreciate your appearance here today to clear up the facts in this case.

The renowned doctor and war chronicler was in his mid-forties. His brown hair lay flat upon his head and his waxed moustache tips extended nearly as wide as his round face. He wore a dark blue suit with waistcoat and a four-in-hand necktie. His skin tone retained the tan he had received during the Boer War, as he still spent considerable time outdoors. He was even known to take his typewriter out on to a patio to work with one of his hounds at his feet.

His voice was clear and confident as he answered, "I am glad to be of service, Mr. Mason, and to your Graces," he added, bowing to the Bishops. "My friend and collaborator, Dr. Watson, must be cleared of these ridiculous charges."

He glared at Parsons as he said this last statement. For the first time I thought I saw a brief flash of uncertainty cross the prosecutor's face.

Mason continued, "We have heard testimony from Mr. Smith, Editor of *The Strand Magazine*, that the typed manuscript pages he received regarding, *The Adventure of the Abbey Grange* and *The Adventure of Charles Augustus Milverton*, were from you and not Dr. Watson. Is this correct?"

"Indeed, sir."

"Why is that? Are they not Dr. Watson's stories?"

The Knight Bachelor used his right hand to emphasise his answer as he spoke, "My arrangement with Dr. Watson is to be his literary agent. As such, I receive his handwritten manuscripts, type them into a submissible format and send them on to various publications, usually to *The Strand Magazine*, but there have been others."

"I see," replied Mason. "Now, in the course of your typing up Dr. Watson's stories, have you ever had occasion to change aspects of the story, or do you merely correct for grammar, punctuation and spelling?"

My friend and agent replied, "Because he often has to change names and locations, I check to make sure that his new data makes sense within the storyline. For instance, if he changes the location from Oxford to Cambridge, I make sure that the travel time is consistent with the difference in miles."

"Do you, yourself, ever change significant details of the story, especially in the two stories which we are discussing today?"

Doyle shifted in his seat and nodded his head, "Yes, I have, on occasion, felt a need to punch up a story line or delve deeper into Holmes's character.

"The stories in question do include such additions. In *The Adventure of the Abbey Grange,* Holmes had deduced an unidentified suspect as an alternative to the gang first suspected, but simply turned the information over to the inspector in charge who failed to act in time to question the man. I felt that the romantic aspect of the case needed to be expanded and so I added the confrontation with the fictitious Captain Croker and the subsequent actions of letting him go."

He turned and faced Parsons, "In my mind it was obviously self-defence and certainly not a matter for police to waste their time on."

My barrister nodded and turned toward the gallery with his hands laced over his waistcoat as he asked his next question.

"And what of the Milverton story? Did my client and Mr. Holmes let a murderer go free?"

Doyle shook his head, "No, Mr. Mason. The story I received from Dr. Watson had he and Mr. Holmes arriving just as the murderer was fleeing the scene, unidentified. In point of fact, the murder was done with a knife, not by the loud retort of a gun. That gave them the opportunity to take advantage of the time to take the actions they did. I added the implication that the murderer was a wronged woman to give it a more appealing nature to our female readers."

Mason glanced significantly at the Bishops and turned toward Parsons, "Your witness."

The Crown Prosecutor put on a brave face, but was clearly uncomfortable having to question such a poplar public figure as Sir Arthur.

Attempting to recoup some dignity from his case falling apart before his eyes, Parsons gripped his lapels and addressed the doctor, avoiding his honorary title in an attempt to lessen his authority.

"Dr. Doyle, is it your testimony that you have taken the facts of real events and real persons and twisted them into these damnable deceptive fictions in order to garner the public's sympathy and dupe them into believing in the extraordinary powers that Sherlock Holmes is supposed to possess?"

I had to admire Doyle's composure under this scathing attack. He merely crossed his arms, cocked his head and addressed the prosecutor as if he were lecturing a schoolboy.

"No, that is not my testimony. While I admit that I did re-imagine certain facts for literary reasons, they had nothing to do with inflating Mr. Holmes's abilities. In all my editing I have never changed nor added to Sherlock Holmes's talents or character. Every observation and deduction that was recorded by Dr. Watson has been faithfully reproduced in its entirety. My edits are merely to enhance or romanticise the story without changing their original purpose, which is to demonstrate problem solving techniques through disciplined training."

Parsons shook his head, "Still, you lied to the public. You, a Knight of the Realm, and a war correspondent. How are we ever to believe anything you ever say again?"

Doyle was unflappable and declared, "I do believe you've lost your focus, Mr. Parsons. I am not the one on trial here."

Parsons replied through gritted teeth, "Perhaps you should be."

Doyle started to respond but Archbishop Bourne raised his hand and commanded, "Stop! Mr. Parsons I find your statement deplorable and insulting. Either ask a pertinent question or sit down!"

Parsons glowered at Doyle and merely said, "I have no further questions of this ... person."

Doyle stood from the chair and in a grand gesture of dramatic flair, pulled a business card from his case and stuffed it into Parsons's breast pocket.

"Should you wish to pursue this matter, sir, here's my card!"

He then strode out, leaving the fellow with egg on his face. I do believe that it was only the solemnity of being on Church grounds that kept the entire gallery from standing up and cheering.

Bourne broke the enforced silence with a question, "Does the prosecution have any further witnesses, Mr. Parsons?"

The man walked over to his table, shuffled some papers, looked toward the gallery where, I noted, there were some officers from Scotland Yard, but finally turned to the Bishops and said, "No, your honours. I believe my other witness's testimony would be moot in light of this admission of Dr. Doyle's deception of the public."

"Very well," declared the Archbishop. "We shall retire to consider our verdict."

He and Bishops Sebastian and Slattery stood and walked out toward the chapel. No one else left. Even the gallery members who were not part of the proceedings were held in place by their curiosity.

We did not have long to wait. Less than ten minutes later the Bishops returned and took their seats. All of us at the tables stood to hear their verdict.

Bourne spoke for the court and declared, "In light of the witnesses and evidence presented here today, we are unanimous in finding that Dr. John Watson is not guilty of any of the charges brought forth by the prosecution. It is our considered opinion that no crime has been committed. Should the Crown Prosecutor persist in this action, we shall make our findings public and be prepared to use the Church's influence on Dr. Watson's behalf."

Turning directly toward Parsons, Bourne asked, "Does the prosecution wish to challenge our decision, or may Dr. Watson be allowed to go free without further allegations?"

Parsons looked down at the papers on the table before him, realising the folly of his faulty evidence, and took a deep breath. At last he spoke, "In the face of the testimony given, the Crown declines to pursue any further action against Dr. John Watson or Mr. Sherlock Holmes in these matters."

Bourne smiled and pronounced, "So be it! Dr. Watson, while we have enjoyed your company and will welcome you at any time, you are free to leave us and return to your family."

A grand murmur spread among the gallery as they left and Parsons and his assistant retreated quietly through the crowd. I thanked the Archbishop as he and the others exited. When we were alone I shook Mason's hand in gratitude for his defensive strategy.

Mason laughed, "It was really one of my easiest cases ever, Doctor. Mr. Holmes did most of the work."

He stepped back and nodded to his assistant, Oldham. The elderly gentleman stood up straighter, adding a good four inches to his height and took off his spectacles, allowing me to clearly see those familiar eyes of my old friend. Grabbing the back of his head he pulled forward the bald cap and grey hair came off to reveal the thick black locks of the world's finest detective.

Chapter Nine

"Hello, Watson. Congratulations!"

"Holmes! What are you doing here?

"Where else should I be, old fellow? Gaining first-hand knowledge of the proceedings was the logical way for me to be ready to step out and take whatever actions might have been necessary to sway things in our direction. Although I was sure Doyle's testimony would take the wind out of Parsons's sails. He deserves your thanks."

I crossed my arms and cocked my head at my old friend. "It was Doyle's re-writes that caused all this trouble. You complain about *my* romanticising your adventures. He nearly got us arrested with his literary license!"

"Agreed, but in the end he laid his reputation on the line to come to our defence."

Mason chimed in, "Yes, but I believe he, and both of you, have made a powerful enemy today. Parsons will certainly hold a grudge and be waiting for another opportunity to pounce."

Holmes smiled, "You are aware of Chaucer's saying about people living in glass houses not throwing stones?"

"Of course," replied the barrister. "Advice I've given several of my clients over the years."

"Well, the glass walls of Parsons's life are not so tinted as he believes. They proved especially vulnerable to one Henry Fletcher who has an unfortunate habit of selling information to persons less scrupulous than himself."

"What have you done, Holmes?" I enquired.

"Let us just say that Mr. Parsons will be forced to relinquish his position of power for the foreseeable future with a devastating case of hypocrisy."

We all chortled at that remark. My friend then gave me even better news.

"Now, pack up your belongings, Doctor! I have a cab standing by for you to make a house call on one Victor John, your grandson!"

Acknowledgements

As with all the stories I put forth about the world's first consulting detective, Mr. Sherlock Holmes, I must give thanks and credit to his original chronicler, Dr. John H. Watson. While not all his notes are complete, or in some cases, orderly, those which were left to Mrs. Hudson's care and subsequently entrusted to her niece, my 'Grandma Ruby' of New York, in the early days of World War II, have provided the essential facts of the tales herein. I have attempted to flesh out historical and geographical details via internet research and networking with other Sherlockians and British associates. I beg the reader's indulgence for any errors and trust that the stories herein shall be entertaining in and of themselves.

I would like to express my appreciation to the following individuals:

To David Marcum, fellow member of the Great Watsonian Oversoul, whose passion is keeping the spirit of Dr. Watson's stories fresh and true to the Victorian times in which Sir Arthur Conan Doyle's guidance brought the doctor's stories to light. His friendship, encouragement and shared thoughts on all things Sherlockian have been of immeasurable value.

And to Joel and Carolyn Senter, publishers of the Sherlockian E-Times (www.sherlock-holmes.com). Their encouragement and courtesy in connecting me with publishers, editors and fellow authors has allowed me to add my contributions to the lore of Sherlock Holmes. This book is now the sixth to be published, in addition to contributions to several anthologies of Holmes stories. This volume brings my published stories to over two dozen.

> As this volume went to press we were sorry to learn that Joel Senter has 'passed over Reichenbach' as was his term for those fellow Sherlockians who have passed on before us. His decades of dedication to perpetuating Sherlock Holmes lore will be sorely missed and we grieve with Carolyn at his loss.

A Sherlock Holmes Alphabet of Cases Volume One (A to E)

5 Star Review by Jack Magnus for Readers' Favorite

The book is a collection of short detective stories written by Roger Riccard. The author's interest in Arthur Conan Doyle's famous detective was in no small part fostered by his own British Isles ancestry, and he has written both novels and short stories featuring Sherlock Holmes. In *The Adventure of the Apothecary's Prescription*, Watson is sent a delivery for an emergency patient that doesn't exist. Watson soon realizes that Sherlock Holmes's assistance is being sought by yet another person in need. This time, it's a pharmacist whose family is being held hostage to ensure his compliance with their captor's demands for drugs. Watson and his wife, Mary, work with Sherlock to solve the case and help Hector Burbage's family escape the clutches of a deadly and determined foe.

Roger Riccard's collection of short detective stories will thrill any fan of Arthur Conan Doyle's classic detective fiction. The author gets the relationship between Holmes and Watson, and his recreation of London in their time frame works quite well. I enjoyed both the stories in which Watson was married and living away from 221B Baker Street and those in which the two sleuths are sharing living quarters. Riccard's inclusion of archival photographs works quite well in giving these stories an authentic and historical feel. The book is highly recommended.

Lightning Source UK Ltd.
Milton Keynes UK
UKHW011950231118
332859UK00003B/98/P